Dragon Knights

The Sea Captain's Daughter Trilogy

Sea Dragon

BIANCA D'ARC

CHAPTER ONE

Hrardorr followed the sound of the gulls out over the crashing waves to where the silence of the sea was broken only by the occasional bird or breaching of a sea creature. This place—the middle of the sea—was safe for him to land without guidance. Here, he could fly and not worry about his lack of vision. And he could hunt...sort of.

Following his instincts and the sounds bouncing back to him from the water's surface, he judged a good place to set down in the water, spreading his wings to help keep him afloat. It probably wasn't the most graceful-looking descent in the world, but he was comforted by the fact that at least nobody was likely to see him this far from shore.

With a mighty splash, Hrardorr set down on the surface of the forgiving waves, sinking a bit until his massive limbs could begin paddling. He had reason to be thankful for the rare sea dragon in his lineage that had passed down the legacy of his powerful, slightly webbed fingers and toes. He was a much better swimmer than most of his brethren, and it allowed him some small measure of peace in his current state.

Hrardorr had lost his sight to skith venom while fighting the large snake-like creatures on the eastern border of his homeland of Draconia. He'd lost his knight partner as well, and the pain of that loss hurt even more than his blindness at times.

He'd been in deep mourning for a long time and had vowed to never take another knight. What fighting man would want to partner with a blind dragon anyway? The forces protecting Draconia's borders were better off without him now. Really, how could he contribute the way he was? He couldn't even hunt on land anymore. They had to bring him slaughtered meat and tell him where it was, for goodness sake!

Hrardorr felt useless and impotent. He'd been one of the mightiest dragons in the fighting corps of Draconia. He'd been in his prime, uniquely skilled in combat due to his mixed heritage. His star had been on the rise, and his future had been bright indeed.

Then, it had all gone to hell. He'd lost his knight and his sight. And now, he had nothing. He *was* nothing. *Less* than nothing.

He'd retreated to the Southern Lair where nothing much ever happened, situated on the sea as it was. He would rather have gone into the mountains to be on his own, but he couldn't hunt on land anymore by himself. He knew he needed help, and he grudgingly accepted it.

How the mighty had been humbled. Hrardorr snorted, knowing the black smoke rising from his nostrils contained nothing of his former flame-filled glory. He couldn't even toast a piece of bread, the state he was in.

He felt something tickle his left hind foot and realized an ocean predator had been attracted by his presence. Good. Finally something he could do on his own. A foe he could still fight. A monster—albeit a small one—he could still hunt and kill. And eat.

Hrardorr liked seafood. A lot.

Diving, he once again had reason to thank his long-ago ancestor who had called the sea home as he went to work. Vision wasn't so very important underwater. The other senses, including the echoes he could sense better than any of the land-based dragons, told him exactly what was nearby and where his prey was.

Then, he struck. And for just that moment, he felt like his old self again. Or as close to it as he could come these days.

Livia saw the dragon splash down into the sea many ship-lengths from her location. Her gaze followed him with great interest. It was unusual to see a dragon from the nearby Lair land in the water. Most of them just flew patrols overhead, rarely bothering to come down and encounter the waves themselves.

One of her father's local businesses supplied massive amounts of fish to the Lair each day, so she knew the dragons and their knights and families liked seafood, but she'd never seen any of the giant dragons fishing...or swimming. She wasn't sure what the massive creature was up to, but she was entranced by his graceful movements in the water.

When he dove beneath the waves, she gasped. He was gigantic, and he appeared to swim like a fish! She never would have expected it of a dragon.

And what a dragon. His coloration was like nothing she'd ever seen before. Most of the dragons she'd seen from a distance were predominantly one color or another. All in jewel tones. Red, green, blue, even gold and bronze. There were a few who stood out, like the lovely spring green dragon that she'd seen once, or the almost purple, dark indigo dragon that had flown a message from the capital that one time.

But this dragon was different. When his wings unfurled, they were multi-hued within an overall dark framework. She couldn't tell if he were brown or bronze, but his wings shone with blue, green, even orange and red when the light hit them just right. He was amazing. Like the kaleidoscope her father had brought back for her from one of his many voyages to far off lands.

She scanned the surface of the sea for any sign of the dragon, but he was gone. How long could a dragon hold his breath? Could they breathe under water? Did they have gills? Like any person who had grown up in Draconia, she knew and accepted dragons as part of her world, but that didn't mean she knew all that much about them.

Most regular people didn't deal with them very often, if at all. When on land, they seemed to stick to the Lairs and the people that lived there, among them.

Livia changed tack on her small sail as the wind shifted, and her little boat began to drift. She wanted to keep looking for the dragon, but her lines were moving in the wrong direction, and she had to check them or she wouldn't catch anything for the dinner pot today.

Not that she needed to fish for her supper. Her father was a rich man. He provided well for her and the household, even when he wasn't here, which was most of the time lately. Since the death of her mother, nothing seemed to keep her seafaring father home. Not even his only child.

She suspected it was because she looked too much like her mother. She was a living, breathing reminder of what he had lost.

Her parents' match had been one of deep love. Although he'd given up captaining his own trading ships for the most part while Livia's mother was alive, now that she was gone, so was Livia's father. Off exploring the world and trading with foreign merchants, only occasionally coming home to Draconia with the hold of his ship filled with rare items from far-flung locales.

He was off on one of his trips again, leaving Livia at loose ends. She was an adult and could take care of herself, but she still missed her father when he was away. The house got lonely, which was when she took out her little boat and passed a few hours on the water, fishing.

Fishing was just an excuse, really, though she was pretty good at it. She'd been fishing for fun with her father since she was a little girl, after all. But it was the beauty of nature and the quiet challenge of the sea that made her come out here. There was nobody here looking at her, wondering if she would ever marry. Nobody asking her for a loan or to support their latest business venture. Nobody trying to curry

4

favor or lure her into some sort of trap for the unwary.

People were tiresome sometimes. Especially all those who wanted something from her because of her wealth or who her father was. She despaired that nobody would ever just look at her and see her for herself and not some means to an end.

Which was probably why she wasn't married with children of her own by now. Her father didn't mind. His business ventures meant that she would be looked after even if he never returned from one of his voyages. He'd made sure she was well provided for before he took to the sea again. And she wasn't without resources of her own.

She'd been working in her father's office since she was old enough to do math. When he was away, she ran the small empire he'd built. She hired and fired. She paid wages and made sure the various businesses had what they needed to keep running at optimal efficiency.

Lines checked and boat settled once more, Livia scanned the sea again. Where *was* that dragon? Had he drowned right in front of her eyes? Was a tragedy about to take place? And if so, what in the world could she do about it?

"Oh, Mr. Dragon?" she said softly, into the gentle breeze that caught her sail once again. "Where are you?" Her quiet voice took on a sing-song quality as she looked out over the calm sea. "I really hope you can hold your breath a long time, Mr. Dragon." She began to fret over his safety. "Mr. Dragon?" she said again after a long pause while the sea remained calm beneath her little boat.

"My name is Hrardorr, not Mr. Dragon," a deep, rumbly voice said directly into her mind, making Livia jump. *"Though I do appreciate your polite form of address. It is much better than some of the things I have been called."*

"Where are you, Sir Hrardorr?" Livia asked aloud, shocked that a dragon had actually spoken to her.

"If you are in the little boat, I am directly below you right now. I will surface off your port side in a few minutes. Do not be alarmed."

"I am in a small boat," she replied, still feeling amazed at this unlikely conversation. "I had no idea dragons could swim like fish!"

A rumbly chuckle sounded through her mind. *"Most cannot. One of my ancestors was a sea dragon. It gives me a little bit of an edge in the water. Now, tell me, are you squeamish? It's been my experience that many female humans do not like watching my kind devour our prey. Will you object if I eat my catch above the surface?"*

"Not at all, Sir Hrardorr. I've been fishing since I was young. I clean and gut my own catch. I don't think I'm squeamish. Unless...you don't do anything...uh...strange to your food before you eat it, do you?"

Again, the dragonish laughter sounded in her mind. *"No, milady. I don't believe you would consider it so. I just eat it, like most beings. Of course, the fish I caught is much larger than those you probably deal with."*

"What did you catch?" The dragon had piqued her curiosity. Did he bag a whale or something?

"Watch and learn," he said, with a hint of humor while, just off her port side, his head rose above water, followed rapidly by the rest of his body.

Her boat rocked, and she reached out to grab the lines to steady herself. In the dragon's mouth was the sixteen-foot monster shark that had been terrorizing the fishing fleet of late.

"Oh, well done!" She knew she was smiling, but couldn't help it. "The local fishermen will be singing your praises for taking old toothy away from their nets. Thank you, Sir Hrardorr!"

He seemed to preen for just a moment, then shook his head up and down, positioning the shark for a few giant chomps. Just that quick, the shark that had menaced the shore for weeks was gone. Swallowed almost whole by the biggest dragon Livia had ever seen.

Of course, she'd never been this close to a dragon in her entire life. Maybe they were all this big close up. Then again, this dragon seemed like he was larger than life from his coloration to his swimming abilities. He was special. She just knew it.

"Was this little shark really bothering people?" he asked, sounding curious in her mind.

"Little?" She had to laugh. "Only a creature as magnificently proportioned as you would think that monster was little." She shook her head. "But to answer your question, yes. It was chewing through nets and chasing swimmers. There seem to be an abnormal number of large sharks in our waters this year, and that was one of the bigger ones. I know for a fact that nobody would mind if you ate a few more of his friends, if you feel so inclined."

The dragon bowed his head. *"It would be my pleasure."* His head turned, but he seemed to be looking up, not down at her in the little boat. *"Now, tell me, whose are you and why do they let you out here all by yourself with such dangerous creatures all around your boat? Old toothy was not alone. There is a school of sharks in this water, and you should know that most of them were swimming circles around your boat until I arrived."*

That was news to Livia. She'd figured her bait might attract one or two of the predators, but she'd had no idea there were so many sharks out there, out of sight in the deeps.

"While I appreciate your warning, and I will be more careful in future, I can assure you that I am an experienced sailor and well able to take care of myself on the water. As to your question, I am nobody's. I don't even know what you mean by that."

"Whose family do you hail from? Which set of dragons are your protectors? Surely, they take your safety more to heart than to let you sail out here on your own. Or is there someone else in the boat with you? Or a dragon flying overhead, watching over you from time to time?"

Livia looked around at her small, empty boat. Only her bait fish and tackle were with her. Why didn't the dragon know that? And why did he ask about dragons flying above? Wouldn't he...?

Oh, dear Mother of All. He was blind.

She'd heard stories of the new arrival to the Lair. A blind dragon. Speculation was rife in the town about what a blind dragon could do. Seems she had just learned a bit more than anyone else knew, but she would never gossip about Hrardorr. She wasn't that kind of person.

"Sir, you mistake me. I am not from the Lair. I live in town. I am a sea captain's daughter. My grandpa taught me to fish and to sail. I have never met a dragon before today. You are the first I have ever encountered."

"Truly? And yet, you can hear me when I speak." He seemed to think for a moment, then continued, *"Human females who can hear our speech are rare, mistress. Your ability to do so would make you welcome in any Lair in the land, simply because you can talk with my kind and do not appear to be afraid of us. You're not afraid of me, are you?"* he asked, seeming to want to be sure.

"Should I be?" she asked in a tone that she knew conveyed her amusement. "Honestly, Sir Hrardorr, I had no idea how you communicated, or that it was rare to be able to hear you. As I said, I'm not well acquainted with the ways of dragons or those who live with them. I've lived on this coast all my life."

"If I were still a fighting dragon, I would bring you to the Lair myself. You aren't mated yet, are you?"

Livia was puzzled by his question, but answered anyway. "No, I'm not married."

"Then you must make your way to the Lair. You could find your mates there. I'm sure of it. A lady of such talent and gumption as yourself would be well suited to our life there."

"Mates?" Livia repeated, surprised but intrigued by the idea.

She'd heard about the strange way the knights lived, of course. When she'd been just coming into her womanhood, her girlfriends had talked of little else than the idea of mating with a handsome knight. Until, that is, someone was told by her mama that matings among knights weren't one on one. No, two knights shared one wife.

Livia didn't know why it was so, only that all the married knights were parts of trios. Happy trios, to be sure. She'd seen a few of the Lair women shopping in the square from time to time, and they all seemed happy enough. Nobody ever claimed the knights were bad husbands. Quite the contrary.

But for some reason, not many of the men who lived alongside the dragons up on the cliffs were married. There were few Lair wives and, because of that, few children.

Occasionally, a knight would form a liaison with a town woman, but nobody had become a Lair wife from the town in recent memory. The affairs seemed merely to be of convenience, not love everlasting.

"Mates, their dragon partners, and eventually children," Hrardorr seemed to answer her question. *"Little dragonettes and tiny human babies, with two dragon parents and three human parents."*

"All of them?" Livia asked, intrigued by the concept.

"Of course," Hrardorr said. *"That is the family unit of the Lair. They all share in the parenting of any offspring, dragon and human alike. It is the way we have always done it, since the first fighting dragon partnered with the first knight."*

"I had no idea. I mean, I'd heard things, but nothing like this. It sounds kind of…nice." She marveled at the idea of a baby dragon being raised equally by humans and dragons, or a baby human calling a dragon papa. "Do you have children, Sir Hrardorr?"

The dragon's mouth tightened. *"No. And now, I never will."*

"Never is a very long time," she said softly, wanting to offer comfort.

"Don't I know it." His tone was bitter.

"Being blind isn't the end of the world," she said, confronting his depression head on.

His great head reared back as if she'd struck him. *"You know I'm blind?"*

"I figured it out. A few of my father's people do business at the Lair, and they bring back news of new arrivals. I assumed you're the new dragon that has come here to recuperate. Am I wrong?"

A sigh gusted out of Hrardorr's mouth, filling her sails for a brief moment. She had to change tack to get back to him, but he didn't seem to notice.

"No, milady. You're not wrong. I'm the damaged dragon who can't even fend for himself anymore."

"Seems to me you just bagged a menacing shark all by yourself and chomped him to little pieces without any help at all," she mused. "You're not helpless. Hopeless, maybe...and that can be changed."

"You're a strange female," Hrardorr said, making her bark a laugh she hadn't expected.

"You're not the first person to tell me that," she allowed, smiling.

"I'm not a person. I'm a dragon." He bared his pointy teeth, as if grinning at her.

"Point taken, Sir Dragon." She regarded him for a moment, searching for the right words, but she couldn't find them. "I like fishing. I do it most days when my father is away. Maybe you'd like to meet me here again sometime? I mean, I need protection from the circling sharks, and I suppose you could make yourself useful in lowering their numbers before someone from the town ends up maimed or dead. The fishermen would be grateful, I'm sure, as would most of the townsfolk."

"You don't say." Hrardorr looked as if he was thinking over her words. *"I like to swim. And I also like the taste of shark."*

"Really? What does it taste like to you?"

"Like victory."

Victory over his disability, she surmised. Well, it was a start.

"Perhaps I will seek you out again. If your little boat is in the water, I can find it from below. My water hearing works as good underwater as my eyes used to work in the sky."

"Water hearing?" she asked, intrigued.

"That's my name for it," he replied. *"I'm not sure what the sea dragons call it, but it's dark underwater. Eyes don't see much. But sound echoes back to me like waves. I can tell where things are using that sense. I don't know exactly how it works. It just does."*

"That's pretty amazing," Livia told him. "You could also

just talk to me, right? I mean, how far away can you get before I can't hear you in my head? Do you know?"

"It depends on you, milady. On how strong your mind is." He tilted his head as if in thought. *"We could experiment, if you like."*

"I think I'd like that. If you wanted to find me at any time, you could just ask, and maybe, if I can learn how to answer you the same way, I could give you directions."

"If you can speak into my mind, you could do more than that," he said, then immediately backtracked. *"But no. I won't get that close to a human again. Even if you're not a knight, it hurts too much to lose friends, and you are too short-lived, unattached to a dragon family as you are."*

She didn't understand a lot of what he'd just said, but the things he was hinting at were intriguing. She resolved to work on him. She'd wear him down in time. Hrardorr didn't realize it, but he'd just become her new project.

CHAPTER TWO

Seth went to check on Hrardorr, as he'd done every night since the blind dragon had arrived. At first, Seth had thought of Hrardorr as a patient, but over time, he'd come to enjoy the caustic dragon's company.

Seth had grown up in the Southern Lair and was apprenticed to the healer, though he wasn't much good at his vocation. He could help stitch wounds and bandage fragile wing bones, but he didn't have a true healing gift. He'd just taken up the job because the Lair's aging healer, Bronwyn, was a friend of the family and had been like a grandmother to him since his earliest days.

Bronwyn was getting on in years and could no longer handle the more physical aspects of her job. Once Seth had seen how she struggled, he'd volunteered to help her and had somehow ended up as her apprentice, though he really had no special gift for the work.

Everyone in the Lair just accepted that the quiet son of two accomplished but elder knights would do well as the new healer, since nobody else had stepped forward for the job.

And Seth hadn't fought it. He wanted to help Bronwyn. If he missed some sword practice to do it, so be it. Bronwyn was more important. People you loved were always more important than anything else, to Seth's way of thinking.

Maybe that had lost him a few opportunities over the years, but that was okay with him.

Hrardorr was becoming important to Seth, too, which was surprising, really. While Seth admired, and was friends with, many of the dragons in the Lair—especially those that needed a healer's help now and again—somehow, this blind dragon had earned a special place in Seth's heart in only the few weeks he'd been in residence in the Lair.

Seth could bespeak dragons. He'd always had the ability. It made him eligible to be chosen as a knight, but he didn't really have the weapons training to go with it. Although he'd taken the basic classes all Lair children were given, he hadn't had the time to pursue his natural affinity for sword work once he'd apprenticed to Bronwyn. That, his mother insisted somewhat optimistically, was why he hadn't been chosen by a dragon yet.

Seth didn't really think that was the reason, but he wouldn't gainsay his mother. She meant well. While he would have loved to have been chosen to partner a dragon, if that wasn't his fate, he was reconciled to it. He was content enough, he supposed, helping Bronwyn in her twilight years and doing good work in the Lair that needed to be done.

They wouldn't turn him out because he could talk with dragons, but he would never really fit in with the knights unless a dragon spoke the words of Claim to him. Which was about as likely to happen as it was that Hrardorr's vision would spontaneously return.

Seth snorted as he approached the massive door to Hrardorr's private suite. It was up near the top of the Lair so he could fly out easily and not have far to walk from the landing ledge to his sand pit when he returned.

Every accommodation had been made for Hrardorr, hero fighter that he'd been. Most of his brethren gave him a wide berth, seeming to not know what to say to their disabled colleague. Dragons were fighters by nature, especially those that chose to partner with knights and fight to defend the borders of Draconia. They weren't necessarily eloquent. And a lot of them didn't know how to deal with injuries—either to themselves or to others of their kind.

In general, they healed fast, and well. There was a phenomenon known as the Dragon's Breath that could be used to heal humans as well as dragons, though a dragon with the gift could not heal itself. Just like with humans, the healing gift only worked on others, not on the healer.

So minor injuries usually healed fast, and the dragon was right out there fighting once again. Major injuries were tended by Bronwyn and Seth. Lady Bronwyn had a true gift and was able to use it to save many lives. Seth did the heavy lifting. He sewed up wounds the conventional way, without the use of magic. He applied poultices and administered healing herbs. He fetched the raw materials from the forest and the town's market for Bronwyn, and learned from her the proper way to brew the various potions and ointments that were her stock and trade.

Because of his work for Bronwyn, Seth had more contact with the town, especially its merchants, than most other Lair folk. There was one woman in particular who had caught his eye on multiple occasions.

Livia. Livia O'Dare, daughter of the most reckless sea captain to ever sail the high seas. Since the death of his wife, he was never home—or so the gossip said. Her father sailed the really dangerous routes and brought back some of the highest quality medicinal components.

Seth had sought her out in the market and had traded with her a few very memorable times. She had no way of knowing who he was or where he had come from. Seth didn't like to boast of his origins to the townspeople. A few of the innkeepers knew he hailed from the Lair, and he had one or two friends among the locals, but Livia wasn't in his social circle.

As far as Seth was concerned, she was so far out of his reach he might as well not even daydream about her. Yet, he found he couldn't help himself.

The richest girl in the town of Dragonscove wouldn't be

interested in a failed knight candidate—a mediocre healer who had only a small room in the Lair. She deserved a man as powerful and connected as she. A man of means who could be a true partner to her.

Not a fellow who was still only an apprentice long after the age when he should have found his true vocation, or at least achieved some higher rank in his chosen field. Seth was a failure in his own eyes, and Mistress Livia O'Dare was much too good for the likes of him.

Seth sighed heavily and knocked on the door to Hrardorr's quarters. No use thinking about the woman he would never have. Hrardorr should be his focus now. He could at least try to help the blind dragon.

"Enter." Hrardorr's voice rumbled through Seth's mind. The single word held a new tone that hadn't been there since Seth had met him. He sounded...almost...happy?

Seth pushed open the massive door with a frown of confusion on his face that Hrardorr couldn't see. Once he could see the dragon, ensconced in the warm sand of his wallow, Seth became even more intrigued. For the first time, Hrardorr wasn't scowling in that way only dragons could scowl—with their whole heads, furrowed ridges of scales making deep grooves on their faces, twisting their horns into strange positions.

For once, Hrardorr's expression was relaxed.

"You look like you had a good day," Seth remarked as he approached the dragon, being careful to make a little extra noise with his feet, so Hrardorr would know where he was.

"I did, thank you."

The politeness was new, too, though Seth didn't remark on it. Most dragons were polite as a general rule, but Hrardorr have been—somewhat understandably—almost surly since he'd arrived in the Southern Lair with such grave injuries.

The lacerations in his wings had been healed already, but the scars had taken a few weeks to fade. The cuts and deep gouges in his body were taking a little longer to heal, but those were coming along nicely, and all had protected scabs. Seth checked them daily, to make sure no infections were starting that could be prevented.

It was the eyes that were the worst of Hrardorr's injuries. Turned milky by the searing burn of skith venom, Seth knew Hrardorr's eyes still gave him great pain each day. They oozed, and though the venom had been washed away, Seth still needed to irrigate them each day with a mild solution of biliberry to help whatever healing might still take place.

By now, Hrardorr knew the routine. He stepped out of his sand wallow and over to the area that would have served as a sitting area for Hrardorr's knight, if Hrardorr still had a fighting partner. All human furniture had been cleared, except for a small stool and ladder that Seth used when administering Hrardorr's treatments.

The empty sitting area was right next to the human bathing alcove, where Seth could access water. He kept his supplies there and went into the small chamber to make preparations while Hrardorr got into position, laying his head near the doorway. They would do the eyes first, then Seth would do a body check on Hrardorr's other injuries before finishing up with a rubdown of his wing joints with protective oils.

Since Hrardorr couldn't see anymore to take care of himself and had lost the knight who should have been seeing to his health, Seth had taken to doing it. Seth had done as much for his fathers' dragon partners, the dragon pair he called Mama and Papa. He even had dragon siblings whom he'd helped in the same way.

Big as they were, dragons sometimes needed help reaching the delicate places on their wings, and a little ointment or fragrant oil went a long way toward keeping wing joints in the best possible shape. Seth was happy to have the knowledge and skill to help Hrardorr, though he knew the dragon resented needing the help.

If his knight hadn't been killed, Hrardorr would've been tended by him. Seth knew the bond between dragon and knight was formed on a soul-deep level. It was a true partnership. A melding of hearts and minds that lasted for the knight's lifetime. And when the knight eventually died, the dragon went into mourning for a period before ever considering picking a new knight to share its life with.

Hrardorr had to be in mourning now. Seth felt for him. It wasn't easy to lose those you loved.

"I went fishing today," Hrardorr informed Seth, breaking into his thoughts.

Seth was so surprised he didn't quite know how to answer at first. "That sounds like fun." Seth figured that was a safe answer. The dragon could elaborate if he chose to speak further.

"It was. I caught a shark which apparently had been harassing the fishermen of the town." An unmistakable tone of satisfaction flowed through the dragon's rumbly words.

"Then you have done a good deed today, Sir Hrardorr. I have a few friends among the fishing folk, and I know they fear some of the truly large predators of the sea, yet they must go out there each day to feed their families."

"So I have been told," Hrardorr agreed while Seth began bathing the dragon's sightless eyes.

Seth was surprised to hear Hrardorr had spoken with anyone. He'd been spectacularly isolated since his arrival, not really speaking to anyone besides Bronwyn—at first—and now just Seth.

"I'm glad you're talking with your brethren," Seth said softly, choosing his words carefully.

"Oh, no. I heard this from a human in town. Or actually, on the sea. She was fishing, and we stopped to talk for a few minutes. For a human female, she is remarkably brave. I have not been around many human females in my time. I wonder if they are all like her?" The dragon seemed to muse on this as Seth worked on his eyes.

If there was a woman in Dragonscove who could bespeak dragons, Hrardorr's discovery was big news. Every single knight in the Lair would want to meet her and try his luck, hoping she might be the one to complete a Lair family and allow the single dragons to pair up as well.

For a dragon couple could never consummate their union with a mating flight while their knight partners were single. The spillover of passion could not be satisfied by a casual liaison. There had to be deep and abiding love between the participants, or the knights could easily run mad with the emotional echoes coming down the connection between themselves and their dragons.

The dragons could not mate until the knights found their match. And women who could live in the Lair, among dragonkind, were rare. Even rarer were those who could speak with dragons. The gift was found more often in males, though even then, it appeared only in a very small percentage of the population. Only a man who could speak with dragons was eligible to become a knight—and only then, if a dragon chose him.

Dragons could see into the soul. They could judge the goodness in a man's heart. They would only pick the best of the candidates to partner with for, once chosen, the dragon bonded to his knight for life. And that life was spent in service to their homeland of Draconia.

"Do you know who this fisherwoman is? Did you get her name?" Seth asked, knowing such information would have to be shared. Women who could hear dragons were just too rare to ignore.

"Did I say she was a fisherwoman?" Hrardorr asked in an insulted tone. *"She is a lady through and through, though she is not afraid of hard work, or of me, as it turns out. She is unlike any human female I have ever encountered."*

"You know the knights are going to want to seek her out," Seth said, laying his cards on the table. "Such women are rare."

"I know that as well as you do, youngster," Hrardorr snapped. *"But something tells me this lady will not be content to accept just any knight. She is special. So must the men be who claim her."*

"You're going to keep her identity secret?" Seth almost couldn't believe what he was hearing.

Then again, this mysterious woman seemed to have brought a spark of life back to Hrardorr. He was much more animated than Seth had ever seen him. He looked as if he was taking an interest in life again, which Seth counted as a great sign.

"Perhaps," Hrardorr agreed. *"For a while, at least. I need to find the right knights and dragons to court her. And since I am new to this Lair, you must help me. You were born here, no?"*

Seth sighed. "Yes, I was born here. I know everybody. And I suppose you'll want me to give you the run-down on who's who?" Secretly, Seth was thrilled with Hrardorr's new interest in his surroundings and in learning about the people of the Lair. Maybe this would be the first step in getting the blind dragon to become truly part of his new home.

"That would be very helpful. Yes. I think we should start there," Hrardorr mused as Seth finished treating his eyes.

After that conversation, every night when Seth treated Hrardorr's wounds and cared for his wings, Seth told him about the people of the Southern Lair. He talked about his family and their close friends. He talked about the prominent knights and dragons. He told stories about daily life in the Lair and who was better at what sorts of tasks among the dragons and knights.

Seth told Hrardorr about his friends—both those who had already been chosen by dragons and even the few younger males who were still living with their parents and hoping to be partnered with a dragon as soon as the right one came to choose them. Seth's motive for that was to hopefully get Hrardorr interested in taking another knight who could help him recover. Seth thought that, if Hrardorr had the care of a true partner, he would heal faster and better, but choosing another knight was totally up to Hrardorr.

For his part, Hrardorr continued to improve. He'd go off each day for a swim and a fishing expedition. Some days, he'd come back to the Lair and mention that he'd met up with his human female friend again, though he never told Seth her name. Some days, he'd talk about the way the fishermen on their little boats had cheered when he came to the surface with a massive shark in his teeth. Each day, Hrardorr seemed to grow stronger and more engaged in the world again. And each night, Seth became happier with the dragon's progress.

At the end of each week, Bronwyn would make the trek to Hrardorr's chamber to check on his progress. After the first few visits, she had taken to sitting with the dragon for a while and bringing him up to date on the news in the Lair. Bronwyn was old enough to get away with such tactics, for a dragon would not be disrespectful to an elder—human or otherwise.

Seth sat by her side, having made tea for them both in the small kitchen area that was mostly bare, except for the jar of tea and a tin box of crackers he'd placed there especially for Bronwyn's visits. He'd taken a comfortable chair out of storage for her to use and sat himself on the wooden stool, near her side.

"You are looking better each day, Sir Hrardorr," Bronwyn pronounced after she'd settled with her tea. She'd already done a thorough examination of Hrardorr's wounds. "I'm glad to see Seth is taking such good care of you."

"That he is, milady," Hrardorr agreed, allowing both humans to hear his words. Dragons could direct their speech to one mind or several. They were highly skilled in such things.

"I would take the credit," Seth said, modestly, "but it belongs mostly to Sir Hrardorr's daily excursions. Since he's been flying out to swim and fish, he's been gaining strength steadily."

"Word of your shark fishing exploits has reached the Lair, Sir Hrardorr," Bronwyn said with a smile. "The townsfolk are grateful to you and have sent word to the leaders of our Lair in formal thanks. You're fast becoming a local hero."

The words of praise didn't have the desired effect, Seth could see, as Hrardorr snorted and black puffs of smoke rose from his nostrils toward the vented ceiling. Hrardorr shifted in the sand pit, ruffling his wings slightly.

"Being known for fishing is not something I ever would have

predicted." Hrardorr let off a mighty sigh that sent more smoke rising upward. *"How the mighty have fallen."*

Seth decided a change of topic was in order. "How is it that you swim so well, Sir Hrardorr?"

Hrardorr wiggled deeper into the sand in his wallow, getting comfortable.

"One of my ancestors was a sea dragon," he told them. *"I'm told my coloration comes from her."*

"I've lived on the shore all my life, and I've never seen a sea dragon," Seth said, surprised by Hrardorr's words.

"I'm not surprised. They do not come up from the depths often. Their domain is the water, and they do not mix with humans or even other dragons, very often. My great-grandmother, Dureen, was injured in a mighty battle with a creature of the deep and washed up on shore, nearly dead. My great-grandsire, Jaranth, and his knight, Edjel, found her and nursed her back to health, but she was never able to swim the deeps again. She and Jaranth fell in love, and she stayed with him, building this very Lair with him after choosing Kael as her knight."

"I had no idea you were descended from them. I've heard the story of Dureen and Jaranth my entire life," Seth told him, duly impressed. "They were legendary leaders of dragons and men."

"I thought coming here, to be in the place that they built, might help me heal," Hrardorr said softly. *"And, if nothing else, I could explore my sea dragon side a bit. Water is one of the few places I do not notice my shortcomings so greatly."*

The conversation was rolling around to unhappy thoughts again, and Seth was at a loss as to how to fix it this time. Luckily, Bronwyn saved the day.

"There's a new pair coming in tomorrow from the Castle Lair," Bronwyn said, changing the subject again. "They're going to be filling in for old Tercel and Ailish while Tercel heals from his broken leg. Ailish was most insistent that her knight be given time off from his duties to spend with his family while he rests. He is the oldest of the serving knights and should probably have been allowed to retire to a less active duty post a few years back, but he is a stubborn man. I think this injury has finally proven to him that he is not as young as he used to be." Bronwyn laughed. "In fact, none of us are. Which is why I have you to help me, dear boy." She reached out to stroke Seth's hand in a motherly way.

"Tercel and Ailish are wing leaders, are they not?" Hrardorr asked, his sightless eyes narrowed in thought. It seemed to Seth that Bronwyn's change of topic had engaged the dragon's interest.

"They command the first flight," Seth answered readily.

He knew all the positions in the battle groups, having grown up with two of the best knights in the Lair as his fathers. They'd always made certain he knew how everything worked among the fighting cadres, thinking he would be a knight one day himself. But Seth had gone down a different path.

He couldn't fault Bronwyn or fate or whatever for his current position. He was doing what his conscience demanded, following a difficult path to help another person whom he loved as family. While he might regret giving up his boyhood dreams of being a knight, he couldn't be bitter about it. He'd chosen this path. He'd made his bed, and he had to lie in it.

Still, he kept up with the fighting units and knew them all. Not only did he help them when there were injuries, but he'd grown up with many of the younger knights and still counted them as friends.

"Who did they get to replace such a strong pair?" Hrardorr asked, breaking into Seth's thoughts.

Bronwyn answered, "A dragon named Genlitha who is partnered with a knight by the name of Gowan."

Hrardorr's head lifted. *"I knew Genlitha when we were children. She is an excellent flyer."*

CHAPTER THREE

"Stop fussing, Gen," Gowan said soundlessly to the dragon who was so uncharacteristically nervous that she'd almost unseated him three separate times during their flight from Castleton to the Southern Lair. Gowan was still learning about dragons, but Genlitha had always been steady and calm with him. Until now.

"Apologies. I'm just…"

"Yes, I know, milady. You're nervous about our new post and about meeting the new dragons and people of the new Lair. You're not alone in that. I may have been a warrior all my life, but fighting with you as my partner is still new to me. Nobody was more surprised than I when the new orders came down, sending us here."

He was, frankly, still confused by the orders. There were many more experienced knights who could easily have taken this post. So why had they chosen him and Gen? They were still bonding. Still learning their way together.

Gen was the true veteran of their pairing. She'd had a knight partner before. More than one, in fact. Dragons lived very, very long lives. Even when they shared some of their magic with their chosen knights, extending their human partner's lifetime by centuries, they still outlived their chosen human friends many times over. Genlitha was considered in her prime years among dragons at about five hundred years old.

That was his best guess at her age. Gowan hadn't asked her exact number of years. He suspected that females of any sentient species would balk at such a query.

"What is that in the distance?" Gowan asked, hoping to distract his dragon partner as they flew toward their destination. He had never been this far south and didn't know the terrain. Besides, Genlitha had much better eyesight than he did, and way more experience in the air.

"That is the ocean, my friend," she said, finally a bit calmer than she'd been for the past few days. *"And that small arrangement of mountains and rock spires is our new home. The Southern Lair. We'll be there within the hour."*

As they flew on, the shapes of the mountain and the dark openings of large caverns within resolved. Not as large as the Castle Lair, this new place was quite different from what he had gotten used to since partnering with Genlitha. Still, there were familiar patterns. Landing ledges and indications of where dragons could come and go freely among the cliffs and many caves.

Some of the openings flickered with light as the sun began its descent. Gowan knew there would be lanterns and watch fires, cook fires and those around which old knights and dragons would share stories and flagons of ale. This was a home. It might be smaller and less distinguished than the fancy Lair up in the capital, but it was still the place many dragons and knights called home and fought to protect.

As they neared the Lair, Gowan also got his first real vision of the water. So much water! He'd never seen anything like it before in his entire life. He'd seen rivers and lakes before, of course. He had traveled many miles as a warrior and soldier for the kingdom of Draconia. He had seen many things that most townsfolk or city dwellers could never even imagine. But he'd never seen anything like the vast expanse of water licking at the sandy shore. It was immense. And beyond his ability to describe in words.

"What do you think of the ocean?" Genlitha asked him when

he'd been silent a long time.

"It is…"

"Yes, I know." A smile seemed to come through in her words. *"I was trained here as a young dragon with my first knight before moving on to other postings. The winds off the water are challenging, so they send the promising flyers here when they're young to learn the air currents. It is considered a plum assignment."*

And now, she was verbally preening. Gowan had learned her moods in the months they'd been together. At least he knew that much.

So much about being a fighting knight partnered with a dragon was still a mystery to him. He supposed he would learn as he went, but with the war on in the north, there was no time for years of training in a safe environment. It was on-the-job training or nothing at all.

It made sense, when he thought of it like that, as to why he and Genlitha had been sent here. They were a new pairing, even though both of them were proven fighters on their own. Genlitha was a veteran, as was Gowan—they just had never had the experience of fighting together as a team. Certainly, there were other pairs more suited to this assignment, with much more experience, but all of those were probably better sent north, to where the real action was.

That made sense, even if it did take the shine off his plum assignment. If the others could have been spared from the ongoing threat in the north, they would have been.

It was a backhanded compliment, at best, that he and Genlitha had been sent here. Everyone knew the Southern Lair never saw any real action. It was known as the knight's retirement home for a reason. Old knights came here at the end of their careers, to enjoy this seaside air, the gentle climate, and routine patrols without any real excitement or conflict.

Gowan wasn't sure what to think. In one way, he was thankful that nothing ever happened here, because it meant he and Genlitha would have more time to learn how to fight together as a team. Leading the fighting wing was an unexpected bonus. Gowan was used to command. He had led regiments and battalions into battle. He was blooded and celebrated in single combat. It was fighting with a fire-breathing dragon at his side, and beneath him in the air, that was new and untested.

He hoped they would work out the kinks in that arrangement during this assignment. If he had a chance to cast his lines in the water occasionally and do a little recreational fishing, he wasn't against that either. Every warrior knew to enjoy life while they could—during the lulls between battles. This seemed to be that time for him and Genlitha, and he would take advantage of it as best he could.

Genlitha needed no guidance from him on the arrival procedure to a new Lair. A patrol came out to greet them, consisting of two spring green dragons that looked almost like twins, both with magnificent wingspans. Even Gowan—as untutored in dragon lore as he was—could tell they would be exceptional flyers. Perhaps that's why they'd been stationed here, much as Genlitha had been in her youth.

The dragons trumpeted a greeting to each other while the knights merely nodded to one another. Gowan suspected Genlitha was communicating with the other dragons, but he was not privy to their discussion. Dragon stuff, probably. Mysterious and arcane. And not for the likes of him.

Before long, they came in for a landing on the wide ledge at the top of the Lair. Genlitha navigated the markedly more powerful air currents with skill, landing with a graceful flare the two younger dragons still lacked. Gowan could feel the appreciative looks from those on the ledge—dragon and human alike.

Genlitha certainly knew how to make an entrance. And by dragon standards, she was lovely. Pale blue with darker blue and gray highlights along her flanks, she was almost perfectly camouflaged in the sky, under all sorts of conditions. A few of the folk in Castleton had nicknamed her the *air dragon*, both for the flawless way she flew and her resemblance to the sky itself.

Gowan greeted the knights who were waiting, relying on the procedures he had learned in the military.

"Gowan and Genlitha, reporting for duty from the Castle Lair, as ordered," he said to the oldest of the knights who had come up to greet them.

The older man smiled broadly, and there was a certain twinkle in his eye as he looked at Genlitha. It looked like recognition.

"Oh, we know who you are, laddie. It's been many years since I've seen the lovely Genlitha. Do you remember me, milady?" The old knight walked slowly toward Genlitha, who had lowered her head to get a better look at the man.

"Senneth! How have you been keeping, my old friend?"

"Old is right, milady," the knight joked. "Yet you look as young and fit as ever. It is good to see you again." He turned back to Gowan as if it was an afterthought. "Get ye to the leaders. They'll want to speak with you. Lady Gen and I have some catching up to do."

That was as clear a dismissal as Gowan had ever heard, but he took a moment to check in privately with his dragon partner. *"Will you be all right if I go check in with the leaders of the Lair?"*

"Perfectly fine. Senneth was the teacher of my last knight, and we spent many years fighting at his side. He is a good man and was a cunning warrior in his time. I would like to spend time with him, if I may."

"Milady, your time is your own when we are not on duty. I'm glad you have found a friend already here in our new posting." Gowan bowed to her and left, seeking directions to where the leaders of the Lair might be found at that time of day.

As it turned out, they were in a cavernous chamber, called simply, the great hall, that was used for communal meals, meetings and celebrations. It was large enough to accommodate all the knights of the Lair at once, and a few dragons besides. Dinner was just starting and the place was full, the leaders sitting at the head table with their lady.

Heads turned to follow his progress as Gowan made his

way to the front of the chamber. He knew he was the center of attention, and gossip, for the moment, but it couldn't be avoided. He had to check in with his new commanders. It was protocol.

The two knights and lady at the head table were older than Gowan had expected, but then again, so were most of the knights he'd seen here so far. They were either very young or very old. Training or teaching…or just plain retiring from the field to a cozy Lair by the sea.

But as they caught sight of him, both knights rose to their feet. Not standing on ceremony, they both came over to meet him as he neared the table. Both were smiling, though to differing degrees. The gray-haired knight seemed the more skeptical of the two, while his brown-haired companion was more open and welcoming.

"Sir Gowan." The brown-haired one took Gowan's hand in a strong grip. "It is good of you to come and fill in for Tercel while he heals. I am Jiffrey, and this is Benrik and our lady, Ilyatha."

Gowan made the proper responses and was offered a place at the table to join the leaders for dinner. He was surprised to find that Tercel was also seated at the large table, and they put Gowan right next to him. All through the meal that followed, Gowan was able to learn more about the duties he'd be expected to perform as wing leader for the first flight of the Southern Lair.

It was a few hours later that Gowan made his way out of the great hall. He'd learned a lot, and his mind was buzzing with all the aspects of his new assignment that he hadn't known about. He had to admit his head was also a little fuzzed by the strong wine they'd been pouring by the flagon all through the meal. He'd have to remember to take it a little easier on the wine, in future, if he wanted to maintain combat readiness.

As for tonight, he was on the way to comfortably toasted as he wandered the halls of the strange Lair, trying to figure out where Genlitha was. Then he remembered she'd wanted to spend time with her old friend. Well, it was easy enough to contact her. He paused his steps outside a doorway and leaned one hand against the carved stone wall.

"Gen?" He sent out the call soundlessly, mind to mind.

"What's wrong, Gowan?" she answered immediately.

"Don't know where you are," he managed. Stringing words together in his current state wasn't the easiest thing in the world.

"Are you drunk?" The tone was only mildly accusatory. She sounded more amused than anything.

"Wine was strong," he admitted.

"Where are you?"

"Don't know."

A dragonish rumble of amusement sounded through his mind. *"I'll send someone to help you. Just stay where you are for now."*

"No knights." He was adamant. *"Don't want to be the laughingstock on my first night."*

"All right, we'll save that for when they know you a little better. I'll find someone suitable. Senneth will know. Hold on."

Gowan wasn't sure if he dozed, but when the door he was nearly leaning against opened, he nearly slid down the wall in surprise. A man stood in the open doorway, looking at him.

"Are you Gowan?" the man asked.

Gowan nodded, but it made his head spin. "I told her no knights," he mumbled, a little upset that Gen had betrayed him by sending this fit young man of about his own age. Maybe a little younger. No doubt this man was a knight, and Gowan feared his drunken state would soon be the hot topic of the Lair's gossip grapevine.

The other man cocked his head to the side, and his eyes took on that slightly dilated look Gowan knew meant he was probably communicating silently with a dragon. Yeah, he was definitely a knight.

"I'm not a knight," the man said. "My name is Seth. I'm the healer's apprentice. Lady Genlitha asked me to find you, but I think you found me instead. You're on the doorstep of the apothecary chamber. Come inside, and let's get you sorted out. Can you walk on your own?"

Gowan did his best to straighten up, but much to his shame, Seth had to help him stand and keep an arm around him to steady him as he walked into the small chamber. Assaulted by the scents of many dried herbs vying for precedence in the small space, Gowan had a moment of nostalgia. His mother had been a wise woman and had kept just such a room in her home, where she stored and prepared herbs for those in the keep who needed them.

He raised a finger to touch a bundle of herbs as they passed. "Feverfew," he mumbled.

"Yes, that's right," Seth said with surprise in his tone. "I have a cot over in the corner. You can rest there for a bit." Seth helped Gowan over to the small cot and held onto his arm to steady him as he sat. Once he let go, Gowan quickly fell over, landing on his side, his head just making the thin pillow. "Or you can stay there all night, if you want. I think you fell victim to one of Tercel's little hazing jokes."

"Tercel. Yeah, he kept refilling the wine," Gowan agreed from his sideways position on the cot. His words were slurred pretty badly, and he kept wanting to close his eyes.

Seth sighed and lifted Gowan's legs up onto the cot, then turned to collect a blanket from a closet. He came back and spread the blanket over Gowan, and that was it. Gowan couldn't keep his eyes open any longer.

"I'll leave a pitcher of water on the table and something for the headache. Drink it down when you wake. I'll be working for a while in the next room and will check on you. You're safe here. If Tercel comes looking, I haven't seen you."

"Damn decent of you," Gowan mumbled as he felt unconsciousness approaching. And then, he knew no more until morning.

Seth didn't know what to make of the new knight, but his dragon was a sweetheart. He'd had a long conversation with Lady Genlitha after Senneth had made the introductions and was utterly charmed by the lovely blue dragon. To call her blue was a bit of an understatement, of course. She was an incredibly pale sky blue with many shades of sparkling gray and violet, like no other dragon he'd ever seen.

And she had a good heart. Her care for her knight partner was evident in every word she spoke, and she checked in with Seth several times to make sure Gowan was sleeping peacefully.

For his part, Seth worked a little later into the night than he normally would have, just to keep an eye on his patient. It wasn't often that Tercel had fresh blood to torment, and he hadn't pulled one of his tricks in a long time. As a result, Seth couldn't be sure Tercel hadn't gone too far and overdosed Gowan on whatever he'd most likely put in the younger knight's cup.

Seth would have words with Sir Jiffrey, though he knew it wouldn't do much good. They had long ago gotten used to Tercel's mildly sadistic ways. They overlooked a lot because he was such a good fighter and had done so much in service to the country, but even his dragon had chastised Tercel on occasion when his pranks had gone just a tad too far.

If Gowan woke none the worse for wear, Seth would see what the knight wanted to do in the morning. If he took a turn for the worse, Seth would be on hand to try to help—and to summon Bronwyn, if needed. But Seth didn't see any truly worrisome signs as the night wore on. Gowan seemed to be resting easily, breathing well and in no distress.

Seth bedded down in the next room—a glorified closet, really—so he could stay near enough to the sleeping knight to be able to hear signs of distress. Thankfully, both slept through the night.

When Seth woke the next morning, it was to the sound of a heartfelt groan from the next room. Splashing water indicated to Seth that the knight had found the water pitcher and was partaking of the headache cure Seth had left waiting the night before.

"There's a privy chamber in the corner, Sir Gowan," Seth

called as he levered his feet over the side of the cot he kept in the closet for emergencies.

"Thanks," Gowan grunted from the other room while Seth scrubbed his hands through his messy hair.

This wasn't the first time he'd been called on to sleep in the tiny cot, but that didn't mean he didn't always wake with a kink in his neck from the too-small accommodations. Seth pulled on his tunic, stretching his protesting muscles as he struggled to wake fully. Seth wandered into the larger outer chamber just as Gowan emerged from the small toilet room.

"How are you feeling?" Seth was sure to pitch his voice in low tones, well familiar with the symptoms of hangover.

"Like Gen sat on me. Twice." Gowan walked closer until he was standing in front of Seth. He held out his hand, and Seth took it in a warrior's handclasp. "Thank you for helping out last night. I would not enjoy being the butt of all jokes my first full day in the Lair."

"No problem. I've run afoul of Tercel's pranks a time or two myself." The handclasp ended, and each moved to lean casually against the countertops, facing each other. "Most of us who grew up here know his tricks and are smart enough to steer clear. When youngsters come in with fast flyers, they get warned, but a few of them usually end up embarrassed before Tercel subsides."

"The man is a menace," Gowan said with some feeling.

"I think he had it in for you especially, since you're—in essence—taking his job," Seth said. "There's been talk of retiring him after his leg heals, but he wants no part of it. He's cornered right now and feeling especially defensive, so just watch out for him. He's predisposed to not like you, simply because of your position. You're a direct threat to him."

"Great. And here I thought a sojourn at the Southern Lair was going to be easy duty."

Seth laughed outright at that. "We may be the Lair with the best scenery and the oldest knights, but it's still a Lair—with all the personalities and intrigue that implies."

"You grew up here?" Gowan asked.

"Yeah. My parents command second flight, so you'll be working with them."

"Have you a healing talent?" Gowan probed, and Seth's heart fell. He knew what was coming. He decided to head it off at the pass.

"No. I'm not even much of an apothecary. I apprenticed myself to Bronwyn, who is the real healer in this Lair, and like a grandmother to me. She was getting older and needed help, so I chose to fill that role rather than pursue fighting practice. As a result, I'm not really fit to be chosen as a knight. I'm not much of a fighter."

Gowan looked him up and down, appraisingly. "You could be. You've got the muscles for it, and the build. I could teach you. It's what I did before Gen came barreling into my life."

Seth shook his head. "Much like you, I do not wish to be the laughingstock of this Lair any more than I already have. They've all given up on me, and I prefer to leave it that way."

"I respect that, but I'm sure to have some free time once I learn my new duties, and you've done me a good turn here. I owe you. I would gladly train you in at least the basics—in secret, if you wish—so that you might have more options than you do at the moment."

"That was well done," Genlitha's voice sounded in Gowan's mind for the first time that morning. It was clear she'd been eavesdropping on him, which he didn't mind. He liked having her in his thoughts. It gave him an odd sort of comfort. *"I've been learning a great deal about Seth from Senneth and the other dragons. He is a good lad, but will never be the Lair's healer. He hasn't the gift for it, though he tries hard to help Bronwyn and does a credible job under her guidance. He should be a knight, but he holds himself back with his kind heart and compassion."*

It was good to have Genlitha's intel backing up Gowan's own observations. Seth's situation was something Gowan could do something about, given the opportunity.

"He has the look of a born fighter," Gowan told his dragon partner. *"It would be a waste for him to never learn how to use his true abilities."*

"Agreed. All the dragons I've spoken to think so too."

"Then we'll find a way," Gowan decided.

"It's very kind of you to offer, Sir Gowan," Seth said, unaware of the silent conversation Gowan had been having with his dragon partner.

"Don't say no. Not now. I probably won't have time to make good on my offer until I figure out my own duties, and by then, you might change your mind." Gowan could see his logic made the other man pause.

"Fair enough," Seth finally answered. "And thanks again for the offer. Now, I'm going to finish waking up, and then, I'll be happy to show you to the quarters you and Lady Genlitha have been assigned. I can give you the nickel tour along the way."

"Sounds like a plan."

CHAPTER FOUR

Gowan and Genlitha settled into the routine of the Southern Lair over the next week, learning their new roles as wing leaders to the first flight—the Lair's main fighting force. Gowan managed to steer clear of Tercel as much as possible, and he found a steady friend in Seth, when the apprentice healer's duties allowed him a little time off.

Speaking of which, Gowan had decided to go fishing on his first day off. He had walked down into Dragonscove, pausing in the marketplace to purchase some bait and new tackle. He also had bargained with one of the fishing boat owners to take him out past the breakers and let him cast his line alongside the professionals.

He'd been out on the water for a couple of hours, having a great time drowning bait and catching a few fish for tonight's pot when he saw something he never expected. A dragon. Emerging from the deep with a thrashing shark in his jaws.

A cheer went up from all the small fishing boats in the area as the dark-colored dragon chomped on the giant predator of the sea. Gowan had never seen the like.

"Gen?" he sent silently to his dragon partner. She'd decided to take some of the younger dragons with good wings out for a lesson in riding the strong air currents.

"Yes, Gowan?" she answered immediately.

"Do dragons like to...uh...fish?" He hadn't even considered that Gen might want to come along on his fishing trip. Had he been wrong not to invite her? There was still so much he didn't know about dragons.

"Not generally. Or, at least, not in the ocean. Give us a river or stream, and we can do pretty well spearing fish with our talons, but the sea is something different. Most of us aren't great swimmers. Why do you ask?"

He told her what he'd just seen, describing the scene in detail. She asked him to describe the color and look of the dragon and he answered all of her questions.

"That sounds like Hrardorr, a dragon I knew in my youth. They always said he had sea dragon in his lineage somewhere, but I never saw him swim, so I couldn't say for certain. But I know he's here, in this Lair, though he's been hiding from me for the past week."

"Hiding? Have you been stalking him?" Gowan asked with some amusement.

"A bit," Gen admitted. *"He was always a bit conceited, to be honest, but I had a crush on him when we were fledglings. His colors are striking, and he's a fierce fighter. Or, at least he was."* Her tone grew somewhat wistful. *"He was blinded fighting skiths on the border a while ago. He lost his knight, and they sent him here to recover. Seth's been looking after him, the dear boy."*

"I'm sorry, Gen." Gowan felt the sadness in his dragon partner's heart as if it was his own. *"If it's any consolation, he doesn't look blind to me. If this is your friend, Hrardorr, he's very able in the water, and the fishing fleet seems to adore him. They cheer him as a hero."*

"He is a hero," Gen insisted, her voice passionate in Gowan's mind.

Gowan followed the dragon's progress as he seemed to seek out one fishing boat in particular. It was a small sailboat with only one occupant. Gowan strained to see, realizing belatedly that the fisherman on that little boat was really a fisher*woman*. And she seemed to be having a conversation with the dragon as he floated near her little vessel.

They stayed that way for some time, the dragon keeping

company with the woman on the sailboat. Her mouth moved as she spoke to him, and from the animation in her gestures, it looked for all the world as if she were holding a conversation with the dragon. Which could only mean…she could hear him.

Gowan might not know everything there was to know about dragons, but he did know that being able to hear their silent speech was a rare gift. It was even rarer among women, for some reason. Which made the sight he was witnessing something to take note of. Especially as it looked like the woman was not from the Lair and all by herself in the little boat, and therefore, might possibly be single.

She was also beautiful, from what Gowan could see from this distance. But being able to hear dragons meant she was uniquely qualified to possibly…just possibly…be a candidate for becoming mate to a pair of knights. From all accounts, it made it easier for the woman to understand the unique relationship required if she could bespeak the dragons involved.

It was yet another thing Gowan didn't fully understand about his new status as a knight and partner to a dragon. But Gowan was of an age to want to find a wife and had queried Gen at length about the particular traits—if any—that he should look for while he was questing for a mate. He also knew that Gen could not take a mate until Gowan had found one.

Gowan asked the fishermen on the boat he was on about the fisherwoman and found out quite a bit. That she was a woman of means bothered him. Gowan had given up much in his life. His comfortable home as the son of a keep lord had been taken from him when his father died suddenly during a hunt and his eldest brother, Lorcan, became the new lord.

One of Lorcan's first acts as lord had been to kick Gowan out with nothing but a horse and a few pieces of silver in his pocket. Gowan had gone quietly for the sake of their mother, who had been torn between her two sons for a very long time.

Though he would have liked to have seen his mother, Gowan had never been back. He'd chosen his trade as a soldier, eventually working his way up into a leadership position where he led men into battle and trained them.

And then Genlitha had come along. She'd seen him teaching a class one day on the plain outside Castleton and had begun shadowing his movements. When she had started talking to him, Gowan had been startled, to say the least. He'd had no idea how dragons communicated, or that he had the special gift required to hear them.

It had taken a few days, but eventually, Genlitha had spoken the words of Claim to him, and his life had been changed forever. From that moment on, Gowan had become a dragon knight, God help them all.

But the woman who could talk to dragons... She fascinated him. Her name, he had learned from the fisherman, was Livia, and she was the only child of the most successful sea captain and trader in the town. She ran her father's various business interests while he was at sea, which seemed to be all the time now that his wife had passed. The fisherman seemed to respect and genuinely like her, which counted in her favor to Gowan's way of thinking.

"Yon dragon now, he's a newcomer. Strange one, but a good-hearted creature. Most from on high never come down to the sea, but he looks as if he were born to it," the fisherman observed as he and Gowan sat, watching the floating dragon and the small boat he sat next to in the water.

"They say he's part sea dragon," Gowan said carefully, not wanting to give away where he'd heard that from.

The fisherman only knew Gowan was new in town. He probably had no idea Gowan was a knight, which was how he preferred to keep it for now. It wasn't all that long ago that Gowan had just been a soldier. Nothing special about him, really. Becoming a knight had been one hell of an adjustment.

"Sea dragon, you say?" The fisherman looked at the distant dragon speculatively. "Aye, that would make sense. I saw a sea dragon once, you know, when I was a wee lad. Smaller than him yonder." The man nodded toward Sir Hrardorr. "But colored near the same. Maybe a bit more blue and green, but very close. 'Course, that sea dragon had no flame. This one, you can see smoke rise from his nose now and again, so I take that to mean he's got fire in his belly."

"You're probably right about that, aye," Gowan agreed good-naturedly. "But I've never seen a fighting dragon swim like him."

"Seen a lot of dragons, have ye?" The fisherman looked at Gowan speculatively, but with a friendly grin.

The fisherman was fishing for information, but Gowan didn't mind. It was natural to want to know about a newcomer.

"I came here from Castleton. There are scores of dragons there," Gowan hedged. "I've seen a few fishing in the river, but none ever swam that I saw."

"Rivers be different than sea," the fisherman observed.

"Fishing's different too," Gowan said, trying to redirect the conversation. "I've done all my fishing to this point on rivers."

"Oh, aye," the fisherman agreed, going on at some length about all the different kinds of fish that could be had from the sea. "And there are worse predators," he said, gesturing broadly as he frowned. "Shark, giant squid and the like. The dragon lord, though, he's made things safer and more profitable for us of late. The warm weather this year has brought more predators closer to shore than usual, but ol' dragon there has been evening the odds for us. Quite a sight it is to see him chewing on a four-yard shark, too. Better than a tavern show!" The old fisherman grinned, chuckling a bit as they both looked at the dragon, still sitting docilely on top of the light waves, apparently chatting with the girl on the boat next to him.

"He brought up a giant squid yesterday," the fisherman went on. "Never saw the like. It was still wriggling. That dragon must be able to dive deep. Such creatures live in the darkest fathoms. The only time we ever see them is if one shows up in a net, already dead. Usually in pieces, with teeth marks on 'em. Ain't never seen one still alive before. But it weren't for long." The fisherman cackled with something like glee.

Gowan was impressed at what he was learning about the dragon known as Hrardorr. Genlitha had been surprisingly tight-lipped about the male dragon, though she had admitted to having a crush on the brute when they were still youngsters. Gowan wondered privately if there was more to it. Maybe Gen still held feelings for Hrardorr. Maybe, if the stars aligned and the Mother of All blessed them, Hrardorr might turn out to be Genlitha's mate.

Of course, that would mean Gowan had to find one first before Gen could consummate a union with whatever dragon turned out to be her match. And whoever that unknown dragon's knight was would be the man with whom Gowan was supposed to share his mate.

Gowan scratched the back of his neck, still uncertain as to how that was supposed to work. He'd never really been exposed to the three-way relationships that were the norm in dragon Lairs. Knights and their problems were about as far removed from Gowan's old life as a simple soldier as the stars were from the ocean he found himself fishing that day.

Feeling a telltale tug on his line, Gowan set to work reeling in the fish who had taken his bait. The fisherman wandered off to check his own gear, and only the lap of the waves against the hull of the wooden boat and the occasional splash could be heard for a long time.

When they'd caught enough fish for the day, the fisherman turned his boat toward the shore, and Gowan helped the man clean up and prepare the small vessel for the next day. It was only polite. And Gowan liked the guy, rough as he was.

The sea-colored dragon and the girl were still out fishing, so Gowan calculated that he could make it to the Lair—to drop off his catch and clean up a bit—and back, to see if he could accidentally-on purpose run into the lady. He wanted to meet her. It was like a compulsion in his blood. He didn't really understand it, except that she intrigued him on every level.

When Hrardorr took off, winging his way back toward the Lair, Livia headed her little sailboat toward home. She would dock at the pier near the marketplace where her father's offices were. There was something she wanted to check before she went home for the night, even though she'd given herself the day off to fish.

She'd been doing that more often since she'd made friends with Hrardorr. She enjoyed his company, and she thought he enjoyed hers as well. He came down from the Lair to fish most days, but she could only spare a day or two each week to goof off in her sailboat. The weekends were hers, though, and she spent those two days with her new dragon friend. All in all, that meant she'd been spending three or four days out of every seven with Hrardorr for the past few weeks.

If she had her way, she'd do that for as long as possible. She really liked spending time with the dragon. He wasn't like any other being she'd ever met. He didn't judge her by the same standards humans applied. Her father's business meant nothing to him. Her wealth didn't impress him. And her social standing didn't matter in the slightest. Which was very freeing to a woman who had spent all of her life being weighed and measured like the stacks of coins in her father's safe.

The day seemed a little darker now that Hrardorr had left. It always felt that way when he took off for the Lair. He made her world a little brighter when he was near her. She didn't question why that was. He was a dragon, after all. They were magic personified, in her opinion. Of course she would miss him when he left each day they were together.

She maneuvered her boat next to the dock and got help from a young boy just waiting to earn a copper for catching her lines. He helped her tie up and agreed to take her catch of fish up to her housekeeper for an extra coin. Livia knew the boy and had hired him to do this same thing on a few other occasions, so she knew her fish would make it to her home—and that her housekeeper would give the boy a decent meal before she let him leave.

Livia smiled as she headed for her father's office in the marketplace. She paused by a public fountain to rinse her hands and tidy up a bit before heading to make her final stop on the way to the office.

Liam's pie stand served everything from sweets to savories and had the tastiest pocket pies in town. He had a market stall close to her father's building, and she wanted to stop by and get a snack before heading into the office.

"That looks good." A deep male voice came from over her shoulder as Liam placed the pocket pie—a creation of meat, onions and spices baked inside a flaky pie crust—in front of her.

She looked back to find the owner of the voice and nearly did a double take. He was handsome. And tall. Exceedingly tall…and handsome. And did she mention handsome?

"Liam makes the best pies in Dragonscove," she answered, knowing she needed to say something and feeling at a bit of a loss when confronted by such a specimen of manhood.

She slid the coin for her pie over the counter while the man behind her placed his order for the same thing she was having. He was affable and polite to Liam, which spoke well of his manners, and he moved back just enough for her to pass when she picked up her pie and headed for the little pots of sauces Liam kept farther down the counter for those who liked to add a little zest to their purchase.

The man joined her by the sauces, a few moments later, with his own pie. He looked over the selections but didn't move to take any of the spoons that were in the various pots.

"What do you recommend?" he asked her, striking up conversation again.

"The red sauce is hot. The orange sweet. The yellow is

primarily mustard seed with dill. The brown is beef gravy. Any of those would go well with what you ordered," she offered.

She noticed he picked two of the sauces and placed a cautious dollop of each on the edge of his plate. A discerning man, then. Not one to jump in blind with both feet. He was more cautious than that.

When Livia took a seat at one of the wooden tables Liam kept for his customers in front of the stall, the man followed. He held his plate in his hand, waiting until she looked up at him.

"I know this is very forward, but may I sit with you? I promise I am not some random stranger. I'm actually from the Lair and on my first day off in a strange town. I'm only recently arrived." He managed to look harmless, which was quite a feat for someone of his size and build. He was clearly a soldier of some sort—probably a knight, if he truly was from the Lair. "My name is Gowan Hunter, youngest son of Lord Dariath Hunter of Hunt's Keep along the River Arundelle."

"Impressive pedigree," she nodded, having heard such things from suitors in the past. Suddenly, the man was a little less interesting. "If it's true," she muttered.

He had the grace to look sheepish. "It's true, though I rarely use any of that anymore. Forgive me, I made assumptions knowing you were a gentle lady."

"I may have been born to a life of ease, but I am not noble," she protested.

"Truthfully, none of that matters to me. I left home long ago and have lived the life of a simple soldier for many years."

He was still standing there, holding his plate as his pie cooled. She took pity and gestured toward the seat opposite her, across the wooden plank table. He sat, placing his plate in front of him.

"I'm Livia," she introduced herself as he sat down. "Something tells me that you are no longer such a simple soldier though," she said, before biting into her pie.

He smiled somewhat ruefully. "My life has taken some strange turns of late. One minute, I was training a company on the plain outside of Castleton. The next, a pretty blue dragon landed beside me and struck up a conversation. My life has not been the same since."

"There was talk of a light blue dragon arriving recently," Livia offered, still unsure if this man was for real, or just a spinner of tales.

"That would be Gen. Lady Genlitha, if you want to be formal. She trained here as a young dragon, and we were sent to take over for an injured knight while he recovers. We are learning our way as a new partnership, as well, before heading into battle. I hope." He added that last little bit almost under his breath, but she heard it.

"You wish to join the fighting in the north?"

"We both want to do what we can to keep our land safe," he replied carefully. "I do not revel in bloodshed. I have seen enough of it in my time." His eyes took on a weary cast that made her heart go out to him. "Forgive me, I didn't mean to stray into such dark waters."

They ate in silence for a few moments.

"The gravy is a nice complement to the flavor," he said a short while later, clearly wanting to change the subject.

She nodded, still unsure of him. Was he a fortune hunter, simply trying a new tack with her? She'd seen it all in recent years. Without her father here a lot of the time, she'd had to learn how to fend off unwanted attentions from scoundrels who thought to marry her and live off her father's money.

"If you're a knight, where is your dragon?" she asked, speaking her mind bluntly. It may not be polite, but she'd learned how to come to the point since running her father's businesses in his absence.

Gowan chuckled. "She is teaching some of the younger fliers today while I went fishing."

"Fishing?"

He nodded. "Yes, milady. I saw you out there with your

dragon friend. I was duly impressed by him. Sir Hrardorr, wasn't it?"

"He doesn't like people from the Lair to study him," she said carefully, not sure what her dragon friend would make of this. Perhaps it would be best not to tell him.

"He's been avoiding Genlitha. She knew him when they were both youngsters. I think her feelings are hurt that he refuses to stand still long enough for her to say hello."

"He's still healing. He doesn't like people to make a fuss," she hedged.

"People, I can understand. I don't much like being fussed over when I'm hurt either, but his fellow dragons?" His voice dropped to a lower, more intimate level. "Is it because he's blind? Does it bother him that much?"

Livia didn't answer. Few, if any, in town knew of Hrardorr's handicap. She didn't think it was her place to talk about it, so she remained silent. She didn't really know this man. She didn't know what his game was, but she refused to betray her new friend, Hrardorr, in any way.

"I cannot say," she said finally, hopefully putting an end to this line of conversation.

Gowan sat back and regarded her. She held his gaze, refusing to give in. Finally, he shrugged.

"I can respect that. You don't know me. We've only just met." He leaned back, looking upward. "But maybe seeing Gen will help you believe me just a little bit."

He pointed upward, and she followed his finger with her gaze, seeing a flight of dragons circling high above. There was an almost invisible sky blue dragon in the lead, several other colorful youngsters behind her.

"Lady Livia?" A strange, rumbly, yet somehow feminine voice sounded in her mind. Was it the dragon? *"Can you hear me?"*

"Yes," she whispered, still looking upward, hoping her words would communicate silently to the dragon high above—if that was who was talking to her.

"Fabulous!" came the feminine rumble in her mind again.

Apparently her reply had gotten through. *"I am Genlitha, and you have met my knight, Gowan. He asked me to communicate with you for two reasons. First, he wanted to see if you could, indeed, hear me. Second, he wanted to provide you with some proof that he really was who he claimed to be. I can assure you, he is a knight, though he is newly chosen and knows little of our ways. He is still learning, which is why we were assigned here—to both teach and learn. I'm teaching these youngsters, and he's learning how to be a knight. We're also learning how to be a team. It takes time when a new pairing is formed."*

"Amazing," Livia breathed.

"Yes, she is," Gowan said softly, drawing Livia's attention from the sky, back down to earth and the man who was sitting opposite her. Gowan was smiling at her, but she wasn't as easy to impress as he thought—or at least, she didn't want to appear that way.

"All right. I believe you are who you claim to be." She shot him a narrow-eyed look. "But you are not the first person from the Lair I've met, and you likely won't be the last."

"Ouch." He winced, smiling broadly. "I see I will have to work harder to earn your regard. Good. I like a challenge."

CHAPTER FIVE

Livia allowed Gowan to walk her to the door of her father's offices, and he left her with a kiss on her hand. It was a courtly gesture from his youth at the keep that just seemed right in this particular situation, though why that was so, he wasn't sure.

He only knew that she seemed to bring out the gallant in him, and making her smile made him feel good. So good, in fact, that he whistled a jaunty tune all the way back to the Lair.

He was happy because she'd agreed to see him again. They'd made a date for the weekend, and he was looking forward to it with a great deal of enthusiasm. If he'd paused to ask himself why he was so excited to be seeing this young woman, he couldn't have answered. There was just something about her. Something unlike any other woman he'd ever met.

She drew him like a loadstone. Her smile made him want to be around her. And her wit challenged him in ways he hadn't known he liked to be challenged. She was the full picture. The kind of woman a man could get serious about and consider spending the rest of his life with.

And the very fact that such thoughts didn't have him running in the other direction was surprising as well. Gowan had known that he would need to start searching for a mate because of Genlitha. It would be unfair to his dragon if she had a mate she could never claim because he couldn't get off his ass and find a woman to share his life. He'd known that academically, but he'd always shied away from commitment before. Frankly, he hadn't been sure he'd be able to adjust his thinking so radically, or so quickly, but it seemed meeting the right woman made all the difference.

When he returned to the Lair, Gowan retrieved his fish from the cool water chamber in which he'd stored them temporarily. He'd been taking all his meals in the great hall with everyone else, but the rooms he and Gen had been assigned had a small, serviceable kitchen. Tonight, he would eat the fruit of his labors and spend time with his dragon. They'd been either working or off on their own since they'd arrived, and he missed just spending time with Genlitha, he was surprised to note.

Gowan cooked the fish and knew Gen had stopped to feed with her small class of young fliers. When she arrived back to their suite of rooms, she went directly to the giant sand pit in the center of the suite, around which everything else had been designed. The sand was warm—heated magically from below, somehow—and sized perfectly for a single dragon. The rest of the circular cavern held chambers for various needs of the human half of the partnership.

There was a bathing chamber, a kitchen, storage rooms, closets, and of course, a bedroom. The quarters for single knights and their dragons were said to be more utilitarian than those designed for families. For one thing, the sand wallow would be double the size to accommodate two dragons and perhaps one or two offspring. The rooms circling the wallow were also larger and more plentiful, for the human side of the family.

Gowan was in the kitchen, cooking his fish when he heard a voice in the outer chamber. He poked his head out and saw Seth standing behind Gen on the edge of the sand pit, looking at her wing. Concerned, Gowan took the hot pan off the flame and went out to see what was going on. He wiped his hands on a towel as he went out into the main chamber.

"What's wrong?" he asked, approaching Seth from behind.

The other man turned his head, keeping his hands on Gen's wing joint, just where the wing met her torso.

"Lady Genlitha asked me to bring some liniment. She may have strained her right wing during maneuvers today," Seth explained, continuing his examination.

"Gen? Are you hurt?" Gowan asked silently, frowning as he walked around to catch Genlitha's eye.

"It's sore," she admitted, somewhat reluctantly. *"I guess I was showing off a bit and over extended. I hope you don't mind that I asked Seth for help. Normally, this is something you could do for me, but you need to learn how, and Bronwyn said Seth was doing all this kind of work for her now that her hands are too gnarled to do it properly."*

"I don't mind at all, Gen. Anything that helps me learn how to help you is all right in my book. I'm just sorry I don't know all these things already. You would have been better off choosing a partner who had grown up around dragons, like Seth."

"Seth will be an excellent knight..." Gen surprised him by saying, *"...but he's not for me. You're the man meant to fight by my side, Gowan. Don't worry. You'll learn. And I'll learn how to partner you as well. I've never had such an able soldier as my partner before. It will be fun to learn how to fight and fly with you so that we make the best possible team."*

"I look forward to that too, milady. Now, I'm going to find out how to tend your sore muscles from Seth here, and please sing out if I do anything wrong. It's been a long time since I was a student, but I'm very willing to learn." Gowan had to hide his smile as he returned to Seth's side and spoke aloud to the other man. "I'm not well-versed in dragon keeping, as you know. Would you mind showing me what to look for and what to do to help her?"

Seth smiled up at Gowan as he manipulated the large muscle that joined wing to body. "I'm glad to show you. It's not all that much different from our own muscles, just on a much larger scale."

What followed was an hour of intense study of dragon musculature. Seth was a thorough teacher, and he showed

Gowan how to check the muscles for integrity as well as the best method for massage and application of soothing salves.

Gowan managed to surprise Seth a time or two by recognizing the herbal scents in the salves and their uses too. They got to talking, and Gowan mentioned how his mother had run the stillroom in the keep and how Gowan had helped her gather and prepare medicinal herbs from the time he was a young boy.

By the time they were finished tending to Genlitha's strained wing, Gowan had invited Seth to join him for dinner, since the meal in the great hall was pretty much over. Plus, Gowan had caught plenty of fish and had more than enough to share. He went back to cooking, picking up where he'd left off, and soon, dinner was ready.

"You caught all this yourself?" Seth asked when he saw the bounty of fried fish on the table in front of him.

"I had a good day on the water," Gowan said modestly.

The more Seth was around the new knight, the more he liked him. Gowan was willing to learn how to treat Genlitha's minor injuries and had paid more attention to Seth's instructions than he was used to getting from knights in this Lair, most of whom didn't take him seriously or saw him as a failure. Or both.

But not Gowan. He freely admitted his own shortcomings when it came to knowledge of dragons and Lair life. He was a willing student, though he was obviously a seasoned warrior.

"Where did you learn to fish?" Seth asked as they served themselves and dug in to the succulent fish.

"Oh, I've been fishing since I was a boy. My father's lands ran alongside the River Arundelle on one side, so there was ample opportunity. It's very relaxing, and I try to get out on the water whenever I can. Sea fishing is quite different from what I'm used to, though. Different creatures and deeper waters."

They ate in silence for a while, but it wasn't uncomfortable at all. Gowan was easy to be around. He seemed to have no preexisting ideas about what or who Seth should be, which was refreshing. So much of his life in this Lair had been spent trying to justify his decisions. It was nice to be around someone who didn't judge him—at least not openly. If Gowan had any opinions about the choices Seth had made in his life, he kept them politely to himself.

"So you come from nobility, then?" Seth asked sometime later.

Gowan took a sip of the ale he'd served alongside the fish before answering. "I'm the youngest son of a lord. When my father died, my brother kicked me out with little to call my own. Noble birth doesn't mean much when you've got nothing to back it up. I started soldiering and have been on that path ever since." He paused a moment, the mug of beer halfway to his lips. "Until Genlitha showed up. She took me in a whole new direction, and I still have a lot to learn about how to be a knight."

"You're doing very well for a newcomer to dragons," Seth said honestly. "Even some of the men who grew up here had a hard time adjusting to their dragon partners when they were newly chosen. But you and Genlitha..." Seth looked out the archway that led to the central sand wallow where the dragon rested. "Your partnership looks to be one of those that was always meant to be. Easy. Pure. Natural. I doubt it will take you long to get accustomed to your new role. You were already a veteran fighter and leader of men. All you have to learn is how to be that with a dragon under you and in your mind."

"Oh, is that all?" Gowan laughed, and Seth joined him. Seth liked the other man's wry sense of humor.

Gowan drained his mug and poured a bit more for both of them. He sat across from Seth, regarding him steadily.

"Speaking of fighting..." Gowan began.

"Oh, no." Seth held his hands up, palms outward. He thought he knew what was coming next, and though one part of him wanted to jump at the chance to learn from this seasoned warrior, another part was adamant that he stick to the path he'd chosen to help Bronwyn.

Was it fear that held him back? That one thought made Seth pause. He hadn't thought he was afraid of anything. He'd thought he was being noble. But what if his refusal to train with the fighters was more due to fear than respect for Bronwyn and the choice he'd made so long ago?

What if he feared being chosen by a dragon? Or *not* chosen?

Fear of either outcome was unacceptable to a man who had always prided himself on honesty—with others, but especially with himself. Was he being honest with himself? Or willfully blind?

"Hear me out, Seth," Gowan went on, quietly overcoming Seth's objections. Though Seth wasn't really objecting anymore. His own thoughts troubled him enough to make him listen to Gowan's proposal.

"I'm listening." It wasn't exactly a gracious response, but it wasn't an outright refusal.

"I need to learn dragon and knight things, and from what I see, you could use some tutoring in the art of war. I propose an equal exchange of information. You teach me, and I teach you in return." Gowan seemed to warm to his subject when Seth didn't interrupt. "Neither of us want to be seen as needing remedial help. I don't think it would help either of our reputations for every busybody in this Lair to know what we were doing, right? So I think we should meet here of an evening—say, every third or fourth day—to train. What say you?"

Seth sat back in his chair, really thinking about it. He wanted to help Gowan learn the things he would have known had he grown up in a Lair. He and Genlitha had been dumped into a position of authority that would put strain on them both until they became a more streamlined team. Seth knew he could help them become better acquainted with each other. He really wanted to help them.

By the same token, Seth had regretted giving up weapons training all those years ago, but he'd been made so uncomfortable by the other boys when he'd apprenticed himself to Bronwyn that it hadn't been worth the hassle. The knights who taught the classes were especially tough on Seth—especially after he'd gone to work with Bronwyn—and there was no real incentive to continue to train.

Still, he missed it. He'd been pretty good for his age and one or two of the knights had unbent enough to give him praise now and again. His hand missed the feel of a sword.

"I'm willing to give it a try," Seth said with surprisingly little hesitation, once he'd made up his mind.

Gowan smiled and raised his mug. "Excellent. Now, you've already given me my lesson on how to care for Genlitha, so how about we work for an hour or so later tonight, after we've had a chance to digest some of this meal? It isn't ideal to fight on a full stomach, though when the alarm goes up, you don't always have the choice."

"I have a few things I need to do," Seth said, already rising to place his empty plate in the sink. "I need to check on Hrardorr and make sure he has everything he needs for the night, but I can return in an hour, if that's suitable."

"Perfect," Gowan said, his eyes shuttered as if he was considering something. Seth could see the moment he decided to speak his mind. "You know, I saw Hrardorr out there on the water today. He was fishing for shark, and he caught a huge one. It was very impressive."

"I don't think he'd be comfortable knowing a knight was watching him," Seth said, worried about how Hrardorr would react. The dragon was touchy about certain things.

"Yeah, I figured as much. Which is why I didn't say anything to him. I only mention it to you because it seems like you have a special relationship with him. He is a magnificent dragon, and from what I saw, his blindness doesn't hold him back in the water. If I hadn't known of his injury, I would never have guessed."

"That's good to hear." Seth paused in scrubbing his plate. "I look in on him each night. He is much better than he was, but Bronwyn doesn't believe his sight will ever return. He is not happy about it and unwilling to mingle with the rest of the dragons in the Lair. He thinks they'll pity him, and he doesn't want that above all."

"Genlitha knew him when they were young and has been trying to see him, but it's like he's been hiding," Gowan admitted, scratching his head.

"I wouldn't be surprised if he has," Seth admitted. "He knows she's here, and he remembers her. He's asked me about her, and about you. He's curious, but I think he's afraid of what she will think of him now."

"Between you and me, I think there was some attraction there, between them, when they were younger," Gowan mused. "I wonder if that's not part of the reason he's hiding from her?"

"Possibly, but he's been hiding from just about everyone since he got here. It could be just that he doesn't want to be around other dragons at the moment." Seth sighed. "He lost his knight. It was a fairly new pairing, so I'm not sure how badly he's taken the loss, though he's definitely in some state of mourning. If he hadn't been so badly injured, I think he would have sought refuge in a mountain cave, away from everyone and everything for a while. As it is, he's trying to be alone in a Lair full of dragons and knights. I'm actually impressed that he's mostly succeeding."

"Except with you," Gowan said quietly. "I know the depth of the bond with Genlitha now, and I wouldn't discount how hurt he must have been when his knight was killed, even with a new bonding. I know if something happened to Gen right now—new as we are as a team—I would never be the same." Gowan looked out into the wallow where his dragon partner was sleeping. She had really stretched her wings today. "I think she'd probably say the same thing."

It hit Seth, then, how much Hrardorr must be hurting. He'd thought he'd understood, having grown up around dragons and knights, but just seeing the look in Gowan's eyes as he gazed at his dragon... It drove it home how quickly the bond was forged in some cases, and how deeply.

"What can I do to help him?" Seth whispered. He felt so badly for Hrardorr. He was a good dragon at heart and had been a hero of his Lair. He'd been one of the best they had in all the land, and now, he was a mere shadow of himself. Seth wished he could fix it. Fix him.

"Just be his friend. Do what you have been doing. It's not good for a dragon to be so alone. I know they like to get all dramatic and live in mountain caves like hermits at times, but everything I've learned from Gen tells me they are really social creatures, like us. They need friends. Hrardorr needs you, Seth. Be his friend."

"I am," Seth said without thinking. He firmed his resolve to make Hrardorr talk to him more. "I will be his best friend."

"Good man," Gowan said softly, praising Seth's determination.

They were united in purpose at that moment, and for the first time in his life, Seth got a glimpse of what it might have been like to be among knights like Gowan. It would have felt a little like this, he imagined, to be one of their number.

They finished their meal, and Seth went to check on Hrardorr. He didn't rush his tasks. In fact, he took extra time with the male dragon, trying to draw him into conversation, but Hrardorr was taciturn, as always. Still, Seth took heart. He would work on Hrardorr. It would take time, but he was resolved to do as Gowan had suggested.

And then, he was back to Gowan's chamber to keep up the other end of the bargain they had struck. In the couple of hours between the end of their shared evening meal and Seth's return to the suite of rooms Gowan shared with Genlitha, the knight had been busy. He'd cleared one of the many side chambers of all obstacles and had added a few things Seth remembered from his early years, training in fighting with the younger boys in the Lair.

Soft mats covered one section of the large room. A couple of practice swords made out of wood with blunted edges were lined up along the wall, along with wooden fighting sticks of various lengths. Lances and pikes—all with blunted tips—were also in the space, as were bits of light armor used for sparring.

"Did you raid the armory while I was gone?" Seth asked with a laugh, looking around the room and taking it all in.

"Something like that," Gowan admitted. "I was discreet about it. I don't think anyone saw me take these things. They were in a dark corner, so I don't think they'll be missed. It looked like the smaller stuff was all in use, but the man-sized bits were covered in dust. From that, I surmise they don't get a lot of full-grown knight trainees here, eh?"

"Not the ones who don't already know how to fight," Seth agreed. "Like you. You were already a warrior, so you don't need this stuff to learn with. What you need is what we have in plenty—tricky wind currents for you to learn to fly with your partner as if born to it. Those are the kind of human trainees we get here, for the most part. And young dragons with excellent wings but a need to learn how to use them."

"Gen was sent here as a youngster for just that reason," Gowan observed as he hefted a practice sword and tested it for balance.

Seth wanted to do the same, but he didn't know what to look for in a blade. Not anymore. Maybe once, when he'd been a lad, he had been learning such skills, but he'd given it all up...

But maybe this was a second chance for him. Maybe he'd learn the things he should have known—if he hadn't made the decision to support Bronwyn instead. He would never hurt her by leaving her side, but he figured it couldn't hurt to learn how to fight. He went down into the Dragonscove often enough that knowing how to defend himself wouldn't be such a bad thing. And, if he was honest, he wanted to know. He *thirsted* to know. It was as if it was a need, deep inside him, that had never been satisfied.

"There's a lot of talk about her already," Seth said, putting aside his thoughts of fighting glory in favor of talking about Gowan's dragon partner. "The older dragons were watching her fly and teach. They say she has a gift for teaching, and all who saw her today approved of her approach with the youngsters. If you're not careful, they may just station you both here permanently."

"Would that be such a bad thing?" Gowan asked, surprising Seth.

He'd thought Gowan was more a man of action. He'd thought Gowan would want to be in the thick of the fighting up north, not stuck down here where nothing ever happened, teaching. Worse—he wasn't really needed for teaching, only his dragon. He'd be rusticating. Fishing. Or whatever else he liked to do in his free time.

Then Seth saw the teasing light in Gowan's eyes.

"You almost had me there," Seth said good-naturedly, laughing along with the knight.

"Not that I mind the sojourn here," Gowan was quick to add. "I know as well as anyone that I have a lot to learn as a knight. I need to be a better partner to Genlitha before we go taking on the enemy for real. If she can do some good with the young dragons while I learn how to be a knight, so much the better, but ultimately, we're going to be fighting, and I need to make sure we're both as ready as possible when our time comes."

Seth caught Gowan's eye, the mood having turned serious. "Then I vow to teach you all I know of dragon craft so that someday in the far future, when you have grown old, you can come back to this Lair and retire to go fishing and watch the waves roll onto the shore."

They both knew he meant that as a good fate—where neither Gowan nor Genlitha was killed in battle.

Gowan nodded with respect. "And I vow to teach you all I can in the time we have together, starting with what to look for in a blade…even a wooden one."

Gowan threw one of the practice swords to Seth and then commenced the lesson. He showed Seth how to check for balance and the trueness of the blade, what weight would be right for his size and ability and so forth. It was an eye-opening hour of verbal instruction that Seth hadn't expected before they ever started swinging the wooden swords.

Even then, Gowan had him go through his paces alone. They weren't fighting against each other at all. Gowan taught Seth a dance of sorts. It was a series of movements with the blade, taking it through a variety of slashes, strikes and even blocks. He made Seth repeat the movements in a specific order, over and over, until he knew it by heart. Then he tasked Seth with practicing that series of movements whenever he could over the next days, until they met again.

They set up a schedule of sorts, working around both of their schedules, so they could trade knowledge on a more or less steady basis. Seth's head was full of the lesson he'd just received as he left, and he was already looking forward to two days hence, when they would do it again.

CHAPTER SIX

Livia was fishing again, scanning the skies for Hrardorr. She'd been fishing more and more of late, keeping the dragon company. Her heart went out to him. He seemed so lonely.

But he was better when he was in the water. She just knew it. She may not have access to him on land, but he was always melancholy until he had swum a bit and caught something tasty to nibble on. Usually a shark, but occasionally another sort of predator, or even an entire school of fish.

He only hunted the smaller fish on days when the town's fishing fleet was elsewhere. He was wise enough not to anger the fishermen by eating their catch right in front of them.

Suddenly, there was a disturbance in the water off the port side of her boat. A second later, Hrardorr's head broke the surface, followed by the rest of him. He'd snuck up on her.

"Good morning, Sir Hrardorr," she said with a grin. She couldn't help but be charmed by his expression. "You just took ten years off my life with your stealthy ways," she declared, laughing out loud so he would know that she was teasing him.

Little curls of smoke wafted upward from his nostrils. Dragonish amusement. He couldn't quite smile—not with all those teeth—but his expression came as close as it could to joy, and it made her heart feel lighter.

"I am practicing," he declared.

"Practicing for what?"

"Good question." He seemed to sigh, a billow of hot air wafting into her sail, driving her little boat slightly away from him.

"Oy," she called out, working to lower the sail. "Give me a minute to put the sail down before you start blowing me all over the place."

"Apologies." He moved his head about, as if looking for her.

It was then that she realized he couldn't see above water. He couldn't actually *see* in the water, for that matter, but his other senses compensated to let him know, with incredible accuracy, what was around him under the waves. Up here, in the air, he was still blind. That thought made her sad, and sorry that she'd drawn attention to his disability.

"No problem, but if you'll paddle about three ship lengths to your left, you'll find me again. I've lowered the sail, so no danger of setting me off again." She tried to inject calm competence into her voice.

"Again, my apologies, mistress. I did not know your vessel was powered by sail. I will be more careful in future."

"Oh, so you thought maybe I had a crew of scantily clad slave boys in the hold ready to row me wherever I wish to go?" She tried for a joke, already knowing that nothing she could say would truly shock the dragon.

"In a vessel so small, they would have to be very tiny," he observed wryly.

"Alas, slavery is properly illegal in this land. Good thing I don't have a taste for slave boys, then, I suppose." She sighed wistfully, prolonging the gag. "Of course, some scantily clad men wouldn't be bad to have around, if they were fit and easy on the eyes."

"You females are all the same, no matter the species," Hrardorr complained. *"You just want males to see to your whims and look decorative."*

"Funny. That's what I thought most males wanted in their

females. Sadly, all my suitors have been gravely disappointed in me on that score." She laughed, but even she could hear the slight bitterness in her tone.

"Why aren't you already mated, Livia?" Hrardorr asked suddenly, a hint of paternal concern in his voice she never would have expected from the dragon.

"I guess I haven't found the right man yet," she admitted. "Though I have tried a few on for size." She laughed, having admitted something to the dragon that she never would have said aloud to anyone else. Hrardorr was good at keeping her confidences. "What about you? Where is your dragoness?"

It was a good thing she had lowered the sail because Hrardorr sighed again. *"There was a pretty young dragoness when I was just starting out, but we both had some growing to do before we could act on our attraction. I fear she is lost to me now that I am...useless."*

Another sigh, wafting cinnamon-scented hot air over her. It was kind of pleasant, though the emotion he was expressing gave her pause. Her heart broke on a nearly daily basis for Hrardorr.

"Never say that again. You are *not* useless. Ask any fisherman in this harbor. In the short time you have been fishing here, you've made this place safer for everyone, and much more productive. Poor families can feed their children because of you, where before they would have subsisted on scraps. You've made an impact here that you don't even realize."

Hrardorr's sightless eyes narrowed in thought, but he said nothing.

"Now, tell me about your dragoness. I bet she was very beautiful," Livia coaxed, hoping to lighten the subject.

"She was. She is," he corrected himself. *"She's here, in fact, but I've been avoiding her. I don't want Genlitha to see me as I am...now."*

"Oh, I've seen her. Sky blue and gray. She fades into the sky and flies like a dream," Livia enthused, ignoring, for the moment, Hrardorr's admission that he'd been hiding from the dragoness. "I met her knight too. Gowan is his name. In fact, I have a date with him on the weekend."

"Do tell," Hrardorr said, sounding both surprised and impressed. *"I didn't know Sir Gowan had come down to the town at all, much less had time to make a date with the prettiest girl in it."*

"You're a charmer, Sir Hrardorr," she replied in a teasing tone, liking the way he had become so familiar with her over the past days. They were friends now, she thought. This giant blind dragon was more her friend than anyone she could remember in her life. Now wasn't that a surprising thought?

"Apparently so is Sir Gowan, if he got you to agree to go out with him so quickly."

"Alas, you're right. He is very charming. The youngest son of a northern lord, if such things matter to you. He has very nice manners, but he is not snobbish, which I like very much. He is also handsome and someone I wouldn't mind seeing in the aforementioned scanty slave boy attire." She knew she was blushing, but Hrardorr couldn't see it. He could probably sense it, though. He was very perceptive. "Of course, he's no *boy.* The man has muscles on top of his muscles, and he's tall. Very, very tall. And a warrior, I have no doubt. He holds himself as if nothing could ever harm him—as if arrows wouldn't dare touch him, but merely bounce off."

She laughed at her own description, but Hrardorr had grown quieter.

"Arrows don't bounce," he said softly in her mind.

"Oh, Hrardorr. I'm sorry. I didn't mean—"

"It's all right." He sighed yet again. It seemed to be a day full of sighs. *"I miss my last knight. His name was Theo. He was a good lad, but he didn't stand much of a chance in that last battle. Neither did I. We both knew the chance of our survival was minimal, but we had no choice."*

"Why was there no choice?" she asked quietly. Respectfully. She wouldn't push too much, but she knew he needed to talk this out with someone. Anyone. She hoped he would allow it to be her.

"A town full of innocent people were pinned down by skiths and a battalion of enemy troops. We were alone on patrol when we saw it. There was no time to waste. We sent word back to the Lair, but knew

they would not arrive in time. We talked it over for just a few seconds, but we both knew what we had to do. I dove for the skiths while Theo hung on for dear life. He was an archer, and he was able to get off a number of kill shots at the enemy commanders during my flame runs. Eventually, though, the enemy archers were all focused on him. Their bolts bounced off my scales for the most part—all except for the special ones that were tipped in diamond. I got sliced up pretty bad, and it affected my flying. And then, Theo got hit multiple times, and we both tumbled to the ground. We still fought on the ground, but there were too many skiths. I'd crash-landed in the midst of them. I flamed and flamed until my flame gave out and their acid hit me over and over..."

Livia wished she could reach out and hug him. Tears flowed down her face at his words. Tears for the loss he had suffered and the noble sacrifice he had made.

"I felt Theo die, and then, I lost consciousness. They told me later that it was only seconds later that help arrived from the Lair. A whole wing of fighters took out the remaining skiths, and the knights and dragons of the Border Lair pushed the enemy back, saving the town."

"You saved the town, Hrardorr," she said, knowing he could probably hear the tears in her voice. "You and Sir Theo, stars bless his soul."

"He was a selfless boy who would have grown into a great knight, had he been given the chance," Hrardorr agreed.

"He already was a great knight," she insisted. "And he should be remembered for his heroic deeds and willingness to put himself in the path of danger for the sake of innocents."

"The townsfolk honored his name and created a shrine where he is buried. They promised me they would remember him and offer prayers to thank him for his sacrifice."

Was it possible for dragons to cry? If so, Livia believed Hrardorr would be weeping right along with her. Regardless, she wept for him. And for poor Theo.

"They sound like good people, worthy of your sacrifice," she said softly, wiping her eyes and nose on a hankie.

"There was a monastery at the heart of the town. The monks there took me in and allowed me to stay while I was healing. My wings were so torn up I couldn't fly. It took a month or more before I was able to get

myself back to the Lair. But I couldn't stay there. I couldn't face the rooms where Theo and I had once lived. I chose to come here because I knew I couldn't be left on my own, as I wished. I need help now. Out of the water, I am useless."

"I told you not to say that," she chastised him in a weak voice.

"It is the truth. I can't even care for myself properly. Seth has to check on me every night."

"Seth? The healer's apprentice from the Lair?" she asked, her interest piqued.

"You know him?" Hrardorr asked.

"He comes to trade occasionally for the rare herbs my father's ships bring in. He grew up here, so I saw him sometimes. I always wished he'd notice me, but he never did." She figured Hrardorr deserved to know another of her deepest secrets, since he'd been so forthcoming with his own today.

"I find it impossible to believe that he never noticed you. He seems like a competent young man. No sign of brain damage or stupidity."

She laughed at Hrardorr's humor. "He could have any girl he wants. Contrary to your high opinion of me, I am plain by most standards. I have a lot of money, which makes me a target for the less scrupulous men in town. And when my father is in residence, he makes me live like a nun. No dating. No male friends. No fun at all. He scared off most of the boys when I was younger. Only now, since my mother died and he's away so much, have I been able to spread my wings a bit, much to my housekeeper's shock. I pay her extra to keep her mouth shut each time Father comes home."

"You are a very cunning young lady," Hrardorr complimented her, bowing his head in her direction.

"Thank you, Sir Hrardorr. I do try."

It seemed the time for serious conversation was over, and Hrardorr excused himself to do a little fishing. He was gone for almost an hour, but when he returned, he seemed more settled. Calmer. A little more at peace with himself.

She knew the water—and his ability to navigate in it as if

he weren't blind—had that effect on him, but this was something more. It felt to her as if speaking of his lost knight had been cathartic. He wasn't over the loss by any stretch of the imagination, but he had started coming to terms with the events of the past. Speaking about it with her had begun a process she hoped would continue to heal his emotional wounds. Either way, she would be there for him as long as he needed her.

She not only respected Hrardorr, but she...kind of...loved him. Not in a romantic way, of course, but in a sisterly sort of way. He felt like family to her—something of which she had precious little. There was only her and her father, and he had mostly abandoned her in favor of his travels after her mother had died.

Hrardorr felt alternately like father, brother and uncle to her. She was coming to depend on seeing him at least a few times each week and found herself counting the minutes until she could get back on the water and rendezvous with the dragon.

"You should talk to Genlitha," Livia said quietly as they sat side by side—she, in her boat, and he, floating on the waves like some sort of overgrown, scaly swan.

"*I cannot,*" he replied quietly. Frankly, she was surprised he'd replied to her impertinent remark at all. "*I don't want her to see me like this.*"

"You don't want her to see the evidence of your bravery or your courage? You don't want her to see how magnificent you are, even as badly injured as you once were?" Livia searched for the right words, hoping he understood.

"*I don't want her to see me helpless.*" His voice was small in her mind. Tragic.

"You aren't helpless. Especially not here, in the waters of your ancestor. You are amazing, Hrardorr. You can do things other dragons cannot, and someday, I hope you'll see what I do when I look at you—a hero who can do anything he puts his mind to. You are far from helpless. You have me, and Seth, and many others in the Lair, I'm sure, who stand ready to help you, should you need it, but you are doing very well on your own. Much better than I think anyone would have believed, in fact. No, my friend, you are far from helpless."

"I'm glad you think so." His tone clearly indicated that he did not agree, but he seemed willing to let her words pass without getting upset about them. *"And I'm glad you think of me as a friend. You are that to me as well, Livia. Which is surprising, when I think of it. Other than my knights, I have had few human friends, and never a female. You are unique in my experience."*

"Well, you're the first dragon I've befriended as well, so I could say the same," she admitted, feeling a warmth in the region of her heart that he'd called her friend. "We're quite the pair, aren't we?"

"Oh, to be sure. A mismatch, if there ever was one, but somehow, it works."

"I still think you should talk to Genlitha. Her knight seems a most reasonable man, and he speaks so highly of her. I think she would surprise you. And she would not make you feel bad about your injuries. Not on purpose."

Hrardorr refused to answer that last attempt, merely sitting quietly, paddling slowly in the waves. They sat like that for an hour more before the light started to fade, and Livia reluctantly told Hrardorr she had to turn for home if she was to arrive at the shore before nightfall.

Surprisingly, he paddled alongside her boat for part of the journey home, making a game of filling her sail with gusts of hot wind from his nostrils. She laughed as her boat surged forward each time he did it, and he seemed to draw amusement from the game as well.

More than one fisherman remarked on it when she finally returned to shore and Hrardorr had flown off toward the Lair. They were fast becoming used to seeing the dragon in the water with her, and they all loved him for the way he'd removed so many predators from the waters near the shore. He was quickly becoming a town favorite, little did he realize it.

Livia went to sleep that night, still smiling at Hrardorr's

antics. They'd crossed a line today from mere acquaintances to true friends. Though her heart still broke for him and what he'd been through, she felt gratified to know that she had helped him, even in such a small way. He was a different dragon from the one she'd met that first day. He was a little happier, she thought. A little more grounded.

She sent up a prayer as she prepared for sleep that he would find happiness again one day. If anyone deserved it, he did.

Gowan was ready to burst with anticipation as the weekend finally arrived. He had a date with the lovely Livia, and he was more than ready to get out of the Lair for a bit and do something enjoyable. He thought spending time with Livia would be immensely enjoyable, and he'd spent the past couple of days planning their outing.

Genlitha had agreed to help, which was both surprising and fantastic. He only hoped Livia wouldn't be too scared to fly. If she was, he had a backup plan for an evening in town, but he'd rather go with Plan A, which was something much more special.

At the appointed time, he and Genlitha flew down to Dragonscove. Gen dropped him off in an open square near Livia's home, where she would wait to see if Livia was game to fly or not. He'd picked a giant bouquet of the prettiest wildflowers for her from a mountain meadow earlier that day, and he brought them with him to her door.

As the housekeeper answered his knock and let him in, Gowan waited nervously in the front hall. The house was impressive without being overpowering. There was wealth here, but it wasn't ostentatious. Everything was of fine quality, but not overblown. Gowan liked it. Very much.

When Livia came down the stairs, Gowan held his breath. She was a vision. Lovely as the morning sky. Would she think him foolish if he said so? Probably.

"You look beautiful, mistress," he offered instead, proffering the bouquet, which she accepted with a huge smile. She bent her head to sniff at the delicate flowers, her cheeks rivaling the pink of the meadow daisies he'd found. Enchanting.

"Thank you, Sir Gowan. I love flowers."

Score. He'd thought she would enjoy the blooms and was glad he'd gone through the effort of tracking them down and selecting just the perfect ones from the field for her. Genlitha had laughed at him a bit, but just seeing the look on Livia's face now made the effort worthwhile.

"I'm glad to hear it," he said modestly. "Now, about our outing. I have a proposition, but you can decline if you wish." The next few minutes would tell him a lot about her spirit.

"I'm intrigued. Pray tell, what dire choice must I make?" She smiled at him, her tone light and teasing. So far, so good.

"Well...you can choose between a quiet dinner for two here in town, or something a little more adventurous. Lady Genlitha, my dragon partner, is willing to convey us up to a lovely meadow where I found those flowers for you. We could have a picnic, if you're willing to try flying. I promise it's safe, but we'll understand if you'd rather not."

"Are you kidding?" Livia's eyes blazed with excitement. "I would love to fly!" Her lips broke into a huge grin. "It would be like a dream. A once in a lifetime opportunity. How could I refuse?"

Well, that answered that question. Livia had heart and a keen sense of adventure.

They walked together to the square where Genlitha waited, being admired by the children in the area. She was very good with little ones, allowing them to climb on her forelegs, giving them little *rides* through the air by lifting her legs upward, slowly, while the children clung to her and giggled and laughed loudly.

The children scattered back to their parents when Gowan and Livia appeared, though a few ran up to Livia for a pat on the head or a word of praise.

"She is good with the little ones," Genlitha observed silently to Gowan. *"That is a good sign in a potential mate."*

68

CHAPTER SEVEN

"Who said anything about mating?" Gowan replied, not quite sure he was willing to go that far just yet...though it was very tempting to think about having the lovely Livia in his life on a permanent basis. At least so far. She seemed like a nice girl, but he needed to know more about her—which is what this outing was really all about.

"Greetings, Lady Genlitha," Livia said, curtseying to the dragon prettily. She had the manners of a lady, which didn't surprise Gowan in the least.

"Hello, Lady Livia. It is good to finally meet you," Genlitha answered in that silent way of dragons, sharing her words between Livia and Gowan equally, including them both in the conversation.

While the two females had spoken briefly before, Genlitha had been high in the sky teaching a group of younger dragons the finer points of judging tricky air currents at the time. They'd never met in person, as it were.

"Thank you for agreeing to take me with you. I have never flown before, but I've dreamed of it. I hope I don't turn out to be a coward." Livia was grinning when she said that last, so Gowan wasn't too concerned by the idea. Still...

"If you're the least bit uncomfortable, we'll bring you right back. That is a promise. Right, Gen?" Gowan was quick to say.

"Most assuredly," Genlitha added her thoughts. *"I have never once dropped anybody, and I promise you will not be the first. If you do not like it aloft, I will return immediately to ground. You have my vow."*

"Thank you," Livia said, blushing slightly. "Let's hope that is not necessary." Gowan ushered her closer to Genlitha, toward the foreleg that was propped up so that they could climb it like a ladder to the dragon's back. "I don't think it will be necessary," Livia added, almost under her breath as she walked.

Gowan showed Livia how to mount and climbed up behind her on the dragon's back. There was a natural *seat* in the area where the wings joined the body and what would be akin to the shoulder area. When Gowan rode alone, it was more than comfortable for him. With them both, it was...cozy. *Very* cozy, indeed.

"Hold on now," Gowan warned her as he felt Gen gathering for a leap into the sky.

With as little jolt as possible, Genlitha launched into the air, her great wings causing only a little disturbance at ground level. She had more power in her hindquarters than most, which allowed her to jump higher before she had to use her wings, allowing her to land in tighter spots than most average dragons. She made good use of her skills now, showing off just a bit as the children below cheered and the adults waved and smiled.

Gowan tightened his arms around Livia's waist, but she seemed all right. He was able to put his mouth next to her ear as Genlitha leveled out a bit, flying over Dragonscove.

"How are you doing?" he spoke loudly, to be heard over the rush of wind, even at this low height.

"This is amazing!" she shouted back, and Gowan felt his shoulder muscles relax. He'd been worried that she wouldn't like flying, but she seemed to be a natural.

"We're going a little higher. Everyone all right back there?" Genlitha asked.

Experimentally, Gowan tried to include Livia in his silent

answer to the dragon.

"We're all good here. Take us up, milady, if you would be so kind."

Livia sat up straight in his arms, her head turning slightly toward him. "I heard that!"

"Then you are even more gifted than I thought," Genlitha said gently, though Gowan sensed the thrill running through her words. *"It is a rare human female that can hear us, much less the silent speech of our knight partners. Even among the knights, most of them cannot hear each other unless they are closely partnered and joined through their dragons. Hold on now. We're aiming for the top of that cliff over there."*

Gowan enjoyed the feel of Livia's back pressed against him as they rose higher in the sky. True to her words, Genlitha flew right up to the cliff top, encountering a strong counter current at the crest that she handled beautifully. She truly was an artist in the air.

Genlitha circled once, giving Livia a view of the pretty meadow Gowan had picked out earlier. He'd already been up there, setting things up. As a result, Genlitha landed very close to the supplies he'd already brought up, knowing the plan Gowan had in mind.

It was late afternoon, and they would have a few hours before sunset. He had a plan, but he wasn't sure how it was all going to work out. A lot depended on Livia, and so far, so good.

Gowan helped Livia down from Genlitha's back. Livia took a moment to offer formal thanks to Genlitha for the transport, proving again how respectful she was of others. Genlitha raised one eye ridge in Gowan's direction in silent approval.

"I took the liberty of pre-positioning a meal for us to share. It's cold now, but Genlitha can solve that problem for us in a trice." He smiled, and Livia followed suit.

"Handy," she commented. "Must be nice having a dragon around, especially when it gets cold out." Livia smiled at Genlitha, who was moving slightly away, finding a comfy spot to stretch out on her belly. "And to be able to fly with her…"

"It is a privilege I'm still getting used to, if I'm honest," Gowan replied, lifting up the basket he'd stashed between two rocks an hour before. "But you're right. Having Genlitha in my life is an amazing experience I wouldn't trade for the world."

"Nor I," Genlitha added gently, a warm moment passing between them. Gowan felt her acceptance and the glow of her regard down the bond that had formed between their souls when he'd accepted her as his fighting partner.

Words could not describe the bond. Gowan had heard knights try to describe it before, but he'd never fully understood it until it had happened to him.

"Can I help?" Livia broke into his thoughts as he opened the basket and started to unload a few things.

"Do you want to spread the blanket over there, by Genlitha? She'll block the wind on one side so we don't get blown off the cliff." He was exaggerating, but having Gen act as a wind break was a good idea. They were exposed to the air currents up here, and as he had learned, they could be unpredictable.

Livia went off with the blanket while Gowan set up a spit with the chicken that had already been cooked in the Lair kitchen. It just needed warming, which was something Genlitha could do with a single breath. Gowan just needed to set it up so that he didn't get toasted at the same time. Hence, the spit, which consisted of two tripods between which hung the skewer with the chicken on it.

Gowan put that up near Gen's head, leaving a few of the stone crocks containing side dishes that could also benefit from her warm breath on some flat stones he'd already selected earlier that day. All he'd have to do was get out of the way, and Gen could do her thing, warming up the whole meal at once.

"If you would be so kind, milady," he said with exaggerated courtesy, bowing gracefully to the dragon.

Genlitha winked at him as he retreated to a safe distance, bringing the basket and the rest of the items in it over to the blanket Livia had spread. He took out the bottle of wine that was nicely chilled by its time on the cliff top, and two hand-blown glasses he'd won in a game of chance with a glass blower some years back.

"Looks like you've thought of everything, Sir Gowan," Livia said as he handed her a glass of wine.

"A man tries to be prepared," he answered, raising his own glass. "Now, for our winged companion's input. Lady Genlitha, do you think it is ready?"

"Almost," Genlitha answered in both their minds. *"Another little tickle should do it."* Genlitha blew out another warm breath and raised her head with a dragonish look of satisfaction. *"There. Dinner is served."*

The entire afternoon—the flight, the meal, the conversation and the company—was well beyond Livia's expectations. She had liked Gowan before, but he impressed her on every level, pulling out all the stops. He showed himself to be a caring, thoughtful person, not just a tall, muscular soldier.

The fact that he was very much the tall, muscular soldier had attracted her at first. She wasn't shy about admitting to her purely physical attraction to the man. At least not in the privacy of her own mind. But the clues to his true character were what made all the difference. The way he talked to and interacted with Genlitha charmed Livia. The obvious care between the dragon and Gowan touched her heart.

Livia couldn't help but notice his physique, though, when he was sitting right there next to her, on a cushy blanket, flanked by a warm dragon. He even smelled good, like strong man tempered with the gentle fragrance of tree resin, for some odd reason. She wondered if it was something he wore or if he came by that uniquely attractive scent naturally.

She'd been courted by overly-perfumed popinjays in the town. Rich men with more hair than wit, and young lotharios looking to score a rich wife by spending more time in front of the looking glass admiring their own appearance than most teenage girls. Neither had impressed her.

Oh, some of the decorative ones were certainly enjoyable for a short amount of time, but none interested her as a potential life mate. Before she made that kind of decision, Livia would have to put them through their paces. She wasn't about to accept any man as a life-long partner without first getting to know them extremely well—in the bedroom and out of it.

Her father might not agree, but then again, he wasn't here. He'd more or less abandoned her for the past several years. She was a woman grown, over the age of her majority, an heiress in her own right. Her father might be the richest man in town, but her mother had been the only child of a prosperous merchant. That gentleman had been Livia's grandfather—the only one she had known, since her father's parents had both been killed at sea long before Livia was born.

Grandpa Jonas and Granny Lynn had doted on Livia, and when Jonas died, Lynn had given her husband's business interests to Livia's father, to be added to the collection of businesses he looked after. But Granny Lynn had been crafty, and she made sure that legally, once Livia was old enough, the business itself would pass to her. She'd wanted to be certain her only grandchild was provided for in the future.

Livia was the legal owner of a small but prosperous fishing fleet, though few people knew it. They all assumed it was one of her father's many concerns, and she preferred to let them think that, even though while Father was away, she was the de facto head of the company. She was the one people came to when they had a problem. She was also the one who made decisions and paid the bills, made sales, collected what was owed, and split the earnings with the workers. She ran all of the businesses under her father's care, but Grandpa Jonas's fishing fleet was truly hers.

And the little boat she took out to go fishing with Hrardorr had been Grandpa Jonas's very own sailboat. There wasn't a day that went by that she didn't think about her grandparents and how very much they had taught her about fishing and running the small fleet of boats that they had loved so dearly. Granny and Grandpa had taken her out so often with the various captains they all knew her and treated her like their own daughter, and the arrangement had worked very well, even after Granny had left this world to be with Grandpa.

It was Granny Lynn who had cautioned Livia to be wary of men and take time before she married. Early infatuations had led to some very frank, grandmotherly advice that she had never forgotten.

Grandma Lynn had been a bit of a maverick in her time. She'd been around the block, as they say, and had taught her granddaughter what to do to prevent pregnancy. She'd given Livia very blunt advice on what to expect from a man and had told her there was no harm in experimenting with a few before settling down with just one.

Livia hadn't been tempted that many times, and really, no man in recent years had caught her eye enough to make her want to take that step again...until now. Until Gowan.

Sure, there was one shy boy from the Lair whom she'd fancied as a younger girl, but he'd never expressed any real interest. If he had, she'd have been all over him in a flash. She'd daydreamed about him in her youth and still sighed wistfully when she happened to see him in town on rare occasions, but she'd given up on him. She had to be practical, like Granny Lynn had taught her. That boy was probably not attracted to her, otherwise, he would've done something long before now. Sir Gowan was here, now. He was real, and it was pretty clear that he was interested.

And she was interested too. So much so that she was contemplating acting somewhat rashly. It had just been so darn long since a man had turned her eye this way. So long since she'd been held in a strong man's arms... So long since she'd had any affection in her life—fleeting or otherwise.

Gowan was sitting there, next to her, on the blanket, the dragon fast asleep, her head stretched out on the grass, facing away from them, as if uninterested in the doings of the humans. And Gowan sat there looking so handsome and strong. Livia couldn't help herself...

She leaned across the space separating them and kissed him.

Oh, yes. His kiss was all she was hoping it would be. She'd surprised him at first, but he soon took charge, wrapping his muscular arms around her gently, tangling his tongue with hers.

He tasted of the fruity wine he'd served with dinner, along with his own unique flavor that made her want more. So much more. The feel of his arms around her sent flames licking down to her core, igniting a fire that she hadn't quite expected, but welcomed nonetheless.

Never had a simple kiss made her feel so aroused. Not this fast. Not this hot. As it was, she felt like she would burst into flames if he didn't move faster, deepen the kiss, claim other bits of her body that were oh-so-ready to be claimed.

All too soon, Gowan drew back. He didn't let her go, but he seemed to be taking stock, searching her eyes for...something.

"I had no plan to rush you into anything when I invited you up here," he said in a quiet voice that touched her deeply. His concern for her feelings meant a lot to her, but if they were to have a chance at any sort of relationship at all, he was going to have to learn a few hard truths about her.

"If I felt you were rushing things, I would let you know," she assured him. "Though I had no expectations today other than to experience dragon flight for the first time in my life and share a meal in order to get to know you a little better..." She gathered her courage. Her next words would make or break this whole thing. "I feel honesty is usually the best policy, and so, I'm going to be honest with you. I'm not a maid, Sir Gowan. I haven't been with many men, and none in a long time, but there's something about you..." She didn't know what to say, or how he was taking her words. Livia looked down, unable to meet his gaze.

Gowan's hand came under her chin and lifted her chin, but it was a moment before she could bring herself to look him in the eye. What she saw there wasn't condemning or disapproving. He was smiling gently.

"There's something special about you too, Livia. From the first moment I saw you, I knew I wanted to get to know you. I will never take advantage of you, but there are reasons it's a relief to me to know you're not a virgin."

He looked so very relieved, she had to ask.

"What kind of reasons? You have me intrigued." She smiled a bit, feeling more comfortable with his easy acceptance of her revelation.

Now he looked uncomfortable. "It is hard to put delicately. Also difficult not to sound boastful."

"Really?" She thought she had an idea of what he might be referring to, and it made her want to find out for sure. She put her hand on his thigh.

"It's a matter of...size." He caught his breath as she stroked his thigh, very close to the large bulge in his trousers.

"You don't say?" she whispered, growing bolder with her hand. "That is something I'd like to know more about." Her words were calm, but as she spoke, she moved her fingers up his thigh to encounter the object of their roundabout discussion.

Bright stars, he wasn't kidding. His cock was hardening under her palm, and it was huge. Not that she'd been in a position to feel many, but Gowan was, by far, the most well-endowed man she'd ever been this close to. And she wanted to get even closer. So close she would no longer know where he ended and she began.

"Unless you want to take this all the way to its conclusion, you should probably stop what you're doing, much as it pains me to suggest it," he said with a tight grin.

"Maybe I like to live dangerously," she teased, squeezing him through his pants.

"You're living on the edge right now, sweetheart. And you're about to fall over it into my territory. Are you sure you want to go there right now?"

She lifted up, moving closer to him again, until her lips were against his. "I want to go wherever you're willing to take me. Take me right now, Gowan."

What followed was hot and fast.

He loosened her bodice, but didn't take the time to remove her dress completely. Next time. She was too eager to feel his large cock inside of her channel. She arched her back as he uncovered her breasts, his mouth latching onto her nipple for a quick, hot, wet tug with his lips.

She squirmed in his arms, moaning as he took command of her body. It felt like they were in sync. She wanted the pleasure she sensed he could give her. Pleasure like she hadn't had in a very long time—if ever. Compared to her few previous lovers, Gowan was a bit rougher around the edges and definitely more mature and gruffer.

But his gruffness turned her on. She never would have believed it before meeting him, but while the decisive way he moved, the bulge of his muscles and the other purely physical attributes were all well and good, it was his commanding presence that really flipped her switch. He was all man. He was almost overpoweringly masculine—sure of himself and of his command of everything in his realm.

She found that devastatingly sexy.

"I can't wait," he whispered against her breast. "Are you sure?"

She moaned in answer, unable to form words right away. She tried again.

"Need you, Gowan," she gasped. "Do it now."

He lay her back against the soft blanket and flipped up her dress, peeling down the undergarments with a skill she should have expected of a man of the world like Gowan. Yet, she wasn't jealous. He was with her right now, and she could feel the way she affected him. Whatever had come before had readied them both for this moment in time, and she couldn't begrudge the other women he'd been with. She thought he would probably say the same about the few men who'd been in her life well before him. What mattered was the two of them together now.

His fingers tested her readiness before he slowly pushed inward with something a whole lot bigger. He wasn't kidding about being well endowed. She could feel it for herself.

So much so, she pushed against his shoulders.

"Give me a minute," she whispered, gasping as she tried to catch her breath. She was desperate for his possession, but her body was balking at accepting all of him so quickly.

"You're so tight," Gowan said, stopping all motion. He waited, placing soft kisses all over her face. "It's all right, Livia. Just let me know what you want. I'll give you anything."

She breathed in little pants, concentrating on relaxing her inner muscles. His words and the caring way he held her helped too. He was a thoughtful man who cared for her comfort. He wasn't going to force anything. He would give her the time she needed to become accustomed to him, and he'd hold her through it all. He'd be there for her.

Her heart melted, and her insides made room for him. What had been a little overwhelming a moment ago suddenly became something she craved like her next breath.

And she wanted more.

"Keep going," she urged him in a breathy voice.

"Are you certain?" he asked, and she could hear the strain in his voice. It was costing him to hold back, but she knew in her heart that he would put her first, no matter what. He was just that kind of man. Her heart melted a little more.

"I want you, Gowan. All of you. Now. It'll be all right."

"I'll go slow," he promised, putting actions to words and pressing inward by small increments.

He kept going until he was seated fully inside her, and then, he stopped. His gaze held hers.

"Are you good?"

"Any better and I'd be in heaven. Take us there, Gowan," she urged.

Then he began to move. Slow at first, his strokes became

more urgent quickly. He held her by the shoulders, surrounding her as he lay over her on the blanket. She loved the way he sheltered her with his body, even as he took possession of hers.

She whimpered with need, and he answered by speeding his strokes even more. He pushed hard, fast, deep and thick, and she began to moan. She cried out as her climax hit, stunning her so much with its intensity she thought she felt the earth move.

Maybe it had. Or maybe it was just her world that had shaken off its foundations for a few moments. Gowan held her throughout, and when she was done with the first climax, he coaxed another out of her straining body before he joined her in a shattering orgasm the likes of which she had never experienced before.

She felt like she could touch the sun, she flew so high in his arms.

And then, it was over. But it wasn't really. He stayed with her, within her, for long moments, just…savoring. Or at least, that's what it felt like.

When he finally rolled away, he didn't go far. He tucked her into his arms as they lay, looking up at the stars. Night had fallen while they'd been wrapped up in each other. The perfect end to a perfect day.

CHAPTER EIGHT

"I hear a certain lady dragon has been seeking you," Seth said one night, while he was tending Hrardorr's eyes. "Genlitha is her name, and I've had the pleasure of making her acquaintance. A very sweet-tempered lady, she is."

"Is she well?" Hrardorr asked, as if worried she might be hurt. Seth could make the connection. He was the healer's apprentice. He didn't usually meet dragons unless they were hurt.

"Merely a strained muscle," Seth admitted, bending the truth a little.

The muscle strain had been quite a while ago. In the time since, Seth had been waiting to see if Genlitha would finally corner Hrardorr somewhere. He'd been avoiding her, and Seth had been hoping he wouldn't succeed in evading her this long.

In the meantime, Seth had been studying with Gowan, and Gowan had been learning about how to care for his dragon in return. They'd struck up a friendship, and Seth enjoyed spending time with both Gowan and his dragon partner. So much so that Seth had grown impatient with Hrardorr's hiding and decided to broach the subject of Genlitha.

"She flies beautifully," Seth added when Hrardorr made no reply.

"She always had good wings," Hrardorr said softly.

"She's been teaching the youngsters," Seth said conversationally. "They say she has a real gift for it."

"I am not surprised. She was ever a patient and kind dragon, even in her youth," Hrardorr admitted.

"So why won't you see her?" Seth came out and asked bluntly. "She wants to talk with you. She wants to help you."

Seth knew immediately that he'd said the wrong thing as Hrardorr rose up to his full height and stalked toward the ledge.

"I do not need her help!"

It was dark out, well past the time that Hrardorr usually settled down for the evening, but he looked like he was going out again. Damn it. Seth's unwise words had driven him into this. Seth ran after the dragon, reaching out for him with his hands, so Hrardorr would know Seth was there.

"I'm sorry, Hrardorr. Truly, I am. I said this all wrong. She wants to be your friend, as you were of old. Please come back. It's late and very dark out. A storm is rising. You shouldn't be out in it."

"Do you think I am so infirm that I cannot smell a storm?" Hrardorr's great head turned in Seth's direction.

"I didn't say that," Seth replied. "I'm just concerned for your wellbeing. If my words have driven you away from comfort, then I am shamed for saying them. I did not mean to drive you out. Please, come back. I'll leave and keep my mouth shut in future. If you'd rather have someone else do your treatments, I'll find someone else. I'm sorry, and I humbly apologize."

Hrardorr released a gusty sign of cinnamon-flavored, warm air that ruffled Seth's golden hair. *"It is not your fault that I am this way, Seth. Do not feel bad. I am restless tonight with the storm coming, and I want to be out in it. I did not want to come back here at all tonight, but I also did not want the entire Lair out searching for me."* He took a few steps away, and Seth knew he was leaving, no matter what Seth said. *"I am going down to the sea. I am more at home there now than I am here. I have made a friend on the*

water that I never expected, though she belongs here. If I do not return…
Her name is Livia, and she is the daughter of a sea captain."

Seth felt the knowledge run through him like a lightning bolt. He knew Livia. Everyone in town knew Livia. She was the most beautiful, kind, intelligent woman for miles around, not to mention the richest. Seth had been smitten the first time he'd seen her as a youngster, but even then, he'd known she was too good for the likes of him.

He'd watched her from afar for a very long time, but he'd never suspected she could bespeak dragons. Seth felt his heart sink. If she could hear dragons, she was doubly not for him. She would be wooed by every single knight in the Lair until she succumbed to a pair of charming knights and went on to start a family with them.

She would be forever out of Seth's reach, though she would be living in the same Lair. Seth would have to leave. He wouldn't be able to watch that.

"I know her," was all he said in reply to the dragon.

Hrardorr's ears perked at Seth's tone, but Seth didn't care. His world of dreams had just caved in. The unattainable woman he'd loved from afar for so long was now, forever, firmly out of his reach. It was almost as if she had died. He felt that kind of sorrow.

"I will not return this night. Do not wait for me." With those parting words, Hrardorr leapt from the ledge into the unknown.

Seth prayed this would not be the last time he ever saw Hrardorr.

It was no good. Seth tried not to worry, but he was sick at heart about Hrardorr being out there in the storm. It had whipped up into a gale just after Hrardorr left, and Seth kept one eye on the outside, listening to reports from knights and dragons who came in just as the storm started to rage.

All patrols were called back. The Lair was shut up tight, with no dragons in the air…that they knew about. Only Seth knew that Hrardorr had left. Apparently, nobody else had spotted him leaving, dark as he was against the dark night sky. He'd been nearly invisible to the human lookouts, and since he didn't talk to any of his dragon brethren, they didn't know he'd left either.

Seth couldn't stand it. He bundled up in his oilskin coat and snuck out of the Lair by the back stairs that led down to Dragonscove. It wasn't an easy trip with wind and rain lashing at him, but it had to be done. He couldn't sit still, safe and cozy in the Lair, while Hrardorr was out there somewhere, in the tempest.

Seth called repeatedly for Hrardorr silently, using the skills he'd had since birth to communicate with dragons, but Hrardorr was either out of range or just ignoring him. Seth suspected the latter, considering the way the dragon had left. Seth tried cajoling, wheedling, commanding, and outright pleading, but to no avail. Hrardorr didn't want to speak to him, and Seth felt about two inches tall for driving the dragon out into the storm.

Making his way through the rain and wind, Seth met no one on the streets of the town, which was highly unusual. Normally, there was at least some foot or wagon traffic along the streets at all times of day. Apparently, the residents were smart enough to stay indoors when a gale was blowing. Not so, Seth.

He went down to the waterfront, looking for any sign of Hrardorr, but he saw nothing. He fought against the wind and driving rain, straining to see even the tiniest ripple of the dragon's passing, but it was no use.

Not knowing where else to look, Seth made his way to the house he knew, but had never visited before. Livia O'Dare's home. The one she shared with her father, the notorious sea captain and the richest man for miles around.

Seth had never dared knock on that particular door before, though when he'd been younger and mooning in private over *the lovely Livia*, as many called her, he'd dreamed of finding the courage to court her. Now that he was older, he knew it would never happen. Not in a million years. Not with his chosen path in life and lack of prospects.

Still, tonight, worry about Hrardorr drew Seth to her door. He hoped she would have some knowledge of where Hrardorr might go. Seth would not rest until he knew the dragon was safe.

He knocked on the door, the wind blowing rain across his face that stung like pellets of ice. This was no fit night for man nor beast.

A tiny door in the center of the main door opened, and a plump woman's face looked out at him suspiciously. It was the housekeeper. A grumpy older woman most in town avoided, but Seth had no choice.

"What business do you have here at this time of night and in such a storm?" She nearly shouted to be heard above the wind.

"I am Seth Nilsson from the Lair. I must speak with your mistress. It is a matter of urgency. Please fetch her." He tried to be both polite and firm. He'd learned you didn't get far with people like this housekeeper by being timid or overly polite.

Sure enough, the woman grunted, shutting the little door in his face with a clatter. A few minutes later—and none too soon—the door opened, and Livia stood before Seth, motioning him to come inside. She looked both concerned and intrigued, and there was a little spark in her eye that he'd noticed the few times they had interacted in her father's business office. He had been there a few times to inquire about rare herbs her father had brought back from his voyages for Bronwyn. But each time, Captain O'Dare had been there, giving Seth the evil eye for even looking at his daughter, and Seth had gone away with only a fond memory of actually talking to Livia.

"Master Nilsson, what can I do for you?" she asked as soon as the door was shut. She was leaning against it, Seth in the great hall that was lit with a chandelier high above their heads. Opulent. Rich. Completely out of his league.

"Mistress O'Dare, I am sorry to disturb you, but do you

have any idea where Sir Hrardorr might go if he was…uh…in a bit of a snit?" There was no polite way to describe Hrardorr's little tantrum.

Livia's brows drew together into a frown. "Do you mean to say he's out there, in this?" She gestured behind her at the closed door through which they could still hear the wind howling.

Seth nodded grimly. "I'm afraid so. We had…a misunderstanding earlier, as I was seeing to his treatment up at the Lair, and he left in a temper. I tried looking for him down by the water, but I couldn't see much with all the rain. He told me that you two had become friends, and without anywhere else to turn, I thought perhaps you might have an idea of how to find him." Seth laid it on the line, allowing some of his emotion to show. "I cannot rest until I know he is safe. The mood he was in when he left… Well…I worry that he might do something rash. And if he did, it would all be my fault for pushing him too hard."

Seth looked just miserable, and Livia's heart went out to him. He was still every bit as handsome as he had been when they were both youngsters, and the attraction she'd always felt toward him seemed to have increased over time, not dissipated.

He had finally come calling. If it had been under any other circumstances, it would have been a dream come true, but her life was…complicated now. She'd begun something with Gowan and didn't regret it one bit. She was as attracted to the knight as she'd always been to the Lair's handsomest son.

"Come into the parlor," she said, pushing away from the locked door. "I have a fire going in there, and you can dry off a bit. You look soaked clear through."

"But Hrardorr…"

Seth tried to object, but she dared greatly, pushing him by the shoulders through the open door into the parlor. She kept pushing until he stood in front of the roaring fire she'd built up when the storm started raging. There was something comforting about the dancing flames when the night was cold and dark.

"You won't do him any good if you catch your death of cold," she said firmly, unwrapping Seth's cloak and hood without so much as a by your leave. She took off his outer layers, spreading the bits before the fire to dry.

Rosie, the housekeeper, showed up at the door with a stack of towels, which Livia took from her with a nod of thanks. Rosie might be gruff, but she was a good housekeeper, attentive to her employers' needs. Livia went back to Seth, placing one unfolded towel over his wet hair without ceremony.

"Rub that over your hair," she instructed. "Do you need help with your boots?"

He grunted agreement, toeing off his boots without a word as he towel-dried his golden hair.

"I'll just put these on the hearth," she said, dipping to retrieve Seth's boots.

They were wet, but not in as bad condition as she'd feared. They were of good quality, and the leather had been treated with something to make it water repellant. The seams though...that was where the water had gotten through. As a result, Seth's socks were wet, Livia could see, as were the bottom half of his trousers.

"We'll have those socks off too." She sighed as she held out her hand for them. "And the pants."

"Now wait just a minute." Seth's head lifted like a shot, no longer following orders.

"No?" She hoped he could see the amusement in her eyes. "Well, all right then, but scoot up closer to the fire, so they can dry out while we talk."

She moved her chair closer so they could both sit by the fire, side by side.

"Now, then. What can I do to help?" Her mind turned to the dragon she had befriended and where he might have gone during a gale. She wasn't worried...exactly...though she was definitely concerned.

"Do you have any idea where he might go?" Seth looked at her, resolution warring with despair in his blue gaze.

"I'm sorry. I've been wracking my brain, trying to come up with an idea, but I just don't know. Did he say anything before he left?"

"Only that he was going down to the water, and that if…if he didn't return…that I should know the name of the friend he'd been meeting to fish with all this time."

"If he didn't return?" She didn't like the sound of that.

"That's what he said." Seth looked grim, and they sat there in silence, watching the fire crackle and burn.

"What set him off?" Livia finally asked, breaking the silence.

"I did, much to my regret." Seth ran one hand through his damp hair in clear frustration. "I pressured him about talking to Genlitha." Seth looked over at Livia. "She's—"

But Livia held up her hands, talking over the explanation he would have made.

"She's Gowan's dragon partner and a friend from Hrardorr's youth. I know. I've met her, and Gowan. And I've talked to Hrardorr about her too." Livia cringed. "Oh, dear." She wondered if maybe her own words had played a part in Hrardorr's upset.

Seth's big hand settled over hers on the arm of her chair, surprising her into looking up into his deep blue eyes. They were so blue…like calm waters on a sunny day. Deep and soothing, she could easily get lost in them.

"Don't blame yourself," he said softly. "I was the one who pushed him over the edge. I'm not very eloquent, and I said it all wrong." Frustration shone in his gaze. Frustration and sadness.

Livia couldn't help herself. She lifted her other hand and touched his cheek, drawing his gaze once more.

"Hrardorr is in a bad place. He has been ever since he arrived. You've tried to help him, which is more than most people have done for him—including his fellow dragons. He likes you a lot, Seth. He speaks of you often."

"He does?"

Seth seemed pleased and kind of stunned at the idea. Livia removed her hand before she started stroking him. His cheek had manly stubble that she could feel, but not really see, since he was fair-haired. It felt good against her palm. A little too good, in fact, for her peace of mind.

"He truly does," she replied, putting both of her hands primly in her lap. "I believe you are his only friend in the Lair. At least, you are the only one he speaks of with any degree of affection. He's mentioned a few others, but mostly because they annoy him." She chuckled at that, and Seth followed suit. It was a weak laugh, but she liked the rich tone of his deep voice.

"I wish I could find him," Seth said after a moment of quiet contemplation. "I've tried talking to him, but he refuses to answer. Either that, or he's too far away. I'm hoping he's just ignoring me."

"You mean speaking…with your mind, right?" she asked, forming an idea.

Seth looked at her, blue eyes snapping with intelligence. "Can you do it too? Do you have the gift?"

"I've been told I do, but I have not really learned how," she admitted.

Seth's eyes widened. "I can show you, if you'll permit me. You might have more luck getting Hrardorr to talk to you."

"All right," she agreed, resolving herself to try whatever she could do to help Seth and the dragon she had befriended. "What do I need to do."

Seth turned toward her and met her gaze. *"Can you hear me?"*

"Oh." She gasped. "Yes, I can hear you."

"Good. Now think your words back at me. Look into my eyes and will me to hear them."

Livia wasn't sure how to do that, but she tried. Squinting hard, she sent thoughts at Seth. At least she thought she did.

Seth shook his head and took her hands in his. "Relax, mistress. This is as natural as breathing for someone like us.

You are meant to bespeak dragons, and so you will. If you are meant to bespeak others like yourself, then you will do that, as well."

"I heard Sir Gowan speak to me in my mind once," she admitted. "That's when they told me I could learn how to speak silently too."

"Then you shall. Just don't try so hard. This should be natural. Just let it flow." His hands had been rubbing hers, then rose to slide along her arms and up to her shoulders, which she only then realized were bunched up around her ears with tension.

She deliberately relaxed her shoulders and tried to let all the stress leave her body. Seth's hands brought a different kind of stress, but that was a welcome feeling of warm lethargy that was as exciting as it was relaxing. She tried again.

"That feels really good," she sent to him, wondering if he'd hear her thoughts, and if so, what he would think of her frankness.

"Glad to be of service," came the intimate reply in her mind. *"As apprentice to the healer, I have mastered many forms of massage."*

Did the twinkle in his eyes mean he was flirting with her, or was it just a trick of the dancing firelight reflecting in his clear gaze? Either way, she was well on the path to being enchanted by the man—which was all wrong, wasn't it? Hadn't she decided on Gowan just the other day? Hadn't she decided to put aside all her girlhood fantasies about Seth? And hadn't Gowan taken up residence in her heart in the place formerly reserved for unattainable Seth?

Only...Seth didn't seem all that unattainable at the moment, and if she examined her heart in depth, she was sort of shocked to find that Gowan hadn't replaced Seth there. He'd taken his place right alongside her long-time crush. How could that be?

Was she really that fickle?

Stars above! She really hoped none of those thoughts were leaking out, making their way from her mind to his.

"So you can hear me?" She had to get back on track

somehow.

"I can. And I bet Hrardorr will hear you, too, if you keep him firmly in mind when you send your thoughts. Want to try it?"

"No time like the present," she mumbled as Seth removed his hands from her person. She missed his touch, but she knew she had to concentrate in order to reach the dragon.

"Hrardorr? Are you there? It's Livia." She kept thinking it over and over, hoping that she was getting through.

"All right, already. I hear you, Livia. Stop repeating yourself," came the grumpy reply in her mind.

She felt a smile bloom on her face as she opened her eyes and looked at Seth. "He answered. He hears me."

"How is he?" Seth asked quickly.

"Grouchy," she replied just as fast. "Let me see what else I can get." She closed her eyes, trying to recapture the feeling of what she'd done before. It was easier this time. *"Thank you for answering me. Are you all right? The storm out there sounds vicious."*

There was a bit of a pause before he answered. *"It is not that bad under the waves."*

"But you can't breathe under water. Can you?"

"No, Livia. I'm only part sea dragon. I don't have gills." There was a pause before he went on. *"How is it you can suddenly speak to me this way? Who taught you? And why now?"*

"Don't get mad at me," she warned before proceeding. *"Seth feels terrible about what happened. He walked down to the water to look for you, but when he didn't see anything, he came here, to my house. Hrardorr, he's more miserable than a wet cat, and dripping all over my carpet. I'll be amazed if he doesn't catch his death of cold from this."*

"I told him not to feel bad..."

"Feelings don't work like that, my friend. He told me he would not rest this night until he was sure you were safe. He feels responsible for driving you out into the storm. He's very upset."

Livia discovered she could open her eyes and not lose the connection with the dragon. The silent way of speaking was becoming more natural to her by the minute. She found Seth watching her intently.

"Well, so am I," Hrardorr said with an almost petulant tone. *"He wants to make things right. He wants to apologize."*

"Yes, I heard. I just don't want to talk to him right now." Oh yeah, that was definitely petulance if she'd ever heard it. Sounded like the dragon was throwing a tantrum.

"Can I at least tell him you're safe, so he won't go back out into the gale looking for you?"

Hrardorr made her wait for his response. When it came, it sounded as if the dragon had gotten over at least some of his snit.

"I'm safe, though thoroughly uncomfortable when I have to come up for air. You can tell him that's his fault."

Livia wanted to laugh at his disgusted tone, but knew that wouldn't be helpful at the moment. She had to think... How could she fix this so that both males would be satisfied?

"Hrardorr, can you find my boat in the dock? I mean, can you tell which one is mine from underwater?"

"Yes, of course. How do you think I find you each day?" Now he just sounded insulted.

"If you can find my boat and follow that pier back toward shore, you'll find my family's boat house. It's small, but it should be able to shelter you for the night. It is sound and has weathered many a storm. You should be safe there, though it won't be warm, unfortunately."

Silence greeted her daring plan until finally, it seemed, Hrardorr relented.

"That could work. I will look for it."

"Let me know when you get there."

Livia squeezed Seth's hands as communication with the dragon ceased for the moment.

"He's all right. He is going to look for my family's boat house, and I think he can shelter there for the night, out of the storm."

Relief showed in Seth's expression. "Where is it? Can I go there?" He stood, taking his damp socks off the hearth as if he was going to leave that very minute.

"It's behind the house, down the hill. Though the stairs will be treacherous in this weather," she warned.

"It doesn't matter. I have to see him. To check on him."

Truthfully, Livia was feeling the same compulsion. She wanted to see Hrardorr and make sure he was really all right. She stood, making a decision.

"I'll get my cloak while you redress. We'll both go."

Seth caught her arm when she spun to head for the door. "Mistress, it's not safe. You said so yourself. Please don't risk it."

She thought of all the things she could say to make him understand, then settled finally on the simple truth.

"I must. I love him. I need to know he'll be safe."

Seth held her gaze, a silent understanding passing between them. Finally, he let her go, with a few words of advice.

"Dress warmly. It is bitter cold, and the rain drives needles of ice right into your face. Wear a scarf over your cheeks, and a heavy hood. I'll protect you as best I can, but it is purely dreadful out there."

Happy he understood, she reached up on tiptoe and placed a quick kiss on his cheek, which shocked them both a little bit. She was acting on pure impulse, but she wasn't sorry she'd done it. She'd always wanted to get close to Seth. This short interlude might be her only chance, and she wasn't going to waste it over-analyzing every little thing. An innocent peck on the cheek was hardly something to feel guilty over, after all.

CHAPTER NINE

Mere minutes later, Seth found himself leading the way down a set of slippery wooden stairs in the driving rain. He could just make out the dark shape of a building at the bottom of the stairs. That had to be the boat house.

He slipped and slid a few feet at one point, but was able to catch himself. He turned just in time to see Livia taking the same little tumble. He caught her in his arms, each of them stopping for a moment, in the pouring rain, to catch their breaths and just look into each other's eyes.

It was as if time stood still. Never had Seth imagined he'd have Livia O'Dare in his arms, looking at him in such a way. Maybe miracles did happen.

"Thanks," she said, dragging him out from under the spell. He became aware of the rain pounding on his shoulders and the way her body curved into his, allowing him to shelter her from the worst of it for a few precious seconds. The top of his hood draped over her head as well, forming a little pocket of peace amid the tempest.

"Livia, I—"

A crashing noise from below interrupted whatever it was he'd been about to say. He wasn't even too sure of what was going to come out of his mouth at that point. A declaration of undying love? A plea for her to notice him? A dinner invitation? It could have been any of those, or a few thousand other things he'd always dreamed of saying to her, but now was not the time.

"One of the boats came loose and crashed into the dock," she shouted, peeping around his head to look out over the water. When she returned, she met his gaze. "I hope Hrardorr realizes it." She looked so worried he took her hand and squeezed it in reassurance as he turned around and started down the last bit of the stairs. They would do this together. He'd watch over her, and she would help him watch over Hrardorr—whether the dragon wanted his help or not.

"Maybe I can catch it and tie it up again," he muttered, already thinking of what he could do in such a dangerous situation. Not much. But then again, maybe he'd get lucky.

They made it to the bottom of the stairs without further mishap. There was a landing at the bottom, where the rock and sand of the shore met the water. A deck made of wooden planks led from the shore, over the water. It was a large square of open space that branched out into different docks. On the right side was open dock space. Two boats were tied up there, happily riding out the storm. On the left was the boat house they'd been aiming for.

And in front of it was a larger vessel that had to have come loose from somewhere else, farther up the shore. It was still intact and afloat, but it was careening wildly, bashing into the wooden piers that held up the boat shed.

"That can't go on for much longer. Something's going to break apart. Either the boat, or the boat house," Livia shouted to be heard above the wind and rain.

Seth silently agreed with her assessment. He had to do something, but he wasn't sure what good is single man could do against such a large obstacle. Still, he had to try.

"Wait here," he called to her as he made his way down to the boat house.

As he worked his way around the side of the structure— there was an open walkway on either side—he felt each jolt of the boat crashing into one or another of the sunken piers that held up the whole contraption. He sent up a prayer that it would hold together, and that he could figure a way to stop the destruction.

He was almost to the front of the boat house when the crashing stopped and he saw something big emerge from the water. It was so dark, but he recognized the gleam of dragon eyes. Hrardorr had come. And he was holding the boat away from the boat house.

"Hrardorr!" Seth called. "Can you hold it?"

"Where would you like me to put it?" came the very welcome and rather wry reply in Seth's mind.

"If you can tow it to the dock, we can tie it up," Livia shouted over Seth's shoulder. He hadn't heard her behind him, but he guessed he should have known that she wasn't the type of lady to stay behind.

"I can put it in the slip right behind your vessel, Livia," came the dragon's reply in both their minds. *"You should not be out here in this weather,"* Hrardorr chastised her, in very real sounding concern.

"Neither should you, my friend," she admonished, already running back down the dock to meet the dragon at the other finger of dock where the boats were tied. Seth followed in her wake. She was really fast for such a little thing.

Seth kept one eye on Hrardorr. He hadn't complained, but he was using all his effort to controls the boat in his claws. He even had his tail wrapped around the bow as he struggled to tow it through the water. Any other dragon couldn't have done what Hrardorr was doing. None of them could swim like that—as if they'd been born to the water. Seth was impressed. Majorly impressed.

And he would say as much to Hrardorr. If they all lived through this little escapade.

Livia reached the slip first and started reaching for lines that had been left there, working busily on the sodden ropes, trying to untie knots. Seth knew a bit about boats, but clearly not as much as Livia. He was more than willing to take her lead on this rescue mission, though he drew the line at letting her do anything truly dangerous.

"One of us needs to jump onto the boat and either find the line that broke—which I think is probably a losing proposition—or secure new lines to it. I know the knots," she said, looking up at him finally as if raring to go, putting herself in danger on a storm-tossed loose ship. No. Way.

"I know knots too," Seth said firmly, taking the coil of line from her hands. "I will jump. You can catch the other end and tie her to the dock, all right?"

Livia looked like she wanted to argue, but finally, she nodded. She looked over Seth's shoulder, her eyes gazing into the distance.

"He's coming," she said shortly, prompting Seth to turn so he could see the dragon's mighty struggle for himself.

It was nothing short of amazing. Hrardorr was swimming mostly upside down, with some of his talons wrapped around the side of the wooden boat, his tail holding the bow. He kept his head underwater except to come up for air once in a while.

"He has senses that allow him to see underwater," Livia commented, standing at Seth's side. "He's amazing."

"I agree," Seth said quietly, knowing it was a huge understatement. What Hrardorr was doing—blind as he was—was nothing short of heroic.

Keep coming toward the dock, Seth sent to the dragon, filling him in on the plan. *When you're close enough, I'm going to jump on board and either tie new lines or retrieve the old, then toss them to Livia on the dock.*

I will hold steady next to the dock as long as I am able. You should know, there is a strong undertow, so speed on your part would be welcomed, came the wry reply.

Understood. I'll hurry.

Seth waited for the perfect moment and then timed his jump to coincide with the rise and swell of the waves. He landed on the deck and rolled as the boat came out of the water for a moment, the dragon still wrapped around it. The storm was intensifying. They'd have to do this quick, for all their sakes.

Seth struggled toward where the bow line should have been. It was gone. All that was left was a tattered shred of rope that was useless for their purpose. But the cleat was still intact. Seth quickly unlooped the coil of rope he'd put over his shoulder and set to work. When it was firmly attached to the cleat, he threw the end to Livia. She caught it and secured it as he made his way to the stern.

That line was dragging in the water, so he quickly retrieved it, getting even wetter in the process as the rope added seawater to the mix of wetness all over his clothing. But he didn't care. He had to get this boat secured so they could all get out of the weather. He found the end. It was frayed a bit, but farther up the line, it was sound. He tossed the end to Livia, and she caught it like a professional.

Of course, she'd grown up around boats and ships her entire life. Of course she knew what to do. Seth spared a thought for how much more amazing she was than he'd even dreamed, but he didn't have a lot of time.

"Both lines are tied to the dock, though they should be snugged up," Seth sent to Hrardorr. *"Can you hold it a moment longer, and perhaps move it a fraction closer to the dock?"*

"Yes, to both questions," Hrardorr replied. *"But do not tarry. It's like trying to hold a sack full of cats."*

"I'm jumping onto the dock now," Seth updated the dragon. *"And when have you ever held a sack full of cats?"*

"I haven't," Hrardorr answered with great dignity in the midst of the storm. *"But my first knight, Loren, had a pet cat named Sue, and she had kittens. Loren couldn't bear to part with the little ones at first, and they grew into adolescents rather quickly. He tried to put them all in a sack to take them out of the wallow on one memorable occasion. Suffice to say, it didn't go well for poor Loren. The scratches took weeks to heal."*

Seth could hear the nostalgia and genuine affection in Hrardorr's voice as he spoke of his first knight. It was good to hear. Gone was the dejection he usually displayed...if only for a moment.

Seth and Livia worked together to tie the boat up as securely as possible. They made a good team, not needing to speak to coordinate their movements.

"You can let go now. We've got it tied up," Seth told Hrardorr.

A moment later, Seth saw the dragon's tail slide off the bow, the claws releasing the sides. Hrardorr must have swum off, away from the clashing near the dock.

Livia took Seth's hand, surprising him, but leading him toward the main part of the dock and then back to the boat house. This time, she led him through a door at the rear that took them inside the boat house proper.

The moment he closed the door behind them, he felt a huge amount of relief. There was no boat in the slip that ran down the center of the structure, and the inside was neat as a pin. There was plenty of room for the humans to walk on either side of the water space, and the part that was built half on land, would be large enough for Hrardorr to get out of the rain and roiling seas.

As if that thought conjured the dragon, Hrardorr's head appeared out of the churning water in the center of the slip, followed by the rest of him.

"If you come straight forward, there is a wooden deck you will fit on. Livia and I will be to your left, by the door," Seth briefed Hrardorr on the layout.

"I could see the pilings beneath the water, but wasn't sure what lay above," Hrardorr admitted. For the first time in Seth's experience, Hrardorr was being matter-of-fact about his disability. He took it as a good sign.

"The roof is about twenty feet above deck level," Seth said aloud, in order to give the dragon some auditory input. Seth had often noticed Hrardorr's ears twitching toward him when he spoke and figured it helped the dragon know where he was.

"That's to accommodate my sailboat," Livia put in. "But I didn't want her in here during the storm. There's not that much clearance in case it gets too rough, and I didn't want the mast poking through the side of the roof. But it'll be perfect for you, Hrardorr. Not exactly warm and cozy, but at least you won't be in the water."

"The cold and wet does not bother me like other fighting dragons," Hrardorr said with a small bit of pride showing through. *"But this shelter will be welcome for tonight."*

"I suppose you'll have to stay here. Flying back to the Lair in this storm would be the next thing to impossible for any dragon," Seth put in, hoping Hrardorr understood that he wasn't discounting Hrardorr because of his blindness.

Hrardorr heaved himself up onto the deck, moving slowly and keeping his wings tucked, as well as his tail. He reached around himself gently, one leg at a time, learning his boundaries. Even his tail helped him discover where the wall behind him was as he arranged himself to face Livia and Seth, who stood against the wall near the door.

"Are you well, Sir Hrardorr?" Livia asked quietly as Hrardorr settled down to a resting position. "Is there anything we can do to make you more comfortable?"

Hrardorr blew out a small tendril of smoke. *"All is well, mistress. I have received no injury. In fact, it was rather invigorating to fly through the storm and dive down into the deeps. Everything is churning down below as well as up here."*

"Still, you should not have had to do that." Seth stepped forward slowly, approaching Hrardorr as he always did— talking aloud so the dragon would know where he was. "It is my fault for speaking out of turn, and I apologize. I will not pressure you again. It is not my place."

A gusty dragon sigh almost swept Seth off his feet. *"But it is. It is the place of a friend to express concern. I am at fault for refusing to listen and flying off in a snit. Even I can see how foolhardy I was."*

Seth moved closer, putting one hand out to touch Hrardorr's sinuous neck. Before this moment, he had only ever touched Hrardorr for purposes of treatment. This was the touch of a friend.

"I consider you my best friend, Hrardorr. Ever since you came to the Lair, my life has been better than it has been for a long time. You changed it," Seth told the dragon honestly, articulating thoughts that had been rolling around in his mind for a while, but never spoken.

"You've done the same for me, Seth," Hrardorr said softly.

Seth felt closer to the dragon in that moment than he'd felt to anyone since his childhood. He stepped closer and rested both hands on Hrardorr's neck. The dragon moved, and then, Seth was hugging him, like he used to hug his fathers' dragon partners when he'd been a child.

When Hrardorr didn't move away, Seth realized the hug was welcomed. That made it all the more special.

"I'm sorry I flew off in anger. It was childish of me."

"Don't say that. You had every reason to be annoyed with me. I'm sorry." Seth could feel tears at the back of his eyes, but they didn't fall. He was deeply moved by Hrardorr's warmth toward him after the tumult of the past few hours.

They stood there for a long moment.

"If I were whole, I would speak irrevocable words to you, Seth," Hrardorr shocked Seth by saying. *"You have been a true friend and have a great heart. Any dragon would be proud to partner you in defense of our land."*

Seth shook his head as he finally let go of Hrardorr's neck. "Not I, my friend. I am a healer, not a fighter. I chose my path a long time ago."

Hrardorr sighed. *"Sometimes, it is not the path we choose, but the one chosen for us, that is the hardest to bear."*

Livia turned away, allowing Seth and the dragon a moment of privacy. It was clear the emotions ran strong between them, and she felt a bit like a voyeur, getting a glimpse of what living among dragons could mean. It was fascinating, but also heartbreaking that Hrardorr had such pain down deep inside him.

She brushed away tears as she looked around the boat shed, trying to make herself useful. Perhaps there were some supplies here that could make Hrardorr's stay—for that matter, her own stay—here, more comfortable. She rummaged around quietly, coming up with a few items that could be of use.

She set up two folding camp chairs near the wall, groping around in the dark for a few lanterns. There were flints somewhere, but she figured she could always ask Hrardorr to light a stick of kindling once he and Seth were done talking. And hugging.

She spared a glance for them and wept anew at the picture they presented. Man and dragon, clearly friends. Perhaps more like family. Like brothers who just wore different guises.

Livia stumbled around a bit more. It was very dark inside the shed, but there were reflections bouncing off the turbulent waves, from Hrardorr's eyes and scales, that sent little sparkles of light dancing all around. It was enough to see by...almost. Yet another reason, she was learning, why it was handy to have a dragon around.

She looked on another shelf, feeling with her hands, and came across some old sail cloth that might be big enough to cover Hrardorr, should he feel cold. It wasn't much, but at least it was some bit of comfort she could offer him. Or maybe he could put it under him to use as a barrier between his body and the wooden deck. She wasn't sure if he'd like that, but she'd at least make the offer. Seth would know how best to help the dragon, and Hrardorr himself could decide what he wanted.

When Livia saw them break apart out of the corner of her eye, she turned with the sail cloth under one arm. She also had a dry stick they could use to light the lanterns in her hand. She approached cautiously, not sure if they were done, but Seth saw her and waved her over.

"I was wondering if you could maybe direct a tiny spark of flame at this stick?" She held the piece of wood out to Seth, who placed it in Hrardorr's foreclaw. "There are some lanterns we could light if you don't mind, Sir Hrardorr."

Mind? Why should I mind? Just guide me a bit, Seth. I don't want to set fire to this little building.

Seth smiled and reached up to touch Hrardorr's head,

which the dragon had lowered. It was a lovely sight—the new cooperation between dragon and man. Seth guided Hrardorr into position gently, with utmost care. It was obvious he loved the dragon and would protect him against all comers, no matter what.

"Just a little puff and direct it downward. Your head is aimed over the boat slip, so the water will douse any extra flame, if you overshoot," Seth coached in a quiet tone.

A flash of light, and the stick in Hrardorr's hand was alight.

"Excellent," Seth praised as Hrardorr held out the lit stick. Seth took it and handed it off to Livia. She took it, delivering the folded wad of sail cloth into Seth's hands in return.

"Great. I'll light the lanterns." She turned to do just that, still speaking. "I thought maybe you could use that sail cloth as a blanket, or a mat. Whatever works best."

She could hear Seth rustling the heavy cloth as she bent to light the lanterns. Within moments, the boat house was almost cheery with light.

"There. That's better." She stood back, hanging one lantern on the hook on the wall closest to her. She took the other over to Seth. She felt a real sense of accomplishment for such a small thing, but in such circumstances, she guessed you took what you could get.

Seth was spreading the sail cloth around Hrardorr like a nest. He asked the dragon to lift a bit of his body at a time while Seth moved the cloth beneath him.

"This'll insulate you from the cold a bit. It's not like your warm, sandy wallow, but it should do for the night," Seth said, standing back to check his work.

"I will do quite well. I told you, I don't feel the cold like most dragons," Hrardorr insisted. *"But the cloth is welcome. Thank you, Livia."*

Livia noticed a bit of steam rising from the dragon's body as he dried. In fact, the atmosphere in the boat house was getting nice and warm. She wasn't quite drying out from her scamper down the back stairs, but at least her teeth weren't

---

chattering anymore. Yet another reason it was nice to have a dragon around. She was learning more about them all the time, it seemed.

"Mistress Livia has set up two camp chairs for us over by the wall. We can stay with you until the rain dies down a bit, but then, I should escort her back up to her home for the night. I'll return and pass the night here with you, Hrardorr, if that's all right," Seth said, apparently wanting to plan everything out.

"It's not all right," Hrardorr surprised her by objecting. *"While I agree you should wait here a bit until the storm lessens, but once you go back up to the house, stay there. Or go back to the Lair, if you wish. I will be fine here for the night and will return to the Lair once the weather clears."*

"Or we could stay down here tonight," Livia offered. She didn't mind roughing it if it meant they could stay with Hrardorr.

"Only if it is too dangerous to go back up to your home," Hrardorr said quickly. *"I would rather you were warm and comfortable after I have dragged you from your cozy parlor, no doubt, with my antics. I humbly apologize for my actions tonight, Livia. I did not mean to cause you such trouble."*

"None of that, Hrardorr. You are my friend. I would do the same for any friend, but most especially for you, because you have been kinder to me in the past few weeks than any being I have ever known." She looked around the boat house, able to see things a lot better now that they had light. "I am quite warm now that you are heating the place," she said with a chuckle. "You are a very handy being to have around, Hrardorr."

"But you cannot sleep on the floor. You are a lady, deserving of soft things. Feather beds and such. Am I not correct, Seth?"

"That you are, but only if it's safe to go back up those stairs. There has to be a lull in the storm before I'll risk her on that slippery wood a second time. If I'd known how treacherous it was, I wouldn't have done it the first time."

"Was it truly that bad?" Hrardorr wanted to know, his brow

ridges drawing together in a frown.

"We both slipped toward the bottom," Seth admitted. Livia felt her cheeks flush with the remembered moment when he'd caught her and their gazes had clashed...and held.

She'd wanted him to kiss her in that moment, crazy as the impulse was. She'd started something with Gowan not even a week ago. She shouldn't be wanting another man's kiss. Not even her childhood crush's.

Right?

"It wasn't that bad," she insisted, joining the conversation.

"Good," Hrardorr pounced on her admission. *"Then you can go back up the same way and spend the night in your own much more comfortable bed. I will be fine, and I promise not to go swimming any more tonight."*

Livia had to chuckle at Hrardorr's wry tone. "Let's just see how it goes, shall we?" she suggested. "The storm out there still sounds rough. *If* it lightens, then we'll see what we shall see."

Seth looked at her for a moment, then nodded. "The lady has a point."

CHAPTER TEN

Livia took a seat next to Seth. The camp chairs weren't too uncomfortable. At least not for short stretches of time. But she had to admit Hrardorr had a point about spending the night down here. It would be uncomfortable for the human part of the group. She wasn't sure how the dragon felt about it, but Hrardorr really had no other choice that to stay here for the night.

It would be much too dangerous to fly out in the storm again, or try to pass the night underwater, only surfacing to breathe now and again. For all his talent in the water, Hrardorr had always been a land-based dragon. He had attributes of his sea dragon heritage, but at heart, he was a land-dweller.

She looked around, now that there was more light, and tried to find ways to make them more comfortable, but there wasn't much else in the boat house. She'd already scavenged all the sail cloth, so there would be nothing they could really use as bedding for themselves.

"It's nice and warm in here," she said, taking off her cloak and spreading it out on several pegs behind her on the wall. Maybe it would dry out enough to use for a small blanket. Then again, maybe she was only drying it out enough to make the trek back up the stairs to the house. Time would tell.

Seth took off his outer gear as well, placing it next to hers. "Heat is a benefit of being around dragons," he said with a grin. "They carry their furnaces around with them."

She chuckled at the small joke while Hrardorr let little tendrils of smoke rise toward the rafters from his nostrils. Dragonish amusement she had come to recognize during her association with him.

"True sea dragons can't flame," Hrardorr stated in their minds, seeming to want to make conversation. *"At least, that's what I've heard. No sea dragon has left the water since my ancestress. Family lore says she never flamed, though she was as fierce in the sky as she was in the water."*

They talked of legends and told stories as the storm raged outside. From time to time, Seth would go out and take a look at the nearby docks, just to make sure none of the other boats had broken loose. Long into the night, the three of them passed the time together, talking as friends.

Livia felt a warmth within her as the night progressed and the storm continued its furor. It was like a magical moment out of time where she caught a glimpse of what it must be like to live among dragons. She liked it. A lot.

Livia couldn't imagine why so few women wanted to live in the Lair. Hrardorr was both caring and intelligent and had a way with a tale that could rival any bard.

Finally, the weather seemed to break, and the pounding of the rain on the roof lessened considerably. Livia immediately regretted it. She knew her time here, in the dimly lit boat house with her childhood crush and their friend, the most amazing dragon, was almost over. Never would she have a night like this again.

Sure enough, Seth checked outside again and came back to report a slight break in the clouds. "We can go up now, but I'm not sure if this is the end of the storm or just a lull between thunderheads," he reported.

"You two had better get going while you can," Hrardorr said.

"I really don't like leaving you all alone down here," Livia said.

The dragon made a scoffing sound that wasn't quite a growl. *"Nonsense. I will be fine here for a few hours more. And in the morning, Seth can help me get back to the Lair without alerting the whole place to my snit."* Hrardorr's head turned toward Seth, even though the dragon couldn't really see him. *"Won't you?"*

"You know I will," Seth replied. "I'd do just about anything to help you out, Hrardorr. You should know that by now."

Hrardorr bowed his head. *"Thank you, Seth. You're a good man."* The dragon's head rose, and smoke trailed from his nostrils. *"Now you two had best get out of here while you can, or I'll worry."*

Touched by Hrardorr's words, Livia wanted to hug him the way Seth had, but she didn't dare approach that closely. She'd never touched the dragon, though they had spent a great deal of time together on the water, only yards separating them—she in her boat, he floating on the surface of the waves.

"All right," Seth said, reaching for Livia's now-dry cloak. "We'll go, but I'll let you know when we reach the house."

"Good," Hrardorr replied. *"Now get going before the wind starts up again. Or the sun rises,"* he added with a dragonish chuckle.

"It's not quite that late in the night," Livia replied, chuckling along with the dragon as Seth helped her into her cloak. "Have a good night, Hrardorr. Be well and don't hesitate to let me know if you need anything."

"Yes, mother," Hrardorr joked. *"Go on now."*

She didn't want to leave him, but she knew she must. With a last lingering look, she allowed Seth to escort her out of the boat house and into the light rain outside. It was a far cry from what they'd faced on the way down. Going up the stairs was much easier as a result.

Livia figured Seth was talking to Hrardorr silently as they made their way up. He was quiet, keeping his hands ready to catch her should she slip, but his attention seemed to be split.

When they reached the top, she was glad to see the lantern at the back door had been left lit by her housekeeper. The woman was crusty on the outside but deft at her job.

"Have you told him we're up yet?" Livia asked Seth when it seemed his attention was finally back fully.

He nodded, smiling a bit. "He kept asking where we were and if you were out of harm's way yet. He cares greatly for your safety, mistress." That smile warmed her to her bones. Seth was so handsome in a golden god sort of way. He'd always made her knees weak when she saw him. Talking to him these past few hours was like a dream because he'd proved himself as nice as he was handsome.

She opened the back door, taking the lantern with her as they entered the small mudroom. There, she shed her wet cloak, glad to be able to hang it up finally and know that she wouldn't have to put it on again until it was completely dry, barring some emergency. She wasn't sure, but it sounded like maybe the storm was beginning to pick up again. If that was the case, she would have an excuse to make sure Seth passed the night under her roof.

And if the sea gods were smiling, she might even have the chance to fulfill one of her deepest, darkest desires. Somewhere during the night, reality had begun to merge with fantasy until she wasn't really sure what was real and what was just a dream. She wasn't really sure she wanted to know. For now, having Seth in her home was a fantasy come to life. Tiny the alarm bells rang occasionally in the back of her mind, but it wasn't enough anymore. She had almost completely forgotten her liaison with Sir Gowan and what she had thought it might mean for her future.

That was also supposition anyway on her part. Seth was real. He was here. In her house. In the flesh. It couldn't be wrong when her heart was singing and her imagination running wild. She had loved him from afar for so very long... Was it so wrong to want one stolen night with him? The man of her many girlhood dreams.

She didn't want to think about right and wrong. All that mattered was what would happen in the next minutes, or hours, if she could convince him to stay.

She tried the direct approach first.

"You should stay here tonight. It's too wet and cold to be traipsing up to the Lair, only to sneak back down again in a few hours to help Hrardorr get back. We have plenty of room."

"All right," he readily agreed, taking just a little of the wind out of her sails. She'd honestly thought he would argue more.

Why had she thought that? Was she preconditioned to expect disappointment where he was concerned? Was that the legacy of her unrequited love all these years? If so, maybe she had it all wrong. Maybe the problem wasn't him, but her expectations.

Well, there was no use regretting the past now. What mattered most was what happened from here on out. She knew him now. She'd spent time working alongside him and talking with him. They had a mutual friend in Hrardorr, and she had discovered he was every bit as nice inside as he looked on the outside. That couldn't be said of most people—that she'd learned from hard experience.

She shed her boots and left them in the mudroom to deal with tomorrow. She had other boots she could wear if she needed to go out again.

"You can leave your things here. Rosie will see to them in the morning, if they need brushing or cleaning. Mostly I think everything just has to dry out, and they can do that here as well as anywhere. Better, since we won't be tracking water all through the house." She smiled at him as he agreed without comment.

He stripped down to his bare feet, electing to keep his tunic and trews on, even though both sported wet hems. Maybe she could talk him out of his shirt, at least, once she showed him the guest room. She wanted to see his bare chest more than just about anything at that moment, her insides heating from the mere thought.

Having sex with Gowan the other day must have loosened something within her. Suddenly, it seemed, she could think of nothing else. But not with just anyone. Until Seth had shown up at her door, Gowan had been the only star in her more lascivious fantasies.

Then Seth had arrived, rekindling all those girlhood daydreams that had never quite died. While she still couldn't figure out whether it was completely wrong to want two men at the same time, she was also powerless to stop the attraction. It raged, uncontrollably. Like wildfire through her system.

When he was ready, she led him through the kitchen and into the hall. From there, they went up the stairs to the second floor where the family bedrooms were located. Her father had the master suite, when he was home, of course. That massive door lay at one end of the upstairs hall. Livia's suite was smaller and located on the opposite end.

Her plan was to put Seth in the room next to hers. It was a guest room they occasionally used for visitors, or extended family members who sometimes came to stay. The advantage of the room was that it had a very large bed, designed to fit a tall man. The bed had been her father's at one time, but he'd brought something new home from his travels, and this one had ended up in the guest room. It would fit Seth, she thought. He was a tall man. Muscular too.

Trying to banish the lurid thoughts that idea conjured, she led him to the door and opened it. She led the way inside, knowing that she'd have to make up the fire. Seth had to be soaked and chilled from their journeys through the rain. A fire was in order, even with the soft down comforter on the bed.

"Give me just a minute, and I'll have the fire blazing," she said as she walked toward the fireplace. The logs were already laid, the room kept prepared for just such emergencies. All it would take was the striking of a match and a little patience.

"I can do that," Seth said quickly, following close behind her.

"Oh, it's no problem." She bent down, lit the tinder, then stood again. Spinning on her heel, she found herself closer than she'd expected to Seth. Much closer.

Time stood still, and he seemed to notice their closeness too.

"Seth?" she whispered as his head drifted lower, his lips approaching hers.

His only answer was to cover her mouth with his. And, oh, what an excellent answer it was.

There was no thinking, just feeling as he began dancing them slowly closer to the bed, his mouth never leaving hers. His kiss was heaven, his touch divine. Her body was starved for the feel of his, it seemed, and she tossed all caution to the wind.

She had wanted him to notice her since they were children. She had wanted to know the feel of his kiss, his touch, his possession, for years. And now was her chance.

She didn't think about right and wrong. Her mind turned briefly to Gowan, but somehow, it didn't seem that big of a deal that she was with both of them in such a short time, which probably should have raised alarm bells in her mind. But she was beyond such thoughts as Seth laid her down on the soft bed, coming over her, kissing her with such sweet tenderness and passion that she couldn't even remember her own name, much less that she was supposed to be involved with Gowan.

Seth's gentle touch seduced her every thought, her every sense. He was the center of her world for those moments, and when he began to undress her, she was his willing accomplice in the deed. She pushed at his clothing, too, wanting no barriers between them. She wanted to touch his skin and have him touch hers. She wanted, finally, to know what it felt like to be with Seth. Seth, the golden god of her youth. Seth, the unattainable. Seth...the sweetest man she had ever known in word, deed, and heart.

She ran her fingers through his golden hair, loving the silky feel of it against her hands. Contrasted with the slight stubble of his cheeks, she was in sensory heaven, and they weren't even naked yet.

But that was soon to be remedied. Seth worked steadily at

the bows and buttons that held her dress and undergarments together, while she did the same for him. His ties were a little hard, since some were made of leather and were somewhat damp from their long night outside in the rain. She persevered though, wanting more than anything to run her hands over his chest...and lower.

He might not be a knight, but Seth was built like one of those mighty warriors. He had strong muscles and was tall and extremely well put together. Like some artist's ideal of what a man's body should look like. A living sculpture of male perfection, though he seemed not at all aware of his almost magnetic appeal.

Livia hadn't been the only girl in town sighing over him when they were younger. He didn't come down from the Lair often, but all the young girls had made it their business to know who he was. When he hadn't been chosen as a knight, but had taken the healer's path, some of the more fickle girls discarded him from their daydreams, but Livia never had. No, Seth was as attractive now as he had ever been, and her longing for him had never waned.

She'd given up, eventually, on the dream of having him notice her, but once he did, the infatuation flared back to life. And it was more than mere infatuation now. Now, it was genuine liking based on respect and shared thoughts and ideals.

Now that she had spent quality time in his company, she liked him even more.

When he was naked, she pushed at his shoulders until he allowed her to roll him over onto his back on the wide bed. Straddling his hips, she removed the last few bits of her own clothing, watching him watch her. It was exciting to see the fire in his eyes as he gazed on her breasts.

"You can touch, you know," she invited with a smile, reaching for his hands.

"I like looking at you. I've dreamed of this many times," he admitted. His words thrilled her. Had he really been thinking of her as long as she'd been dreaming about him?

She'd have to ask him…later. Now it was time for action, not so many words.

When his hands cupped her breasts and started playing with her nipples, all thought fled her head except for those connected to pleasure. Seth's touch was warm and strong, gentle in a way that spoke of his inner nature and his respect for her as well. It was a heady combination.

Seth was proving to be a considerate lover, but Livia didn't want to take it slow. Not right now. Maybe later, but not now.

She slid lower on his body, rubbing her wet pussy over his hard cock while lowering her torso so that his hands never lost their connection with her breasts. She craved his touch and didn't want to lose it. Not for a second.

Yet, she wanted more. She wanted him inside her. Later, she would take time to examine him, touch him and lick him the way she wanted, but at the moment, she wanted nothing more than to know what it would feel like to finally have him inside her.

Rubbing her slick opening over him, she grasped him in one hand, guiding him into her core. He was long and thick, and clearly ready, judging by the hardness of him. She felt him slip inside, and then, she slowed her motions. Almost perversely, she wanted to savor this moment. She wanted to feel every inch of him as he joined with her for the first time.

The first of many, she hoped, deep in her heart. She realized she had never completely let go of the dream of being with Seth. The thought warred with her recent time spent in Gowan's company, but she was too involved with Seth right now to give that much thought. Later. Later, she would try to figure out what in the world she was going to do about all of this.

But for right now, taking Seth into her welcoming sheath was like coming home to a place she had never been but had dreamed of often. She had spent many an hour dreaming more innocent girlhood dreams of kissing Seth and spending time with him. As she'd aged, her dreams had turned more carnal.

Being on top and riding him like a pony was a fond daydream that was now coming true. If she had her way, they both would be coming in short—well, not *too* short, she hoped—order.

She slid down him until he was fully seated within her and then began to move, rocking back and forth, up and down, in the riding motion she had dreamed about. His hands left her breasts and went to her hips, helping her rise and fall, aiding her trembling muscles.

He was so strong. She hadn't expected that, but she probably should have realized after all they'd been through that night. He was built like any knight, even if he didn't have a dragon. He had the muscles. And the body.

And my-oh-my, what a body it was. He was long and lean. Golden all over, from his rich hair to his lovingly bronzed skin. She wanted to cover him like a blanket and never let him go. After, that is, she had wrung every last bit of pleasure out of their joining humanly possible.

She began to move faster, her instincts guiding her to places she had never gone before. Oh, she'd been with other men—at least one, very recently too—but the experience of sharing her body with Seth was unlike her other encounters. Seth was unique.

As was the pleasure she got from riding him. A dream come true.

She quaked as her climax hit, losing rhythm and coordination as the pleasure overtook her with almost alarming urgency. She lost track of where Seth ended and she began as he rolled her over, taking charge as she pretty much lost her mind.

She didn't care. Seth began pumping in a fast rhythm that set her alight and kept her orgasm rolling in waves of pleasure. It went on and on until, finally, he joined her in ecstasy, calling her name as he came within her, clutching her close to his body as he possessed her fully.

It was beautiful. *He* was beautiful, though she would never use that word aloud with him, knowing most men would object to such a thing. But he was. Inside and out. And he made love even better than all the daydreams she'd ever had about them together.

They made love again and again, throughout the night, catching sleep here and there, between encounters. They laughed at times and at others were serious and without words. Their bodies did the communicating, and their hearts seemed to be on the same page of an account they seemed to be writing together.

It was an idyllic night for Livia, where fantasies were fulfilled and thoughts of the past became reality in the present. The future? Well, she preferred not to think too much about it, because it was just too confusing at the moment.

She'd figure it all out tomorrow. Tonight was for loving. And Seth. And loving Seth...

And on that rather surprising thought, she fell into a deep and dreamless sleep.

CHAPTER ELEVEN

The next morning, Livia woke to the feeling of motion. The bed was moving as Seth slid out of it and began to dress. Memories of the night before came back in a rush, and she could feel a huge grin spreading over her face as she stretched.

"Good morning," she said to Seth between yawns.

He paused, looking up from tying his trews. "Morning." He looked panicked for a moment, but then, his gaze softened. "I have to go. If we don't get back to the Lair before the sun rises, everyone will know that Hrardorr wasn't there last night. Much as I'd prefer to stay here with you..." He prowled forward, stalking her playfully as he boxed her in with his arms, pushing her back into the bed slightly. He kissed her then, a lingering kiss that was all about joy and tenderness, with a bit of rekindling passion thrown in for good measure.

And then, it was over. He looked deep into her eyes.

"You will never know how much last night meant to me, Livia. I would very much like to see you again. That is..." He trailed off, looking a bit insecure, which puzzled her. "If you want it too. I know I'm not your social equal. And I'm not anywhere near good enough for you, but after last night, it will be hell to keep my distance from you, Livia. I'm not sure

I can."

She was so very confused by her feelings for both Gowan and now Seth. She didn't know what to say or how to handle the situation. But she did know she didn't want to let him go. She didn't want to give him up that easily.

"I want to see you again too," she whispered. "You've always been the man of my dreams, Seth. Since we were both youngsters. I've wanted to be close to you for a very long time, and I don't want it to end with just one night."

He smiled as if she'd handed him the world and dipped forward to kiss her again.

A door closing rather loudly out in the hall broke them apart before they could get sidetracked into making love again, though it was a close thing.

"Rosie," Livia whispered when Seth's head rose and he looked over his shoulder toward the door. "That's her version of being discreet. That was her letting me know she knows I didn't sleep in my own bed last night." Livia smiled at his confusion. "It means I'll owe her a bit extra before Father comes home, or she'll go telling tales. Father likes to believe I'm still a child when it comes to sex, and if he had his way, he'd probably want me to join some awful religious sect that makes you promise to be celibate for the rest of your life."

Her words sparked a laugh out of Seth as he rose and finished dressing. When he was done, he paused by the door and just looked at her.

"I hate to leave," he said in a quiet voice that touched her deeply. There was something in his eyes that spoke directly to her heart.

"But Hrardorr is waiting," she finished for him, reminding them both of their friend and his promise to help the dragon.

Livia loved Hrardorr, but just at that moment, she wished he'd been able to fly up to the Lair on his own. Ultimately, though, she cared a lot about the dragon and wanted him safe. Today, that meant parting with her new lover long before she was ready to let him go, but it had to be done.

"I'll be in touch. I want to see you again, but I don't know when I'll be free. I'll find out today and send word to see if you're available." He said it in a rush, as if he was somehow worried that she would say no.

"I'll find time. I want to be with you, Seth."

He gave her a huge smile on his way out the door, and she realized what she'd said sounded a bit more committed than she'd meant to be. Not that she had lied. She wanted to be with Seth.

But the problem remained: she wanted to be with Gowan too.

How in the world could that work?

The stark reality was that, if Seth had also been a knight, it might have been possible, though Livia wasn't completely sure how that all worked among Lair families. She supposed the dragons might have some say in the matter.

Regardless, the fact was Seth wasn't a knight. So she couldn't have them both—strange as it was to admit to herself that she wanted exactly that.

What was she going to do?

Genlitha had had just about enough of Hrardorr avoiding her. So on her very next free morning, she decided to stalk him. She loitered in the hallway outside his suite, planning to ambush him on his way out. She didn't want to be too obvious about it, but she definitely wasn't going to stand around waiting any longer. It was clear to her by now that the male dragon was avoiding her, and if she didn't do something proactive, they would never have a chance to be reacquainted.

She remembered him as a dashing dragon, with the most attractive coloration she had ever seen. He was unlike the rest, both in color and temperament. Sure, he was as brash as the other males of their generation, but his bravado had been tempered by compassion. Genlitha hadn't blossomed fully until her wings came in completely. That happened a little later for her than for the other dragons of her age because her wings were so very long.

They made her a fierce flyer, but while she was growing, she had been clumsy. Some of the others had been mean to her about it, but not Hrardorr. Even though he was right there at the top of all their classes, he had found time to speak kindly to her. and she had never forgotten it...or him.

They'd gone off to different assignments after their training days were over, and they hadn't crossed paths again. Until now.

She knew he'd been badly injured. She knew he was blind. It didn't matter to her. The dragon she remembered had a big heart, and no crippling injury would have stopped him.

Maybe Hrardorr had just forgotten that for a while. Maybe Genlitha could help remind him. At least, she hoped she could help him in some way.

When they were younger, she'd always felt at a distinct disadvantage because he was such a fierce fighter and had skills from his sea dragon heritage that most of the rest of them had not. She'd felt like a bit of a failure next to him—at least until she gained her full wingspan. Over the years, she had come into her own in a way that gave her much greater confidence in who she was as a dragon and as a warrioress. She thought maybe she could face Hrardorr on equal footing now, where she never had when they were younger.

She wanted that chance. But he'd been avoiding her.

Well, no longer.

She paced in the hallway, trying to stage an *accidental* meeting with the male dragon she remembered so fondly. She spun on her tail when she heard the large door down the hall creak open. She looked, and yes...it was Hrardorr's suite.

She saw him pause in the doorway as if testing to see if the hall was empty. She saw his head crane out, his nostrils flaring as he sniffed. He was using his other senses to help him discover if the way was clear.

He shuffled out slowly, spreading his wings slightly in the confines of the hall so that they just brushed the walls on either side. His sensitive wingtips were telling him through touch where he was situated in the hall.

Every hesitant step he took toward the nearby ledge broke her heart a little more. He was a shadow of the confident dragon she'd once known, but at least he was moving on his own, allowing his other senses to compensate for the loss of his eyesight. At least he was doing that much.

He sniffed in her direction as he neared and came to a halt. He looked so unsure she spoke first.

"Hrardorr?"

He let out a long, smoky sigh. *"Genlitha."*

He didn't sound happy, but she didn't let that deter her.

"I have been looking for you, my old friend. It has been a long time." She measured her words carefully, not knowing precisely how to approach him.

"You have found me, despite my best efforts to avoid exactly this situation," he stated rather rudely. His tone, though, said he was weary. Maybe even embarrassed. She tried not to take offense.

"I thought we were friends once," she whispered. Apparently, the hurt was speaking, even though she had wanted to play this first meeting much, much cooler.

"We were, Genlitha," Hrardorr seemed to backpedal. *"But things are different now. I am different now."*

"Your blindness doesn't make one whit of difference to me, Hrardorr. You will always be the kind dragon I knew as a youngling. You were nice to me when others weren't. I remember that, and I would like to renew our friendship."

"I was kind to you, so you want to be kind to me, now that I am crippled?" he challenged with a smoky huff.

"Don't you put words in my mouth, Hrardorr," she said, getting angry. Little flames were flaring from her nostrils.

Hrardorr backed off and sighed. He sat on his haunches right there in the hall, looking defeated. She watched to see what he would do next. So far, this encounter wasn't going at all the way she had envisioned.

"Still the feisty little Genlitha," he mused, almost contemplatively. *"You were a pretty little thing, in the middle of a growth spurt. I wanted to see what you would look like when your wings*

finished coming in fully, but I was sent away on my first assignment. I heard you'd done well for yourself over the years, though."

"And I got sent here, to the Southern Lair, for my first assignment because my wingspan was so broad. I really learned to fly here," she reminisced. *"But you look as you always did. You still wear the colors of your sea dragon heritage. I never told you how fascinated I was by that, and by your skills on the river."*

If she were human, she would be blushing. Genlitha had never told him any of this, and she hadn't really intended to do so now, but she wasn't really following her plan anymore. Hrardorr was much different than she'd expected. So much about him had changed, yet he was still the dragon she'd once known. He was still the same...inside...where it really counted.

"I may look the same, but I am not the dragon I once was," he said with a strong flavor of melancholy.

"None of us stay exactly the same," she told him quietly.

"And some of us change more than others—not for the better," he challenged.

Silence stretched for a long moment before she tried a different tactic.

"I would like to fly with you again," she said in a soft tone. *"Now that I am not tripping over my wings, I would like to share the sky with you, as we did in the old days."*

"You may not trip over your own wings, but I am a hazard in the sky, and you may end up tripping over me, since I cannot judge distances anymore. I find it impossible to fly in any sort of close formation. I am useless as a fighting dragon."

He stated his deficiencies with a mixture of anger, sorrow and frustration that hurt Genlitha to hear. She wished she could do something to help him, but she didn't really know what. Maybe she should just try being his friend.

"I am here to teach the youngsters with exceptional wings how to fly in these turbulent currents. I'm sure I can manage to keep out of your way, Hrardorr." She tried to inject a bit of dry amusement into her tone, along with confidence.

Hrardorr's head tilted as he seemed to consider her words.

Finally, he nodded. *"Maybe you would at that. Well..."* He stood and shuffled forward a few feet. *"If you want to fly with me, I'm going down to the water. I have a date with a young lady to go fishing."*

"A lady?" Genlitha was caught off guard. Was he seeing another dragon? Was he involved with another female? Genlitha certainly didn't want to be a third wheel on an outing he was going on with another woman. *"I wouldn't want to intrude. Perhaps another time?"* Genlitha was already backing away, searching for a deep hole in which to hide from her embarrassment.

"A human lady," Hrardorr clarified with unmistakable amusement. *"Strangely enough, I have made a human friend in the town. She goes fishing in her little sailboat, and I keep her company several times a week."*

"Oh, well, in that case..." Genlitha felt the most incredible wave of relief. He wasn't involved with another dragoness.

And that, right there, told her more than she had known about her own mixed feelings. She was still attracted to Hrardorr, even after all these years. More attracted than she'd realized.

"Come on then," he said, passing her in the hall.

His wingtip slid over her scales in a whisper of a caress that sent chills down her spine. Had he meant to touch her like that? Was it necessity or teasing? She had no idea as she followed him to the ledge and launched into the sky behind him.

He led her down to the water, and she flew little patterns around him, playing with him in the sky, though he couldn't really join in the fun. He was aware of her. She could tell. His head and ears followed her wingbeats. She was sure he knew exactly where she was, even though he couldn't see her.

When they neared the water, he finally spoke again.

"Do you see a little sailboat?"

"I see two boats with sails. One has a green stripe on its sail. One is plain."

"That doesn't help much, Genlitha," Hrardorr seemed more amused than upset at her unthinking reminder of visual clues

that would be useless to him.

"My apologies. How do you usually find her boat?" she asked, truly curious.

"I find it from below."

"Truly? How in the world does that work?"

"Watch and learn."

Hrardorr flew farther out and made a cautious approach to the surface of the water. Somehow, he knew there was nothing on the surface to obstruct his landing, and he made a graceful descent to the surface, and then...below it.

Genlitha stayed aloft, watching from above, awed by the sight of him just below the surface, swimming along almost faster than she could fly. From below, he took only a moment to get his bearings, then made a beeline for the boat with the striped sail.

He popped up a moment later, to sit on the surface of the water like some sort of giant duck, making not a ripple to disturb the little wooden boat. Genlitha saw a human female turn to greet Hrardorr, and there was something very familiar about the woman. Genlitha decided to fly down for a closer look.

"Hrardorr? How do you float like that?" she asked, not sure she could emulate his posture on the surface.

"Splay your feet and use your tail for balance. You might also need to hold air in your bellows to keep you buoyant and maybe use your wings a bit. I'm not sure how a purely land dragon would manage this position, but I think it is possible with some adjustments."

Now, he sounded both contemplative and amused. She liked the change in his attitude, but she was a little afraid she was about to make a huge fool out of herself.

"I'm going to try it. I'll land a short distance away, just in case. I don't want to cause trouble for your friend, or her boat."

"Good thinking," he agreed. *"Let me know how you get on."*

Genlitha spent a few minutes panicking until she finally figured out how to keep her balance on the surface of the water without either sinking or capsizing. After another minute, she learned how to move through the water, using her feet to paddle. She made her way over to Hrardorr, feeling a sense of pride that she'd been able to figure it out, though of course, he couldn't see her.

She heard clapping from the sailboat and looked over to find a smiling face she recognized.

"Mistress Livia?" Genlitha asked, including Hrardorr in her thoughts as well.

"Lady Genlitha, it is good to see you again. You have done marvelously well learning how to float like our friend here. Well done." Livia's good cheer made Genlitha feel better. At least someone had seen her accomplish what no other dragon in the Lair seemed to know how to do.

"Thank you, mistress. It is good to see you again as well. I did not know you were friends with Hrardorr."

What followed was an eye-opening afternoon of conversation and fishing. To be fair, Hrardorr and Livia did the actual fishing. Genlitha merely did her best to stay afloat while Hrardorr was gracious enough to share his catch with her.

Genlitha was shocked to realize that Livia was on such close terms with Hrardorr. She was also fascinated to hear Hrardorr tease Livia about being sweet on Seth, the Lair's healer apprentice. Pieces began to fall into place in Genlitha's mind as a pattern began to emerge.

If Hrardorr were to choose a new knight…and if that knight happened to be Seth…and if Hrardorr was as attracted to Genlitha as she was to him…

It all made a neat sort of sense, but she didn't speak any of her thoughts to anyone. Genlitha thought she saw a way to happiness for all five of them, but only time would tell if Hrardorr could ever get past his limitations enough to accept another knight.

For now, Genlitha would try to be patient. She would watch and wait, and bide her time. She'd work from the shadows, doing all she could to make the pattern in the mist solidify into a beautiful future for them all.

Seth had invited Livia up to the Lair, and tonight was the night. He went to get her and escort her up to the Lair, having secured dinner for her in a private room.

She was gracious company and looked around the Lair with enthusiasm. He noted that she wasn't afraid of the dragons they passed in the hallways. She wasn't frightened by the knights in their armor, weapons on their person. She was accepting of it all and met each new sight with an eager sort of interest that he thought was a very good sign.

After dinner, Seth showed her around the Lair, sticking to the areas where they wouldn't run into too many single knights. Seth figured he would lose her soon enough. He wanted to spend this time with her, away from the possible suitors who would be after her like a shot once they realized she could bespeak dragons.

For just this little while, he wanted to keep her all to himself. Well...to himself and Gowan. He'd heard about their date from Hrardorr, who had heard it from Genlitha. He even sort of understood Livia's attraction to the knight. Seth wouldn't be surprised if she ended up mated to Gowan and whatever knight ended up as his fighting partner.

Seth hadn't had the nerve to ask Genlitha if she was interested in any of the male dragons in the Southern Lair. For whichever dragon was her mate—that dragon's knight would be Gowan's fighting partner and the third in the human threesome. Seth hated the man already, even though he had no idea who he might be.

CHAPTER TWELVE

Oddly, Seth didn't mind Gowan so much. How could he? Gowan was a brave and honorable knight. Seth counted him a true friend, and heaven knew, he'd had precious few of those since he'd made his choice to apprentice with Bronwyn.

They both knew the other had been seeing Livia. They hadn't talked about it openly, but the dragons made sure each knew about the other. And the dragons—particularly Genlitha—seemed to want to make sure there were no hard feelings. She'd spoken to Seth directly about it after Hrardorr had told him. She'd asked a few probing questions about his feelings and made Seth recognize that he wasn't angry or jealous, just...sort of sad that he'd never be part of Livia's ultimate destiny, which he knew lay here at the Lair.

How could it not? She could bespeak both dragons and knights. She was a generous, beautiful, smart woman that any knight would be proud to claim as wife. Seth had admired her from afar for too long to pass up this opportunity to get to know her, but he knew—much as he could wish it were otherwise—that she would end up with knights. And Seth would never be a knight.

Never had he regretted that decision more.

Seth took Livia to all his favorite spots in the Lair. Spots that most of the knights didn't frequent. The kitchens, the inner workings of the place where the magic happened, and of course, the healing rooms.

Bronwyn had long since retired for the night when Seth and Livia arrived at his little corner of the apothecary. He'd taken it over when the climb up the stairs had become too much for Bronwyn. He did all the heavy lifting now, including tending the heavier plants and bulkier items in this corner of the healing suite.

Seth showed Livia the wide balconies built right into the side of the cliff, where he tended hardy bushes and small trees that provided various healing herbs. There were also many, many potted plants and an ingenious irrigation system that Seth operated on a daily basis, taking care of his leafy charges.

He also just loved the view out here. He spent many nights on the balconies, looking out at the stars and contemplating the infinite. Never before had he brought a woman here. It was his special place.

"This is really beautiful, Seth," Livia said in a hushed tone of reverence. "You can see for miles from up here."

"I often think this is how a dragon must see. I've been aloft a number of times in my life, but even for someone Lair-born like me, it's a rare experience."

"It's wonderful, isn't it?" she asked candidly, gazing out at the stars. "When Genlitha took me up that first time, I thought I'd be afraid, but it was so beautiful up there, among the clouds..." Her thoughts trailed off, but Seth understood. He'd felt much the same things the times he'd been invited onto a dragon's back.

"It's truly magical," he agreed. "And I just wanted to say..." He wasn't sure if this was a good idea, but he really wanted the air clear between them. He forged ahead. "Genlitha told me about you seeing Gowan. If you prefer him to me, I want you to know I understand."

Livia looked at him, her mouth open in shock. She seemed so caught off guard by his statement it took her time to figure out what to say. His heart sank. She was probably going to try to let him down easy, but he waited to hear what she would say. He wasn't a coward. He could take it if she rejected him. He hoped.

"It's not like that. I never planned any of this to happen, and to be honest, I'm confused about it all. I've watched you from afar for years, Seth." He took heart from her words. "I started seeing Gowan, and then suddenly, there you were, and I couldn't pass up the opportunity to get to know you the way I'd dreamed about for so long. I know it's not right to keep you both on a string. It's not fair to either of you." She looked away, her expression tortured. "I'm very confused by it all. I don't understand how I can be with both of you, or how this could end any other way but badly."

"Well, I don't know about the ending for you and me, but it's pretty clear that you are destined to be a Lair wife. If that's the case, it's only natural that you be willing, even eager, to take on two lovers, so don't doubt yourself. You're following your instincts. The only real problem I see here is that you've chosen one knight and me, who will never be a knight. I'm the one who should bow out so that you can find the mates you were meant for." He had to look away, gazing out at the dark sky. The pain in his heart was enormous. Almost too much to contain.

"Is that what you really want?" she asked in a small voice.

"No." He had to tell her the truth. "I've admired you from afar for years, too. I didn't think you ever noticed me, though I dreamed of you often enough." He shook his head, almost not believing he was laying his deepest secrets out before her. But it was so easy to talk to Livia. The reality of being with her was better than any dream he'd ever had of her.

"We've both been foolish," she said finally. "I liked you, and now, you say you liked me. Why did we never act on it before?" She didn't wait for an answer to her question, but went on. "I'm sorry, Seth. We've wasted a lot of time. And now, there's Gowan..."

"I don't mind Gowan. I actually count him as a friend. I know he's a good man, and I respect him."

"I didn't know you were close," she said softly.

"Not close, exactly, but he's probably my best friend in the Lair right now." Seth didn't talk about the way they'd been helping each other. He didn't want anyone to know about his secret training. He didn't want to be a laughingstock among the knights if word should somehow get out.

"I'm glad you two are friends, though it does seem to complicate an already complicated situation." She made a face, and Seth had to smile.

"Actually, it makes this easier. I couldn't bear to see you with anyone I didn't respect as much as Gowan."

She shook her head, but she had a soft smile on her face. "I don't really understand the way you look at life. I wasn't raised with Lair sensibilities, I guess."

"You'll adapt," he said, shrugging. "Lair life is freeing in many ways. And so full of love and care between dragons and humans. Growing up in a Lair family was a really great experience."

"You're assuming I'll end up as a Lair wife."

He shrugged again. "It makes sense. Women who can talk to dragons are a rarity."

He let that statement hang in the air for a bit as they both looked out at the sky. Silence reigned for a few minutes while they each processed their own thoughts.

"I suppose Gowan knows about us too, if you know about me and him?" she asked finally, surprising him.

"Well, yes. Genlitha has been talking to us both, I'm sure."

"And what does he think?"

She bit her lip as if worried, and Seth wanted to kiss her, but he dared not at that moment. There were things to discuss and settle between them to ease her worry.

"I haven't talked to him directly about it. Mostly, it's been Genlitha talking to us individually. Dragons have been known to meddle in their humans' lives from time to time." He had to chuckle at that. It was truer than she knew. "Genlitha seemed to indicate that Gowan was learning to accept that, if and when he does find a wife, he would have to share her. He grew up much as you did, with even less exposure to the ways of the Lair. I got the impression that he sees me as a worthy competitor for your favor." He had to smile at that.

"Competitor?" Livia shook her head. "I never meant to pit you two against each other."

"Not at all," Seth was quick to reassure her. "It's not a competition in that sense." Especially since he knew who would ultimately win, and it wasn't Seth. "More like a friendly rivalry. And we have stayed friends. There are no hard feelings. We both want whatever—or whoever—you want. You are the one who decides, Livia. Not us."

"That's very generous of you," she said after a moment's thought. "I'm not sure, in your place, I could be as selfless."

Seth didn't know what to say to that, so he kept silent.

"Seth…" Livia turned away from the balcony rail to face him, her cheeks lit by starlight. He hadn't lit the lanterns out here, and the only illumination came from the sky and the open doorway that led back to the apothecary. "I really like you, Seth. A lot."

Seth felt his heart racing as he wondered where she was leading the conversation.

"I really like you too, Livia."

"That's good." She smiled at him and moved closer. "Because I really don't want to go home tonight. Can I stay with you?" She looped one arm over his shoulder, tangling her fingers in the ends of his hair at his nape. Little thrills of sensation went down his spine.

"Are you kidding?" He smiled, putting his arms around her and drawing her closer. "Of course you can. You can stay forever, as far as I'm concerned," he whispered, closing in for a kiss. If he'd been too candid, then so be it. Maybe she'd chalk his enthusiasm up to the heat of the moment.

He kissed her, loving the feel of her in his arms. Her mouth welcomed his, her tongue enticing, tangling, tormenting in the most delightful way. But Seth wanted more. No. He *needed* more.

He dipped, lifting her into his arms, and carried her back

into the apothecary, through a couple of archways that led them eventually to his private quarters. His room was attached to the apothecary on one side and a small side hall on the other. He entered from the apothecary side, glad to not have to go too far to get her to his bed.

He was a tall man, so he had a large bed, thank heaven. He placed her upon it, then paused. He just wanted to savor the moment, but Livia had other ideas.

She scooted forward until she was sitting on the side of the bed, facing him. Facing his belt buckle, to be exact. With a saucy smile, she set to work, her nimble fingers making short work of his belt, his ties and then his trews. Before he knew it, he was naked from the waist down, cock out, hard and pointing at her.

"For me?" She made a show of surprise, but the way she licked her lips made Seth's breath catch. And then, she was touching him. Stroking him.

Seth yanked off his best tunic, throwing it into the corner. He wanted to see what his little vixen had planned.

A moment later, his knees threatened to buckle as she put her lips on his cock. She placed little teasing kisses all over his hardness, then batted her long, lustrous eyelashes as she looked up at him a moment before opening that luscious mouth and taking him deep. She held his gaze, and he just about came right then and there.

Only force of will kept him upright. He'd never had a woman go down on him before, and this was an experience he didn't want to miss. He would remember every moment of this encounter until his dying day, he knew, because he was with Livia. The one woman who had always made an impression on him, even though he knew it was impossible to be with her on any sort of long-term basis. Especially now, when he knew she was destined to be a Lair wife.

But all that didn't matter right now, with her tongue swirling around his cock, teasing and tantalizing. He wanted to bring her the same kind of pleasure, and he knew he had to slow things down before he got too excited. He placed gentle but firm hands on her shoulders. Livia looked up at him as she backed off, releasing him by slow degrees until the head of his cock left her mouth with a little pop.

"What? Don't you like it?" she asked with mock innocence.

"I like it a little too much, and you're wearing too many clothes," he answered. He knew he had to be grinning like a fool, but Livia was the most amazing woman he'd ever been with. She made him feel things no other female had ever given him. She was one in a million, and he felt blessed to be with her in this moment.

"Well, we can fix that easily enough," she said, putting action to words and unlacing her bodice.

A few tugs and her breasts were free. Another shimmy and a whoosh of fabric over her head and the dress was gone completely. With a few more pulls of ribbons and bows, the last of her undergarments went sailing into the corner to mingle with his tunic, forgotten for the moment.

And she was gloriously nude.

Livia enjoyed stripping for Seth. If she'd been any less excited, she would have taken the time to draw out the striptease, but as it was, she was too hot to wait much longer. She needed him, and she needed him soon.

"Come down here and join me," she invited, rolling to one side of the bed and patting the sheet next to her.

Seth didn't disappoint. He climbed onto the lovely, large, cushy bed and surprised her by taking a position between her knees. Was he going to...?

Oh, yes. He *was.*

Livia lay back for a moment and just enjoyed the feel of Seth's surprisingly talented tongue in her folds. He stroked lightly over her clit, arousing sensations that made her moan. Oh, yes. He certainly knew what he was doing down there.

But she didn't want to come without him. No, she wanted him inside her when she came.

She sat up on her elbows and met his gaze.

"Want to try this together?" she challenged.

Seth lifted his head away, quirking one blonde eyebrow at her. "What did you have in mind?"

She felt a moment of triumph. She loved the way Seth was game to try things. Some men got a little odd about a woman being somewhat bold in the bedroom. It was refreshing to find Seth wasn't that way.

"Get up here and lie on your back. I'll show you," she told him.

Seth did as she asked, moving slowly and stroking her body as he assumed the position she wanted. "How do you know about such things, milady?" The title was exaggerated in a way that made her feel exceedingly naughty, just as Seth had intended. The accompanying wink made her want to blush, but it also heated her blood to an even higher level.

"My father sails all over, you know. And he brings back all sorts of things. In his library, there are many books in foreign tongues. Some with drawings. Very interesting drawings," she said as she positioned herself over him so that her knees were on either side of his shoulders and her head was above his jutting cock. Perfect.

"I think I'd like to learn more about these strange books," he whispered against the soft, sensitive flesh of her inner thigh. And then, he moved into position, and his tongue lapped at her clit.

Oh, yeah.

She couldn't speak. She could only feel as she lowered her head and took his hardness back into her mouth. With the intense sensations coming from his tongue stabbing softly into her channel, she renewed her suction on him, using one hand to fondle his sac, making him moan. The rumble of sound from his mouth against her most sensitive place caused tingles to shoot up and down her spine.

It was almost too good.

All too soon, he was pushing her higher, but she didn't want to come this way. Not this time. No, she wanted him inside her. She craved it. She had to have it.

Livia pulled away, moving upward over his body until she could seat herself on him, facing his feet. It was a different angle, but it felt like heaven the moment she slid down onto him fully.

And then, the door opened.

Gowan had come looking for Seth, hoping to score a pot of ointment to use on Genlitha's scales, but it wasn't an urgent mission. Still, he had a free hour and thought he'd check in on his friend. When Gowan couldn't find him anywhere, he grew concerned enough to check his quarters, just in case something was wrong.

But the sight that greeted Gowan when he opened the door to Seth's bedroom had him stopping in his tracks.

Livia was naked, an expression of pure bliss on her face as she rode Seth's cock. She was facing the foot of the bed, and the doorway through which Gowan had come. For just a moment, she didn't see him, and that image would remain forever etched on his mind. That free abandon of a woman thoroughly enjoying getting fucked by a man. It was beautiful, really. And intensely arousing.

Damn.

Then she looked up and saw him. *Caught.*

But whether he was more concerned that she'd caught him watching or that he'd caught her fucking his friend, he wasn't sure. He'd have to think about that.

Then Livia smiled.

What in the world?

"Join us?" she said, shaking his world to its foundations. Livia O'Dare was inviting him to…to what, exactly?

"You mean…?" He couldn't even put it into words. His brain was leaping to all sorts of conclusions, and his body was so far ahead his cock could be used to drive nails at this point. That's how hard he was.

"Well, this is the Lair, isn't it? What better place for three?" She looked back at Seth, sitting up on his elbows behind her. "If you don't mind?" she asked him, his cock still showing hard between the folds of her pussy. She was pulsing softly on him, slowed from what she'd been doing when Gowan walked in, but still moving as if she couldn't quite help herself.

Seth apparently had to clear his throat before he could answer. "I don't mind," he said, then flopped back on the bed. "Just make up your mind quickly. This is torture."

Livia reached back to pat Seth's ass. "Delicious torture," she agreed.

Gowan thought he heard a muffled *hell, yeah* from Seth, but he couldn't be sure. All he knew at the moment was that he wanted in that pussy spread so delectably before him, servicing Seth at the moment. His mind might be confused by it all, but his body knew what it wanted.

Gowan stepped fully into the room and shut the door, locking it behind him. Then he leaned back against it and folded his arms.

"Fuck him hard, Livia," he ordered softly, wanting to see what she'd do. Would she respond to his order with eagerness, or just do whatever she wanted?

Gowan knew himself well enough to know that if she obeyed him, all bets were off. He'd want to keep her forever, and damn the consequences. She'd already proven compatible with him in most ways, but if she passed this little test, then there was no doubt she was the perfect woman for him.

"This hard?" she asked, playing along as she rocked on Seth's cock.

Gowan watched her pussy sliding on Seth's hard pole. He hadn't engaged in all that much voyeurism over the years, but he'd seen enough to know that this situation was special. These people were special.

"Harder," he ordered, and she complied, sending a secret little thrill through him. "Spread yourself for me. I want to see you take him," he went on, wanting to see how far she would go in answering his demands. But she didn't disappoint. She did as he asked with one hand, using the other for balance as she moved faster now. "Rub your clit for me, Livia."

That was it. She touched herself, and then, a keening cry came from her lips as she came on Seth's cock. Seth followed, pumping up into her, and Gowan could see it all.

He examined his feelings on the matter for a moment while they rode themselves to completion and determined that he was more aroused than he could ever recall being. Gowan hadn't lived a sheltered life. The uncertain life of a soldier meant you took your pleasure where you could and whenever you could. He'd been with a lot of women over the years, and he'd developed certain...tastes.

The main one of which Livia had just proven to enjoy. Gowan was a dominant man in everything he did, and if he liked giving orders in the bedroom, he figured that wasn't so bad—as long as his lady friends liked it.

Livia liked it. She'd come beautifully for him.

And it *had been* for him. She might have been fucking Seth at the time, but she'd been following Gowan's orders, and that seemed to make all the difference to Gowan's mind.

He felt no jealousy. How could he? Seth was his friend, and Gowan had known they were dating. If Livia hadn't told him in so many words, Genlitha certainly had, though she hadn't gone into detail.

For one thing, he hadn't realized Livia and Seth were lovers, but he probably should have made that connection. Livia was a lass of hearty appetites, which was something Gowan respected. He knew she hadn't been fucking every man in town prior to his arrival. She'd been way too tight for that, for one thing.

For another, her reputation was a good one, even though her father spent so much time abroad. There was no scandal associated with her name, but even if there had been, he would have courted her regardless. She was a special woman in so many ways. He'd do just about anything to be with her.

And that was the crux of the matter, right there.

He cared. As he hadn't cared for a woman in a very long time, if ever. He couldn't really recall ever feeling this deeply for someone. Not in all his years, and not for any of the women who had graced his bed in all that time.

Livia was unique.

And right now, he had to be inside her. He didn't care of Seth had just fucked her. As far as he was concerned, that just meant she was nice and wet and would be able to receive him easier.

Gowan shed his clothes in a few quick movements, crawling onto the bed, on the side where Livia had laid down on her back, breathing hard after her exertions. Gowan framed her head with his arms, holding himself above her.

"Do you want this?" he asked, lowering his cock toward her belly.

Her answer was to spread her thighs and lift her hips toward him.

Gowan spared a thought for Seth. This was his bedroom, after all. Not to mention, his bed.

"You all right with this?" Gowan asked, looking over at Seth.

Seth just waved him on with a tired hand, too spent to talk much.

And that was all it took. Gowan pushed downward, sliding deep into Livia with one solid thrust.

Livia thought for a moment she'd died and gone to heaven. Never in her wildest dreams had she been with both of her perfect lovers at the same time. Sure, she'd thought about what it would mean to be mated to a pair of knights. What girl hadn't?

But she'd never expected...

Conscious thought fled as Gowan slid inside her. He was huge, but he fit so well, now, after she'd gotten used to him. Seth's come helped, too, she was sure. And that thought gave her a thrill as she realized the ramifications of being with both of them. In the same bed.

Stars above, she'd never imagined this when she accepted an invitation to dine at the Lair.

Gowan began to move, fucking her harder than he ever had before, and all she could do was feel. He was so massive he hit that little spot inside her that rocketed her to the moon on every thrust.

She held onto his shoulders for dear life, her nails making little indentations into his skin, but he didn't seem to mind. Her body strained against his, reaching for the peak that was just out of reach.

Gowan sat back on his haunches, changing position slightly, looking down at her, watching the way they came together. His hands were on her hips, guiding her.

That was when she noticed that Seth was sitting up at her side. He was watching with a lazy half-lidded gaze that spoke of his renewed hunger.

They were both watching her. Her mid-section clenched as excitement built. And then...

"Rub her tits," Gowan told Seth. "She needs something more to make her come."

She looked at Seth, saw him look sharply at Gowan, then watched the silent communication between them and Gowan's slight nod. Then Seth looked back at her, and his hand rose.

She anticipated his touch, excitement cresting as Gowan pounded into her below and Seth's hand came in for a landing on her breast. The moment he touched her, she exploded into a million pieces, crying out as Gowan's finger found her clit at the exact moment that Seth palmed her nipple, using his hand to rub over the hard tip.

And then, his other hand joined in, and both of her nipples were rubbed between his fingers as she came. And came. And came.

She could feel Gowan's body pump into her once, twice, and then a final time as he came with her. Pleasure mounted until it was a living, breathing thing that threatened to consume the world.

At some point, she must have passed out or fallen asleep, because when consciousness returned, she was lying in the center of the large bed, a man on either side. It was deep in the night, several hours later, if she had to guess. Seth was awake, running his fingers over her skin, watching her.

"Are you all right?" he asked, her tender lover.

She smiled in reply. "I'm fine. How are you with all of this?"

Gowan stirred, yawning on her other side when she spoke.

She was worried maybe she'd pushed him—both of the men—a little too far, but really, she hadn't known this would turn into a threesome. She'd only intended to snare Seth tonight, not Gowan too.

CHAPTER THIRTEEN

Seth scratched his head. "Can't say I expected this, but I grew up among trios. It's not all that shocking to me as a concept. I just haven't ever been part of one before. Never expected to be, as I said."

Because he wasn't a knight, she knew. Only knights had triad marriages, because of their bonds with their dragon partners.

She looked over at Gowan to find him stretched out on his back, his hands folded beneath his head as if he hadn't a care in the world. He was watching her from under sleepy half-lidded eyes in a way that made her insides clench.

He was a commanding presence, and he'd brought out a side of her she hadn't known existed. She'd never experienced anything hotter or more exciting with any of the men she'd been with before. Now that she'd seen a bit of what he liked—and realized she liked it too—she feared she might be ruined for any other man. Except maybe Seth. He affected her in another way—equally as exciting.

"How about you?" she asked Gowan.

He grinned slowly. "If this is what it means to be a knight, I'm all for it." He glanced over at Seth. "Though I will admit, I didn't count on it being like this."

"What did you think?" Seth asked, sounding curious.

"Frankly, I didn't see how it could work. I knew most knights died bachelors, and I figured that was probably going to be what happened with me." He spoke matter-of-factly, and Livia's heart went out to him. "But now that I've seen how it could work, I'm inclined to rethink my conclusions. If it's always like this, I can see why the families I've seen in Lairs are so happy."

"I can attest to that," Seth added. "My parents are happy, as are all the families that I grew up around. But I'll never be a knight, so I had no expectation of ever experiencing this. You've given me a glimpse of what it could be like, and I'm not sure if that'll ultimately be a good or bad thing. For right now, though, I wouldn't have missed this for the world."

"Me either," Livia said softly, gazing into Seth's eyes. They were so blue she could get lost in them.

"Me three," Gowan said, rolling off his side of the bed, rising and stretching. "And much as it pains me to leave this happy moment, I have to go. Gen and I are on duty in about ten minutes, and I've got to get into my armor." Gowan bent over to kiss Livia once, tenderly, then walked around the bed to retrieve his clothing.

She watched him go with a sad feeling. Would they ever have a chance to share this again? She thought not, which just seemed wrong.

"I should probably be getting you home before the sun rises," Seth said, and she heard a note of reluctance in his voice.

"I don't want this to end," she admitted, "but you're right. I have to be in the office later this morning. I've got ships coming in, and I have to be there to meet with their captains."

Seth walked her all the way to her door in the dim light of false dawn. The sky was bright red, which boded ill for the weather.

Under the watchful eye of her housekeeper, who had met them at the back door with a frown, Seth couldn't draw out the goodbyes. Overall, though, he couldn't complain about their *date*. He'd gotten way more than he'd bargained for out of inviting her to dinner at the Lair.

As he walked back through the town, he saw a flight of dragons maneuvering overhead. He looked up, recognizing Genlitha's gorgeous blue hide. Gowan and she were leading first flight in practice runs. Seth watched them as he headed back to the Lair. They were learning. Genlitha was an excellent flyer, but she hadn't lead a wing before.

Seth also knew Gowan was a skilled fighter and leader of men, but he hadn't fought from atop a dragon before. Both had things to learn, and it looked like they were doing a good job.

Seth's mind was heavy with conjecture, even as his heart was light after the amazing experience of the night before. He made his way back to the Lair, and his chosen life, thinking deep thoughts.

"Seth?"

Livia's voice sounded in Seth's mind later in the day. To say this kind of contact was unexpected was a huge understatement. As far as he knew, she was still down in Dragonscove. She had more reach than he'd thought.

"Is something wrong?"

"It could be. I've had reports from two ship captains that are very troubling. I know Gowan and Genlitha are working today, and Hrardorr is…well…not who I would approach about this, but I thought maybe you could…" Her thoughts trailed off, and Seth wasn't sure what she wanted him to do.

"How can I help?" he asked gently, hoping to alleviate some of the anxiety that came through in her tone.

"I need to talk to someone in power in the Lair. These reports indicate we may soon come under attack by a fleet of war ships— probably pirates—that have been menacing the coast. They're heading in this direction."

Sweet Mother of All. And she was coming to *Seth* with this? What in the world did she think he could do about it?

He was just the apprentice healer, he thought, in a moment of near-panic. She should have brought this to Gowan! But she was right. He and Genlitha were working and interrupting them while they were learning tricky maneuvers could be detrimental.

Seth calmed down. His fathers would know what to do. Quickly, he queried the two dragons who had raised him and learned that his parents were off duty today. Asking the dragons to quietly get their partners to meet him in the great hall, Seth made his way there as quickly as possible.

"All right. I'm going to get advice on how to proceed," he told Livia. *"I'll be in touch shortly."*

Seth joined his fathers in the hall, sitting at the table in one corner they had claimed.

"Thanks for coming," he told them as he took the flagon of ale laid out for him.

"What's wrong?" Gerard said, frowning. "Randor said you had an urgent problem."

"Are you acquainted with Livia O'Dare from the town?" Both Gerard and Paton nodded briefly. "She just contacted me. She had two ships make port today and both of their captains delivered grave news about a pirate fleet traveling this way. She said she needed to talk to someone in power here, but I wasn't sure how best to proceed."

"Is she here? Or did she send a letter?" Paton asked quickly.

"Neither, actually." Seth tried not to fidget. His communication with Livia was extraordinary—especially when he'd never been able to speak mind to mind with anyone else. Just dragons. He could talk to dragons easily. But Livia... She was something special all the way around.

"Seth..." Paton said in a warning tone. His fathers knew him too well.

Seth sighed. "She can bespeak dragons and, it turns out, me as well. She told me in here." He pointed to his temple. "All the way from Dragonscove."

Both older men sat back in their chairs, clearly shocked.

"That's..." Gerard seemed at a loss for words.

"She needs to come here, to the Lair. She belongs with us with such a gift," Paton declared.

"We've already told her so," Seth said baldly, then realized he had to explain. The raised eyebrows from both his fathers demanded an answer to the unspoken question. "She's already involved with Sir Gowan."

"And you?" Paton challenged.

Seth sighed. "Yes, all right. And me. But it was Sir Hrardorr who befriended her first. They've been fishing companions for weeks now."

"Amazing," Gerard muttered, shaking his head.

When silence fell for a moment, Seth tried to get them back on track. "What about the pirate fleet? How do we get the information to Sir Jiffrey and Sir Benrik? As leaders of this Lair, they need to know, but I don't think they'll give much credence to my words." Since he wasn't a knight. That last bit didn't need to be spoken. They all knew Seth wasn't taken seriously by many of the knights in this Lair. It was sore spot the family did its best to ignore.

"Where is Mistress Livia now?" Paton asked, as if skeptical of Seth's claims.

It was so damned typical. Ever since he'd given up warrior training to become a healer, Paton had doubted his every move. Well, Seth would prove he was telling the truth.

"Give me a moment," Seth said, then refocused his thoughts toward Livia. *Where are you now, Livia? I think they're going to want you to come up to the Lair to make the report yourself. Can you do that? Should I come down and get you?*

I thought so, she sent back. *I'm already on my way. I should be arriving at the lower entrance in about ten minutes.*

You're a treasure, Seth sent to her, not bothering to censor his words. *I'll come down and meet you.*

All right. See you in a bit.

Seth brought his attention back to his fathers as he stood. "She's already on her way. Bright girl, is Livia. She thought you'd want her up here, so she started walking probably even before she contacted me. She'll be at the lower entrance in about ten minutes. I'm going to go down and meet her."

"Bring her back here. We'll have Jif or Ben—or both—up here by then," Gerard told him.

Seth made to move past, heading for the door, but Paton's hand on his arm stopped him. He looked down to meet the blue eyes so like his own.

"Good work, lad," Paton said quietly but with conviction behind his words.

"Thanks, Dad." So often Seth had seen only despair in Paton's eyes when he looked at him. This moment was special.

Paton let go, and Seth went on his way to meet up with Livia.

He was so impatient to see her he left the lower doors behind and met her on the road, sweeping her into his arms for a quick kiss before the final bend in the road. Nobody could see them, but there was no time to tarry. There was a threat to the town, and the Lair needed to know.

"My fathers are corralling one or both of the lead knights," he told her as they walked briskly along. "I'm to take you to the great hall to meet them."

"Thank you, Seth." Livia wasn't the least bit out of breath from her quick trip up from town, but she did look a bit anxious. "I wasn't sure how to approach them."

"To be honest, neither was I, but my fathers are wing leaders. They knew what to do," he admitted.

"It's good to have friends—and relatives—in high places, sometimes," she quipped.

He smiled as he led her through the main entrance that led from the road to Dragonscove into the base of the mountain. Stairs and ramps would take them upward. He was able to take her past the guards, right up to the great hall, with little fanfare and only a few odd looks from some of the knights who weren't otherwise occupied.

"Mistress Livia O'Dare, this is my sire, Sir Paton." Seth made the introduction after finding only Paton left at the table in the great hall. Paton bowed politely over Livia's hand while Seth watched impatiently. When the pleasantries were done, he had to ask. "Where is everybody?"

"On their way," Paton said with a calming gesture. "Please, be seated, mistress. My son is remiss, keeping you on your feet after your journey up from town."

Livia smiled politely, but Seth could see she was a bit impatient with the delay. So was he, for that matter. It was at that point he realized that her anxiety had communicated itself to him somehow. *Strange.*

"Seth tells us you can bespeak dragons," Paton started right in once Livia was seated.

"Father..." Seth said warningly, but Paton paid him no mind. Why was Seth not surprised?

"It's all right, Seth," Livia told him, reaching out to cover his hand with hers on the tabletop.

Seth felt the contact all the way to his toes. She'd touched him. In public. It was almost like she was staking a claim. Or, at the very least, letting anyone who cared to look that they were more than mere acquaintances. Seth felt so proud he was afraid the buttons on his shirt would burst.

"Hrardorr warned me what would happen once my secret came out. I suspect I'll be popular with the single knights after this." She gave a long-suffering sigh that was both playful and genuine.

"Seth tells us you're acquainted with one pair already—Sir Gowan and Lady Genlitha?"

Seth rolled his eyes. Paton was about as subtle as dragon fire.

"Yes, I've been flying with Lady Genlitha. She is very sweet."

"Sweet?" Paton tried to hide his bark of laughter with a cough, but he wasn't fooling anyone. "Forgive me. We've been training with Gowan and Genlitha for the past few weeks, and she is formidable. A cunning flyer and a wicked fighter. I never would have applied the term *sweet* to her, though I have nothing but the greatest respect for her."

"Nevertheless," Livia insisted, "she is exceedingly sweet-tempered and kind."

Paton was saved from crafting a response by the arrival into the great hall of Sir Jiffrey, accompanied by Gerard. Both walked quickly over to the table in the corner where Livia waited. Seth rose and made the introductions, wondering privately why Sir Jiffrey's partner hadn't also come.

"He is aloft," said a dragonish voice in his head that he knew well. It was the female dragon who had been as a mother to him, Alirya, partner to Paton. *"When they land, he'll most likely join you, depending on what your lady has to say."* Seth heard the unspoken speculation in Alirya's voice and knew questions would be coming. *"Do you believe her story is as urgent as she claims?"*

"Livia is not a woman given to flights of fancy. If she is concerned, then there is definitely something to be concerned about." Seth defended Livia to the dragon, knowing he was probably damning himself by doing so.

Now the dragons would know for certain he had some sort of feelings for Livia, and they'd no doubt be asking him all about it at their earliest convenience.

Well, then. So be it.

Sir Jiffrey had been exchanging greetings with Livia while Seth was communicating with Lady Alirya. Finally, they were down to the crux of the matter. All were seated around the table, and Livia leaned forward, imparting her news.

"Two of our fleet made port today," she was telling Jiffrey. "As a matter of course, arriving captains make routine reports to either my father or myself, if my father is on a voyage. I have been receiving these reports for many years, and I can tell you, I've never heard two more alarming accounts in all that time." She paused to take a breath and scan the faces of those gathered.

Seth could see she still hadn't convinced the older men, but she would. He knew Livia well enough—trusted her judgment enough—to know that she wouldn't raise a false alarm. He would sit back in silent support unless she needed him. This was her show, and he knew she wouldn't welcome his interference unless there was no other way to make the older men listen.

"What is the report, and from where?" Paton asked quietly when nobody else posed the obvious question.

"First to report was Captain Andrews. He does the eastern trade route that includes Ouray, Penilula, Sabatos and Zealanta. He first heard reports of a large fleet massing east of Zealanta, but didn't think anything of it until he heard more in Ouray. Sightings of a large force, made up mostly of known pirates and heavily armed warships, was confirmed by at least three captains he has known for many years. Tales fill the seaside taverns and are spreading up and down the coast in that land. Captain Andrews is an older man of solid character. He believes the most reliable count is something in the realm of fifty to one hundred ships. Of that, he believes about three quarters have multiple cannons, and some are kitted out with catapults. Whether or not they have any of the diamond-bladed weaponry we've heard is the bane of dragonkind, he does not know."

Now they were listening, Seth saw. All three older men leaned forward and had looks of grave concentration on their faces. None interrupted Livia with objections or questions. Not yet.

"An hour later, Captain Illers of the *Sonova* came tearing into my office in a lather. He has just come from Ouray. His ship left a day after Captain Andrews, and he's been chasing the wind to get here as quickly as possible. Word came to Ouray that the pirate fleet had attacked Listerna, which is just down the coast from Ouray as the crow flies. Fears are that, after Listerna is sacked, Ouray might be next. Whoever was ready to sail took off with all possible haste. The port emptied in record time. Captain Illers had reports direct from messengers sent from Listerna to warn the other coast cities. I have a copy of the missive sent out by Listerna's governor to all its allies. I had our scribes make up several copies and sent them to all the prominent businessmen in town, as well as the Dragonscove town council. And this copy..." She pulled a rolled parchment out of her pocket and handed it across the table to Sir Jiffrey. "This one is for the Lair. If we are soon to come under attack, I think the town council is going to want to know what support we might count on from your knights and dragons."

"We will have to review this information and confirm our readiness," Jiffrey said, scanning the document with a frown.

"As I thought. Which is why I came directly here to give you some time to examine the facts as far as we know them, before the town council comes calling." Livia nodded, and Seth could see she'd surprised Jiffrey with her level-headed actions.

Seth wanted to gloat, but he just sat back and watched her in action. He loved this competent, businesslike side to Livia. Then again, he loved all her moods and facets.

And that was a dangerous train of thought.

"I've sent out two ships. Some of our fastest, not our largest. They are only lightly armed. Their task is reconnaissance. They will make frequent stops along the coast and return with all speed, but even that is going to take days. I was hoping..." Livia's voice dropped to a deceptively innocent tone. "Maybe some of your scouts could fly out a little farther than usual and pay particular attention to the coastline?"

Jiffrey looked up at her sharply. Seth could see the wheels turning in his mind as he, no doubt, talked things over with his partners—both the dragons and the knight who shared responsibility of running this Lair with him. Jiffrey might be sitting at the table, but the other three were listening through him and conversing with him, Seth knew.

"We can do that immediately," Jiffrey confirmed after a few moments. "Gowan and Genlitha are scouting in the east today with first wing. We're sending them farther out toward Ouray. It should take them about an hour to get there from their current location." Jiffrey stood abruptly from the table. "Perhaps you would like to refresh yourself here, Mistress

Livia? I would like to send word back to Dragonscove with you, if you are amenable, since I have no doubt you have a network that far exceeds our own among the local business owners."

"I would be honored to help in any way I can," Livia replied demurely.

Paton and Gerard rose as well. "Perhaps Mistress Livia would like to visit with your mother while we wait for word," Gerard suggested rather overtly before going after Jiffrey.

Livia giggled softly, and Seth knew she understood what was going on. Suddenly, he wasn't embarrassed. A shared joke with the woman who had starred in so many of his dreams was a treasure.

"We're going with Jif," Paton paused to say. Gerard was already halfway across the room, not letting any grass grow under his feet, as usual. "Tell your mother we'll probably be late for dinner, and not to worry. We're just doing the planning now, nothing dangerous."

That was classic Paton, always putting others' worries before himself.

"I'll tell her," Seth promised. And now, they'd *have to* go to his parents' suite. He reached out to shake his father's hand. "And don't think I didn't see what you did there."

Paton winked, smiling at them both, then followed after his fighting partner in double time.

Seth held out his hand to Livia. She rose, taking it, and smiled at him.

"Mistress Livia, now that we have no real choice in the matter, would you like to meet my mother?"

She grinned up at him, making him feel like the king of all he surveyed.

"As a matter of fact, I believe I would like very much to meet your mother. The question is…" she leaned closer, conspiratorially, "…is she going to want to meet me?"

CHAPTER FOURTEEN

All Seth could really do was sit back and watch as Livia and his mother, Enid, got to know each other. Livia was understandably tense, given the news she'd come here to impart, yet his mother did her magic and set Livia at ease. Enid had that way about her. She was unruffle-able. No matter what happened, she took things in stride and was able to convey that feeling of peace to everyone around her.

Currently, she was pouring tea for Livia and Seth around the family table. Seth tried not to squirm when his mother insisted on relating anecdotes from his childhood. Luckily, Livia seemed to think his mother's stories were cute.

They started talking about the market in town and various changes that had been made in the past few years. Seth's mother didn't go down into Dragonscove much anymore, but she went with a group of her female friends—mostly other Lair wives—every now and again.

"I grew up here, you know," Enid told Livia. "The town has changed a great deal since I was a girl. It was much smaller then. Just a fishing village, really. Now it's a small city with industry and craftsmen that weren't here before. Your father seems to have had a lot to do with that, Livia."

"Did you know my father as a child?" Livia asked over the rim of her teacup.

Enid laughed. "Oh, no, dear. It's not generally known, but when you share your life with dragons, they tend to impart some of their magic to their chosen families. I was born over three hundred years ago. Seth is our last child. We have two other sons, both of whom are knights in the Northern Lair. Gerard Junior is nearing two hundred and is mated with grown children of his own. Paton Junior has been a knight for about a hundred years, though he is still unmated. Seth was named for my father." She smiled at Seth. "Our dragon children, Llallor and Mowbry, are also partnered. Mowbry chose Gerry as her knight almost from the time she hatched, which was a beautiful thing to witness. Llallor is partner to a nice young man named Karlac. They're currently assigned to the Border Lair and doing quite well."

To say Livia was shocked would be an understatement. She knew dragons had very long lives, but she had no idea they could also lengthen the lives of their chosen partners and their wives. Yet another perk—if it could be called that—to being a Lair wife.

"You must have seen so much in your time," Livia offered, fascinated with the idea. "Have you always lived here?"

"Oh, gracious, no. We moved around to different Lairs, the way most knights do. Gerard and Paton were both stationed here when we met. I was a local girl, and those two just swept me off my feet." Enid smiled softly in remembrance. "When my parents passed on, I felt free to move away, and the boys took a posting to the Northern Lair. I never saw so much ice in my life, I can tell you! And it's cold up there. Colder than I had ever experienced before. It took some getting used to, but it was quite an adventure. Gerry Junior was born there, as was Llallor. Then we moved to the Castle Lair as my husbands moved up in rank. We lived in the capital for many years. Patty and Mowbry were born while we were there, and Mowbry was old enough to officially choose Gerry right before we left to help set up the

Border Lair."

"You were on the border? Have you seen a skith?" Livia asked, interested.

One of the rarest things her father had ever had in his warehouse was a skith skin. Most skiths who encroached on the border of Draconia from their native land of Skithdron were incinerated by dragon fire, but very occasionally, one would die in another way, and some brave soul would find the courage to skin it and remove all the venom. Skith leather was in high demand from those who worked with caustic chemicals, since it was impervious to almost everything. It would have to be, since skith venom was one of the most corrosive liquids known to man. That one skith skin had been enormous and had been parceled out and sold over years to specialty buyers from all over Draconia.

"I have seen skiths." Enid shuddered. "It is a sight I will never forget. It's one for nightmares, believe me. Those things are just nasty."

Livia would have asked more questions, but the arrival of a large female dragon halted her words. She was red in color, every shade of red in the palette, with hints of golden shimmer and even silver sparkle here and there. She was lovely and fierce, and looking at Livia with a critical eye.

"Livia O'Dare, may I introduce Lady Alirya," Seth said, standing to make the formal introductions. Livia stood, as well, then did her best curtsey to the imposing dragon.

"It is a pleasure to meet you, Lady Alirya," Livia said politely, then her anxiety got the better of her. "Have you any word?"

Alirya nodded her great head. "It is why I have come. First, to meet you, Mistress Livia. I wanted to see for myself the young woman who has befriended my boy. And next, to relay the message that you are wanted in the war room."

Livia exchanged looks with Seth. "That sounds very serious, indeed." Livia turned to Seth's mother and thanked her for the tea and conversation, then followed Seth out of the chamber, leaving the two mothers to gossip.

Livia had no doubt Lady Alyria would be well aware of all that transpired in the rather ominous-sounding *war room*, but she would probably also be comparing notes with Enid about Livia. She almost chuckled. She had often been the topic of gossip in the town, but to her best knowledge, she had never been gossiped about by a dragon. The idea gave her little thrill as she contemplated how her life had changed since meeting Hrardorr.

She thought about contacting him, but decided against it. He was blind. There was no escaping that fact. When and if it came time to fight, he would feel awful for not being able to fly alongside his brethren. Livia set one part of her mind to thinking up ways Hrardorr still might be able to help. He could see underwater—after a fashion. Maybe that could be useful in some way? She promised herself she would think more about it later, when she had time.

For now, she and Seth were walking swiftly through the halls on their way to the mysterious war room. She was glad he knew where it was. She was hopelessly lost in the maze of tunnels and corridors that was the Lair. She did notice an increase in activity from just over an hour ago. Before, the Lair had been almost a sleepy place, of slow-moving people and lazing dragons, basking in the heat of the sandpits she could see through open doorways as they passed.

Now, it was like an anthill kicked into wakefulness. People were scurrying here and there, and the knights were walking around in armor, with purpose to their strides. The dragons were moving around, too, walking through the largest of the hallways, where the humans had to stand back against the walls to give way to oncoming dragons.

Livia was glad to see they were taking her warnings seriously.

One of Seth's fathers—Gerard—met them in the hallway and escorted them the rest of the way to their destination. He looked tense as they strode quickly through the halls.

"What news?" Seth asked.

"Grave news, I'm afraid." Gerard frowned and looked at

Seth. "Stanius was shot out of the sky. Tilden landed in the water and was able to swim to shore. Stanius crashed on a hilltop."

"Send me out," Seth demanded. "I can help them."

"It is already taken care of. They are closer to the Border Lair, as the dragon flies, and the princess has already flown out to help them both. She is a true dragon healer, and based on the huge tear in Stanius's wing, the enemy have at least a few diamond-tipped spears on their catapults."

"Grave news, indeed," Livia said, into the silence that followed.

There wasn't time to talk more as they ushered her into an enormous chamber with a large round table in the center. Knights were standing around the table, looking at what had to be a map, and Livia was amazed to see an equal number of dragons arrayed behind the knights, around the perimeter of the round room. It looked as if they were all discussing battle plans together.

Well, what else? These were dragon-knight pairs. They would go into battle together and depend upon each other. They each had a stake in the outcome and should both be in on the planning. It made sense to her, once she thought about it.

Having never been so close to so many dragons or knights, Livia had never before considered how they must work so closely together. It was really kind of wonderful to see the way they treated each other, and respected each other's opinions. This was a meeting of equals. No species was subservient to the other. They were true partners.

"Ah, Mistress O'Dare," Sir Jiffrey greeted her as they walked to the center of the room to stand around the table with the other knights. He went on to introduce her to his fighting partner, the co-leader of the Lair, Sir Benrik, and the dragon leaders, their partners, Sir Tiluk and Lady Anira. Tiluk was a green dragon, and Anira was a lovely dark blue.

"I have spoken with Genlitha," a low voice rumbled in Livia's mind. It was the female dragon, and apparently, she was

including all the knights in her communication, as all eyes focused on Livia. *"She tells me you can hear us."*

"Yes, milady, I can," Livia answered with proper respect given Anira's position and age.

"Good. Then, if you are willing, we would like you to act as liaison with the council in the town below. We understand you are highly placed in the merchant guild and command sufficient authority and respect that the others would listen to what you have to say. We need such a person, who can also communicate without the use of couriers and written messages, which are far too slow, to act as our conduit to the leaders of Dragonscove."

"I would be honored to fulfill such a duty," Livia answered. Inside, she was hopping in excitement. She'd be able to help, which was what she had wanted. Livia wasn't one to sit idly on the sidelines while others did the hard work of protecting her.

"We would also like to place a dragon with you. While I assume you'd rather have someone you know, Genlitha and Gowan cannot be spared. They are wing leaders and must lead in battle—"

"Hrardorr!" she burst out, interrupting the dragonness, which wasn't entirely polite, but Livia didn't want any other dragon the leader might suggest. She wanted her best friend.

When Anira merely blinked down at Livia in surprise, Livia went on.

"My apologies for interrupting, but Sir Hrardorr is already a favorite of the townsfolk for his part in clearing predators from the water since he has been here. The townsfolk respect him and—pardon my bluntness—he cannot fight in your wings of dragons the way he is, but he can be of enormous help in town. It would be good for him to feel useful, and it would allow those who can fight to do so and not be stuck in town with me."

Tiluk, the male dragon, craned his head forward. *"An elegant solution, and one that honors our sightless brother. Your heart is true and your wits sharp, Mistress O'Dare."* Tiluk actually winked at her, and Livia felt a blush coming on at his praise.

"Then Hrardorr it shall be," Anira agreed. *"But he has no*

knight. Whom shall we send to accompany him?"

"Send me," Seth declared, stepping forward. "I can help Hrardorr if he needs it, and I know everyone in the Lair and can communicate with every dragon." Seth stood at Livia's side, looking up at the leader dragons. "I'm not a knight, but if what we've heard is true, you'll need every knight to fight. Send me to Dragonscove, so I can do my part and allow the knights to do theirs."

"We cannot guarantee the town will be safe. You will be in danger there," Anira said to him, as if testing his resolve.

"I may not be a knight, but I will fight to defend my land, its people and its dragons. I would rather be where I might do some good than hide here in the Lair with the elders and children."

Livia could see Seth's ire was up. He didn't like his courage being questioned.

Then she noticed smoke curling up to the domed ceiling from the dragons' nostrils. They were chuckling. It *had* been a test.

"Be at ease, young one," Tiluk said. *"You may not be a knight, but you have the heart of one. You do your family proud."* Tiluk seemed to look around at the other dragons before he said. *"You will go with Hrardorr and tell us what goes on in Dragonscove while we fight from aloft. With three of you there who can speak with us, we will be well informed of the enemy's movements, and so will you, on the ground."*

"Now all we have to do is get Hrardorr to agree," Anira muttered.

The war council went on for an hour more. They discussed what had happened to Gowan and Genlitha's patrol. Apparently, the enemy fleet was closer than they'd thought and definitely heading this way. When one of the younger dragons flew too close, he'd been shot down, so the intent of the pirate fleet was clear. They were hostile, in the extreme.

Eventually, orders were drawn up and communications

written to the town council, naming Livia, Hrardorr and Seth the official liaisons between town and Lair. Hrardorr grudgingly agreed to do as the dragons asked and accompanied Seth and Livia down to Dragonscove.

Livia and Seth walked back down the hill toward town, while Hrardorr flew. He landed in the water and then swam to Livia's boat house to await them. From there, Seth had to guide him with many hasty words, into a little harder landing in the courtyard in front of Livia's home.

Hrardorr was pretty good at following someone's commands now. He had to get the dragons on watch to guide him into the Lair each time he flew back there, but the landing ledges were wide and clear. Landing in a tiny courtyard without the use of his eyes was a lot trickier, but he managed it with Seth's help.

The meeting hall wasn't far from Livia's home, and it turned out to be a good location from which to coordinate the action. The town's business leaders were already gathered, trying to find ways to protect not only their business interests, but also the town itself. On the whole, they were good people who just wanted to keep the really bad things that were possible from happening.

The town council had mostly deployed to help the weaker and more vulnerable people in Dragonscove either shelter in place, if they chose, or to evacuate. The Lair was taking in as many people as they could, hiding them deep in the mountain chambers, away from possible trouble.

The Lair would be a last line of defense if the town was overrun. Its massive doors could be shut, and even if only a few dragons survived, they could prevent any enemies from entering with their flame. There were also vast storerooms underground where food was kept, as well as a water source that would be impossible to contaminate or stop from outside.

Then there were the dragons, of course, and the fact that they could carry more than one person to safety, if they had to. They could also summon help from other parts of

Draconia.

In fact, the first news that came down from the Lair that Livia was asked to relate to the town's leadership had to do with what they could expect in the way of reinforcements. And the news wasn't good.

"Hostilities in the north and east are at a peak," she told the assembled merchant leaders and the few representatives of the town council that weren't busy elsewhere.

They'd left the mayor to coordinate things, while the younger and more energetic members of the council were out and about, helping folks. The mayor glared at her, and Livia did her best to stand up straight as she continued her report.

"The Border Lair will send as many knights and dragons as they can spare," she went on. "In fact, Princess Adora and General Armand are on their way with the dragoness, Lady Kelzy. They will be in talks with the leaders of our Lair shortly." She didn't mention the fact that Princess Adora was a dragon healer and was coming in with the injured young dragon, Stanius, and would probably be leaving again once he was settled.

The mayor seemed somewhat mollified, but many of the merchants realized the news was, indeed, grave. If the only hot spot in the country had been in the south, they would've sent everyone they could, but with the defenders stretched thin on three borders, the south might have to take care of itself more than it wanted to.

As they started planning the town's defense, it became clear they needed input from the harbormaster. Livia went to get him herself, since he'd already ignored three separate summonses from the mayor. She also needed a little break, and some fresh air.

"I'm going to get the harbormaster," she told Seth, who was seated at her side. She spoke low, keeping the conversation just between them.

"Do you want me to come?"

He was in the middle of describing the kind of support dragons could provide to Dragonscove if it should come to all-out assault. He was fielding questions and had knowledge nobody else could provide. Livia knew it would be a bad time to take him away from those most worried about what was coming next.

"No, it's all right. I'll ask Hrardorr if he wants to accompany me."

Seth quirked one brow at her. "Do you think that's wise?"

"I think it's probably the only way to get the harbormaster out of his office," she replied with a grin.

Seth smiled back. "Well, let me know if you need me, and I'll come right away."

She patted his shoulder as she turned to leave. "Thanks, Seth."

Livia went outside to found Hrardorr surrounded by children, though they all kept their distance.

"Sir Hrardorr?" Livia approached him slowly, not wanting to startle him. She also wanted to show the townsfolk—especially the children—that he wasn't dangerous.

Hrardorr lifted his head toward her. He was lying down on his belly in the middle of the square, looking for all the world as if he'd been dozing.

"I didn't want to move in case I accidentally hurt someone," he confided in the privacy of her mind. *"I can feel them around me, but I don't know exactly where they are."*

"Does it bother you? If so, I can tell them to leave. Most of them live nearby. All the other families have been evacuating to the Lair or elsewhere down the coast, but these will be among the last to leave. The children are scared, and I think you represent safety to them, even though they're a little frightened right now."

"Then, by all means, I do not want to hurt anyone."

"How about I introduce you? I'm on my way down to the harbormaster's office. Would you be willing to give some of the braver children a ride, if I walk beside you? The road is wide from here to the harbor, and it would be a highlight of their lives, I'm sure. It might also help them be less afraid." Livia had to hold back a chuckle. *"You can also help me wrangle a recalcitrant harbormaster who has been ignoring all our requests to come up here to the hall."*

"It is a good plan," Hrardorr agreed, a few tendrils of smoke rising merrily from his nostrils. *"I will trust you to be my guide...and theirs."*

Livia soon had the children riding merrily on Hrardorr's back. He seemed to be in his element as he walked slowly beside her down to the harbor. It wasn't far, and Livia had assured the worried parents that she would keep an eye on their offspring. Many were grateful, since they were in the final stages of packing up what they could carry.

It wasn't a far journey, and it was downhill all the way toward the harbor. Livia made the children promise to stay on Hrardorr's back while she went into the harbormaster's office. There were wide windows, so she could keep an eye on them...and so the harbormaster could see the dragon on his doorstep.

That got his attention. Finally. Livia didn't have to do too much convincing to get the man to accompany her back up to the town hall.

They reversed direction and headed back up to the square, the harbormaster practically running ahead, while Livia walked more sedately with Hrardorr and his little passengers.

The harbormaster didn't stay long at the town hall, insisting that he had to see to the evacuation of the smaller vessels, while he prepared the few armaments they had on shore and on the small number of ships that were big enough, or fortified enough, to be used in battle.

When he left, Seth went with him to get details on the harbor's defenses requested by the dragons. It had been a long time since any of the harbor cannons had been fired, and some were showing signs of problems. Seth was asked to verify the readiness of each cannon and catapult, and update the Lair regarding the locations of the working armaments and any bald spots where things weren't quite working as they should.

CHAPTER FIFTEEN

"I would like to go for a swim, and maybe a short hunt," Hrardorr announced in Livia's mind sometime later. His tone was somewhat speculative—as if he was trying to figure out how to make that happen.

"I'll walk with you down to the boat launch, if you like," she volunteered. *"Can you swim out safely from there?"*

Hrardorr seemed to think for a moment. *"It is a good plan. I can sense obstacles underwater, and can avoid them without aid."*

"Good. I need a break from these guys," she admitted. *"A little walk and some fresh air are in order."*

Livia excused herself from the ongoing discussion and headed outside. She knew the situation was serious, but she also knew that, at this point, the men inside were mostly spinning their wheels. Everyone who could actually do something to prepare was already doing it. Sitting in the town hall and just talking about it was getting them nowhere.

Besides, Seth was down by the water somewhere. Maybe she'd go find him on her way back and steal a few minutes with him, away from the others.

This time, when she went outside, there were far fewer children waiting in the square. Most had been whisked away by their parents to head for a safer place. Livia knew the remaining few would be leaving soon. The Lair had taken in as many families with children as had wanted to go there. Most did. Only a few sought family or friends either farther inland or up the coast.

"Ready?" she said, stopping just to the left of Hrardorr's head. "You're in the clear. Nobody is lurking in your immediate vicinity."

"*Lurking?*" Hrardorr asked with a hint of humor, smoke spiraling upward from his nostrils.

"Some children can be crafty," she replied in a teasing tone.

"*Oh, I'm sure.*" Hrardorr allowed. "*Shall we walk down to the harbor? I'm looking forward to a little exercise and some fat fish for a snack.*"

They set off at a sedate pace, Livia keeping one hand on Hrardorr's neck, guiding him down the wide lane. They'd done this once before already, so it was easier this time. Hrardorr was good at following her lead and she was learning how to better guide him. All in all, it was a harmonious moment...if not for the threat of a possible invasion hanging over them.

"Other than being hungry, how are you holding up in your role as liaison?" Livia asked, making small talk as they walked along.

"*So far, it has been an uneventful job, but I see the sense in sending me here. I hear I have you to thank for this assignment.*" The eye ridge nearest her quirked upward. She was getting better at reading dragon body language and facial expressions. She thought he was mildly amused, inquisitive, or maybe a little of both.

"I thought it would be a good use of your time," she admitted. "Plus, I wanted to spend time with you, Hrardorr. If they were going to send a dragon here, I wanted it to be you, because you're my friend," she told him with unplanned candor.

Hrardorr stopped walking and turned his head toward her.

"*It warms my heart to hear you say it. You are my friend too, Livia. No matter what happens, you will always hold a special place in my heart.*"

Livia stepped closer to him. She'd never been quite this close to Hrardorr. Even touching his neck as they walked down to the harbor was a new experience. They'd always been on the water—her in her sailboat and him swimming a short distance away.

The moment stretched, and she felt a caring tenderness overcome her. She dared to raise her other hand to the other side of his neck, the way she'd seen Gowan do with Genlitha.

"I'm going to hug you," she warned him, emotion swelling in her. "Is that okay?"

In answer, Hrardorr bent slightly, bringing his neck into her embrace. She wrapped her arms around him, clinging to his heat. It was a magical moment of friendship and love between two beings.

There were tears in her eyes when Livia finally stepped back and let Hrardorr go. She didn't bother wiping them away. She wasn't ashamed of her feelings, and Hrardorr couldn't be embarrassed by what he couldn't see.

"Thank you for being here, my friend," she whispered. "No matter what comes, I'm glad you are with me as we try to prepare. You're the best friend I've ever known."

"*You honor me,*" was all Hrardorr said. It sounded as if he was feeling the same level of emotion as her. Or maybe that was just wishful thinking on her part.

"Are you two just going to stand here all day, blocking traffic?" Seth's voice pulled Livia out of her reverie.

Livia moved farther away, keeping just the one hand on Hrardorr's neck to guide him. She found Seth standing in front of them, an indulgent smile on his face.

"But sir, there isn't any traffic to speak of, except yourself, of course." She smiled back at him, feeling playful. "Are you on your way back to the town square, or are you still working down here?"

"I just have two more things to check on the waterfront before I can make my report. Where are you two off to?"

"*Fishing,*" Hrardorr answered with a little growl.

Seth's head quirked to the side, and Livia was quick to clarify. "Just Hrardorr. I'm staying ashore. I wanted to get some fresh air, is all. They're talking in circles up at the hall."

"I guess they haven't had any new information since the last scouting mission we relayed," Seth allowed as Livia nodded. "They'll have fresh data once I finish my survey of the harbor armaments."

"Want some company?" Livia asked.

"I was just going to ask you the same thing. My next stop is in this direction, as it happens."

"Then I think we would love to have you tag along. Wouldn't we, Sir Hrardorr?"

The dragon rumbled his agreement, and they began walking again. This time, when they neared the harbor, Livia led Hrardorr toward the boat ramp that led down gradually into the deeper water.

"How are the preparations going down here?" Livia asked Seth as they walked along. "I don't remember the last time anyone serviced the cannons."

Seth shook his head. "It shows. Many are rusted, and the fire crews must first unstick the moving parts. Most have been broken open, but a few are in worse shape than the others. I doubt anyone will be able to get them working anytime soon. If we have enough time, I've already relayed a request to have one of the smiths from the Lair to come down and have a look. The town smiths are stretched to their limits already."

"This is grave news," Hrardorr commented.

"I had hoped the situation would be better, but there hasn't been a threat on this shore in generations," Livia added.

"We still have a little time before the enemy fleet arrives," Seth said. "Perhaps we'll be able to affect repairs. Either way, it's best we know now what the defensive capabilities are from the shore." Seth's brows drew together in concern. "The dragons are going to have a rough time of it. If those pirates have a lot more of those diamond-tipped weapons, casualties will be unavoidable. Even the best flyers can't avoid everything, and most of our dragons are either very young, sent here for training, or their knights are very old, sent here to retire."

Hrardorr emitted a smoky growl, clearly displeased by the notion.

"My apologies. I did not mean to be so negative," Seth said. "We will prevail, somehow. That's what we do, here in Draconia. We don't let the odds deter us, right?"

Livia shook herself. "You're right, of course. We have no choice but to repel the enemy. Any other outcome is unacceptable."

They stood in silence for a moment more before Hrardorr finally moved. He walked tentatively down the boat ramp, a few shuffling feet at a time.

"I'm going for a swim. Keep me informed. If I am needed, I will return forthwith. Otherwise, I will probably stay down here for a bit, in the fresh air. The sun feels good on my scales after a swim."

"You are always welcome in the boat house if you wish to take a nap after your fish feast," Livia offered. "I doubt anyone will need the ramp today, so if it is sun you are seeking, then this area will also serve. Whatever you prefer."

"I'll be back in an hour or two. Try to keep the humans up at the hall out of trouble while I'm gone," Hrardorr joked as he slithered into the water. He dropped his head under the surface and was gone with barely a ripple.

"He's amazing in the water," Seth said as they both watched after the dragon.

"Out of it too," she murmured. "He is a very special dragon."

"No argument here," Seth agreed. "I think he's probably my favorite dragon in all the Lair, but don't tell my family that. They all think they're my favorites." Seth winked at her, and she smiled back.

"It must have been pretty amazing to grow up with a set of dragon parents as well as human ones. And dragon siblings. It seems so magical to me." Livia turned away from the water and began walking back up the boat ramp. "I always wanted a brother or sister, but it wasn't meant to be, I guess."

"Even though I had siblings, none were near my age. We talk about it sometimes—on the rare occasions when we're together—and it feels like we were all raised as only children because of the age differences. But there were other kids in the Lair for me to play with, and dragonettes. It was a good way to grow up," he admitted.

They started walking, and Seth led the way toward another spot on the shoreline where Livia could see a small group of men clustered. As they drew nearer, she could hear the clank of metal on metal and saw that most of the men were standing around, scratching their heads as one of them worked on something at the center of their group.

"There's an old cannon there," Livia said as they walked. "I thought that was just a statue, but I guess all the things down here that I thought were monuments of some kind are really supposed to be functional, right?"

"That's about the size of it," Seth agreed. "Nobody seems to have bothered keeping the things functional. I hope we don't end up paying for that inattention."

As they approached, the scene became clearer. There was, indeed, the cannon Livia remembered, and a group of local men was trying their best to unstick rusted parts on it. Another group was busy stacking cannon balls and bringing in oak barrels filled with what she assumed was gunpowder and placing them nearby. Apparently, they were optimistic about getting the cannon to function and were setting up the supplies they would need to take on the enemy.

Someone spotted them as they approached, and the small knot of people around the cannon opened up. Seth stepped forward, taking charge in a way that impressed Livia. He might not be a knight, but he was definitely a born leader. Every man in that group looked to him for his opinion, and when Seth took up a heavy hammer from the blacksmith and began hammering on the rusted metal in carefully placed blows, they all watched and waited for the results.

Which weren't long in coming. With one final whack of the metal hammer, the part popped open to the great delight of the people gathered all around. The men actually cheered as Seth straightened and handed the hammer back to the smith with his thanks.

Seth gave the group a few words of advice and encouragement before rejoining Livia.

"That's one more in the functional column," Seth said as he came up to her. "Just one left to check, and then, we can go back to the hall and report in."

They set off walking again, heading a little farther down the shore. Livia was glad to be outdoors. The sun was beginning its slow descent, and there was only a slight chill in the air as night began to fall. She had spent most of the day closeted in the town hall with a group of very nervous men. It was good to escape that atmosphere of fear and anxiety, if only for a few minutes.

"So how many working cannons does that make?" she asked as they walked along.

"Not enough," Seth answered, his expression grim. "The big problem is the weaponry of the opposing side. If they can take out a lot of dragons—and they will, if they have enough diamond-tipped blades, because the dragons won't stop defending Draconia, regardless of the danger—then with this few guns, Dragonscove will most likely be overrun."

"I wish we could talk to Gowan," she said wistfully.

"He and Genlitha are most likely out of range, and if not, they're too busy preparing to risk interrupting them." He wished he could change that, but those were the facts.

"I know. I wouldn't want to distract either of them right now, but I just...miss them."

Seth took her hand and squeezed it. "I know. Me too."

"I had Rosie pack a few keepsakes and evacuate to the Lair," Livia thought out loud, trying to change the subject, but a pang of regret ran through her at the thought of losing her home and belongings. Of course, lives were more important than things. Things could be replaced. Lives couldn't.

"You should evacuate to the Lair too, Livia," Seth said, stopping in his tracks to look at her, emphasizing his point.

"I will, but not until I have to," she assured him.

He put his hands on her shoulders. "Promise me."

"I promise," she replied, holding his gaze.

He drew her closer, and she went willingly. When their lips met, it was in a kiss of solemn union, of caring, of worry and of promise. The promise was for later, when the danger was past. And the rest of it reflected all the emotion of the moment, and what was to come. The feeling was intense and special, and she gladly went into his embrace, feeling more secure just being held in Seth's strong arms.

When he drew back, it was as if something profound had changed between them. Not only had they shared pleasure, but now, they were sharing more serious things. Life and death. Threat and preparation. Anxiety and hope.

Seth *was* hope to her.

They checked the last cannon with good results. The crews had already gotten the rusted parts unstuck and were preparing the ammunition. Seth went over the process of firing with them and left them going through the motions, practicing for when, and if, they would have to actually fire the cannon.

All in all, Seth was satisfied with the outcome of his weapons review. The harbor wasn't as well-defended as it could be, but at least they had some functioning cannons and crews to man them. It wasn't ideal, but he'd heard from his fathers enough times that battle conditions were seldom ideal. They'd just have to make do with what they had available and hope for the best.

When they were on their way back up to the hall, Hrardorr contacted them.

"There shouldn't be any boats out by the headwaters right now, right?" Hrardorr asked.

"Only the two scout ships I sent out. But I wouldn't expect either of them back until tomorrow," Livia answered.

"Can you tell me about their hulls?" Hrardorr said, his tone skeptical.

"The Belinda *is about seventeen feet in length and has a long keel for a boat her size. She is fast under sail and won last year's harbor races. Her hull is narrow compared to her length and she is built for speed. The* Cassiopeia *is a sister ship, built along the same lines, but smaller, at only about fifteen feet long. They were built by the same shipwright,"* Livia told them.

"Would either of them be riding low in the water and have something metallic sticking out just above the water line on either side?"

"Cannons?" Seth was quick to ask the dragon.

"I can't be sure. It isn't in the water, but I am perceiving long, thin outlines of something that tastes metallic on either side of the boat. It's about twenty feet long and wide in the middle. I don't think it's either one of your scout ships, Livia."

Seth and Livia exchanged glances, and then, she took off running up the hill to the hall. The enemy was a lot closer than they'd thought. He took off after her.

"Don't engage them, Hrardorr," Seth warned the dragon as he ran. *"Just watch them. Be our spy. That's what we need most right now."*

"I would like to chomp on their rudder, but I understand the need for stealth." The dragon sounded disappointed, but Seth was relieved Hrardorr wouldn't try to fight them. Hrardorr was brave and a proven warrior, but in his condition... Well, Seth didn't want to see him get hurt. Or worse.

But the idea that Hrardorr could do damage to a ship from below was something worth considering. The enemy wouldn't be expecting that.

Seth and Livia arrived back at the meeting place in record time. Breathless, they ran into the hall, and Livia began to tell those gathered what Hrardorr had reported. People started scrambling and asking questions. Seth offered his take on what was happening when asked, then saw a familiar face entering the hall.

He went to meet Petr, one of the smiths from the Lair that he'd requested to help with the cannon. Introducing him to one of the men who had been leading the efforts with the broken installations, he asked Petr to do what he could in the time they had.

As he was about to leave, Petr stopped him, pulling a sheathed sword from the folds of his cloak and holding it out toward Seth. Not sure what to make of the gesture, Seth was puzzled.

"Sir Gowan sent word to bring this to you, with his compliments," Petr utterly surprised him by saying.

Slowly, Seth took the sword from Petr's big hands. It weighed about the same as the weighted practice blade he'd been using when sparring with Gowan. It was like the sword had been made for him. Seth looked up at Petr, catching an amused look of satisfaction on the smith's face.

Only then did Seth connect the fact that Petr was, perhaps, the finest sword smith in southern part of the country. This blade was one that he'd made. And Seth knew he didn't just give his works of art to anyone. He had a waiting list a mile long. If he had made a blade just for Seth, someone must have...

"Gowan commissioned this?" Petr nodded as Seth pulled the blade partway out of the scabbard. As he'd suspected, this was one of Petr's beauties. It gleamed in the low light of the meeting hall, its edge honed to perfection.

"He said you were ready." Petr was beaming when Seth looked up at him.

Petr was an older man. A master craftsman who'd had his choice of positions and chose the Southern Lair because he'd been raised nearby and loved the sea.

Petr had been like an uncle to most of the Lair kids, and Seth had taken his turn at the bellows in Petr's workshop when he'd been a teen, given chores to help out around the Lair. Seth had seen Petr making swords very much like the one he now held and knew the amount of labor and love that went into them.

Seth had seen Petr present his masterpieces to knights, knowing they would carry the weapons into battle in defense of their homeland. Such occasions were special. Like this. This felt very special, indeed.

"I don't know what to say," Seth thought aloud. "Are you sure...?"

"Aye, lad." Petr put a fatherly hand on Seth's shoulder. "If Sir Gowan thinks you're ready, then you are. He's a good judge of men, is Sir Gowan. He's been overseeing the making of this sword, and I've gotten to know him. He knows his blades." From Petr, there could be no higher compliment. "Use it well."

Seth felt the weight of Petr's approval and was glad of it. He'd never expected such generosity and kindness. Overcome with emotion and unable to speak, Seth merely hugged the older man, pounding his back a couple of times while he brought his emotional state under control.

Stepping back, he bowed his head, holding Petr's gaze—a sign of the greatest respect among warriors.

"Thank you," Seth said, simply, unable to put into words the intense feelings he was experiencing, but Petr seemed to understand.

There was no time to say more, but Seth hoped Petr understood. He probably did. He'd bestowed many swords over the years and knew how much a warrior valued a gift such as his. And that's when Seth realized he was thinking of himself as a warrior for the first time since childhood.

He'd been training with Gowan for a while now, and the early lessons had come back to him as if he'd never had a break from training. He felt confident enough to accept and use a blade of this caliber, and more than that, Gowan had felt the same. Otherwise, he never would have commissioned Petr to make it for him.

As Petr went off the with cannon crew, Seth took a moment to just absorb that new knowledge. He had changed drastically in the time since befriending Gowan. He'd become something he'd never thought he'd be. He'd evolved.

Seth wondered if he'd be able to stuff the genie back into the bottle after this was all over, on one hand. On the other, he wondered why he would even try. He liked the new man he'd become. He suddenly realized that his desire and ability to help Bronwyn hadn't changed, even though he'd reclaimed his heritage as a warrior. Maybe it didn't have to. Maybe he could continue to train—out in the open, after this—and still be there for the woman who'd been as a grandmother to him. Maybe he could do both, and the two desires were no longer mutually exclusive.

Maybe things had changed for the better.

Although…there was still the pending invasion to deal with. Which reminded him. He had work to do.

Seth buckled the sword belt onto his waist as he moved back toward the small group that surrounded Livia. He caught up to them as they were discussing the information he'd brought them about which cannons were working and which weren't.

"Livia, Seth, there are more ships arriving." Hrardorr's voice sounded urgently in their minds. *"I swam out a bit, and their fleet is not far. I've counted twenty ships already. All of a larger size than the first I described to you. I think this is their main fleet, though how they got here so fast, I do not know. I have already informed Gowan. He and Genlitha are going to scout from above."*

"They must've been at full sail since the encounter with the patrol. Even then, they'd have to have favorable winds to reach us so quickly," Livia told them. *"Tell Gowan and Genlitha to be careful,"* she added, worry clear in her tone.

"Genlitha is perhaps the only dragon who could fly above them without being seen," Seth assured her. *"Her natural coloring will keep her well hidden."*

Seth broke away from the silent conversation to announce Hrardorr's observations to the room at large. Without giving it much thought, he gave the orders to set the plans they'd been working on over the past hours into motion.

When Seth realized that even the mayor was looking to

him for leadership, the weight of responsibility suddenly descended upon his shoulders. But it was all right. It actually felt good. Like that's what had been missing from his life for a very long time.

Seth shouldn't have been so surprised. He'd been born to a fighting family. His fathers were leaders of men and dragons. He'd been going against type since deciding to help Bronwyn and turning his back on his heritage. Maybe he'd never be a knight, but he could still be a warrior and hold responsibility for helping keep the town safe. That was right in his comfort zone, and something he had almost been born to do.

The fulfillment of a life's potential. Right here. Right now.

Who would have believed it?

CHAPTER SIXTEEN

Gowan and Genlitha flew far above the mass of enemy ships. The view from above did not look good. Fifty ships or more were heading, at great speed, for the mouth of the harbor. From there, it would only be a quick sail right into the heart of Dragonscove

Oh, the town could mount a small opposition, but the sad state of their defensive armament meant it would be short lived. With this number of ships coming at them, they'd be overwhelmed all too quickly.

On one hand, Gowan was glad Seth and Livia were there to pass on accurate information on the town's defenses, but on the other, he didn't want them in danger. Though Gowan was sure Seth could hold his own in a fight—especially with the sword Gowan had commissioned as a gift for his student and friend—but he was very concerned about Livia. She was so devoted to her hometown and its people Gowan wasn't sure she would retreat in time.

He wanted her in the Lair. Safe. Protected.

He knew better than to say that to her before the last possible second, but he was counting on Seth to make her see reason and seek the safety of the Lair. Until that time, Gowan knew he could definitely count on Seth to protect her out in the open. Seth cared for her. Of that, Gowan was certain.

Which made the whole relationship issue somewhat...interesting. It would all be so much easier if Seth was a knight...

But that was a thought for later.

"I hope you're prepared to get Livia out of there," Gowan sent directly to Seth, impatient with having to go through the elders back at the Lair who were then relaying his information to Seth and Livia. The time had come for more direct communication, and they'd fill in the planners in the Lair as they went along.

"Of course I am," Seth scoffed. *"The only problem I foresee is getting her to go."*

"Tell her Hrardorr needs her to lead him back," Gowan suggested.

"No can do. Hrardorr is in the ocean, scouting the enemy ships."

"He's what?" Apparently, nobody in the Lair had felt it necessary to tell Gowan and Genlitha where, exactly, the information was coming from on land—or in this case, in the water.

"Didn't Genlitha tell you he's part sea dragon? He swims like a fish. A really big, really silent, really smart fish."

Gowan almost laughed aloud, but the situation was a little too dire for that. *"Well, your dragon fish is right to be sending up the alarm. You've got an entire fleet on your doorstep, and about half again as many ships some distance behind. Probably a reserve force. This battle is going to be very one-sided if your cannon count is correct."*

"It's correct," came Seth's grim voice. *"I did the count myself. Even if Petr can get a few more of them up and running in the time it takes the enemy to get here, it's still not enough. Thank you for the sword, by the way."*

"It was time. You still need a little polishing, but you're more than capable of wielding it with more skill than most of the young knights. I hope it serves you well." Gowan felt good that his gift had gotten to Seth in time. Seth was an able warrior and could be of great use to the townsfolk—and in defending Livia, if she didn't get out of there in time. *"I'm counting on you to take care of Livia,"* Gowan reminded Seth needlessly.

"I will. I promise you."

"Good enough. Now, the enemy ships are lining up in rows of five across to enter the harbor. I believe that's all that will fit through the entrance at once."

"Too many," Seth said immediately. *"We can take on maybe three at a time with the cannons we have positioned there. We have plenty of ammunition and able-bodied folk willing to man the guns, but the cannons themselves are the weak link."*

"Let's get the dragons in on this," Gowan thought, immediately linking Genlitha and Hrardorr into the conversation.

He hadn't expected to be working with the blind dragon on this, but if he was their scout in the water, then he needed to be in on the planning. He might see something from below that Gowan and Genlitha couldn't see from above.

Gowan recapped what they'd discussed so far about the number of ships the cannons could fire on at once, bringing the dragons up to speed. Gowan had never been in command in battle with Genlitha as is partner, so he was unprepared for how quickly they analyzed the situation and came up with creative answers.

"I can try to scout for which ships have the diamond bladed weapons, but it won't be one hundred percent accurate, I fear," Hrardorr offered. *"I believe I have a more accurate count of number of cannons per ship. I've been experimenting with what to look for, and I believe I have it sorted out now. The first five ships lining up at the harbor are all heavily armed. At least ten cannons per ship. The two on the ends have more than that. Maybe fifteen or twenty."*

"That's not good," Seth replied, speaking to the entire group and linking Livia into the discussion so she would know exactly what they faced. *"The batteries near the harbor entrance can take on about half that."*

"But they'll be under sail, with more behind, right?" Livia offered. She was the nautical brain in this gathering. *"Chances are, they plan to blow right by the harbor guns, getting off a broadside on their way, but otherwise clearing the entrance for their companions who'll be speeding along right behind."*

They were all silent for a moment while they thought

about that scenario. *"Makes sense,"* Genlitha finally offered. *"They have no shortage of ships, and a reserve force too. Their strength is their overwhelming number."*

"And ours has always been the limited opening to the harbor. If we can stop them at the mouth of the harbor, they'll pile up," Livia said, a hint of cunning in her tone.

"But how? The cannons won't even make a dent in that number of ships in such a quick encounter." Seth reminded them all.

"What we need to do is stop them at the mouth of the harbor," Livia insisted. *"We need to make them fight it out with our gun, and not streak past, letting the rest of their forces in."*

"I can do that." Hrardorr's calm voice surprised them all.

"What?" Gowan demanded as the same time Seth asked *"How?"*

Hrardorr's voice in their mind sounded both amused and eager. *"Remember when I joked about chomping on the rudder of the spy ship?"* He paused, letting that picture sink into their minds. *"I can disable the ships' steering mechanisms from beneath. I might also be able to poke a few strategic holes in sensitive spots below the water. The rest will be up to you above."*

"Stars!" Livia was the first to recover. *"That's ingenious."*

"Are you sure about this, Sir Hrardorr?" Gowan asked. He hated to be the voice of doubt, but it was his job as leader to ask. He noted that Genlitha said nothing.

"Water is my element more than air now, my friend. I can manage the fight below. You take care of the battle above. And keep the dragons clear of the ships I alert you to. I think I have a system for sensing the diamond blades, but we'll have to have a few fly before I'm sure I've got it right, unfortunately. I'll need you and Genlitha to let me know when you see them and where they came from."

"We will, Hrardorr." Genlitha sounded utterly confident, which went a long way toward calming Gowan's mind.

"All right then," Gowan took control of the planning session once more. *"Livia should go to the Lair now, for safety. Seth, will you be overseeing the batteries of guns?"*

"Of course." Seth sounded a little affronted, but Gowan had had to ask. He couldn't take anything for granted, though

he'd assumed Seth would want to be right where the action was.

"Good. We need someone who can communicate with us from the ground. You're it," Gowan confirmed.

"I'm staying. I can relay information to the council." Livia tried to find a reason she had to stay in town, just as Gowan had suspected she would.

"Livia, I must insist that, once you finish briefing the council on this conversation, you head for the mountain. They won't be able to do anything once battle is engaged. You risking yourself by staying would be pointless. In fact, they should evacuate all the non-fighting people to the Lair immediately. Please, Livia. Promise me? I won't be able to concentrate knowing you're in danger."

That seemed to convince her. *"All right."* She gave in with a distinct lack of finesse. *"I'll go. And I'll take those who can't fight with me. You're right. We can't do any good here once the battle starts."*

"Thank the Goddess for that," Seth summed up Gowan's feelings exactly.

Seth made sure Livia was well on her way to the Lair before he moved down to the harbor gun emplacements. The harbormaster would coordinate the attack from the guns along the innermost sections of the harbor, but Seth was going right out to the edge, to the guns that had been placed decades ago inside a rock wall three feet thick, with only small ports out which the barrels of the cannons poked.

There were several batteries of them, all functional, thanks to the guns being inside the rock enclosure, out of the weather. They were well supplied with shot, and plenty of fresh gunpowder had been stocked next to each cannon.

What they lacked was someone to lead them. To organize the various gun crews and signal them to fire at the right times. Seth stepped into the breach and was ready to fill that role. He really was the only one who could do it—besides Livia, which Seth wouldn't even contemplate—because he could communicate with Hrardorr and coordinate the guns with the dragon's action below water.

The enemy wouldn't know what hit them.

Seth hoped.

Otherwise, this wasn't going to be a long battle, and Dragonscove would be forfeit in short order.

"Livia, are you safe?" Seth paused long enough to ask, even as his feet kept him running toward the guns.

"We're almost to the Lair."

"Almost?" Seth wanted to curse. Why wasn't she inside the mountain already?

"We stopped to help some old timers who were having trouble with the climb. We're almost there."

It made perfect sense. Livia would not pass someone in need of help, though Seth could have wished otherwise at the moment.

"Let me know the minute you're safe. We're about to have company in the harbor, and I'd rather have one less thing to worry about."

"Not sure if I like the way you phrased that, but it's nice to know you care," came the rather sarcastic reply.

He didn't really have time for this right now, but he couldn't leave it alone. He didn't want her mad at him now. Not when there was a good chance he wouldn't make it out of this alive.

"I do care about you, Livia. I've had a crush on you since we were youngsters. You were always they prettiest girl in the world to me, and I never thought I'd ever stand a chance with you. Not with your father glowering at me every time I came into the shop." He tried to inject a bit of his current amusement and past frustration into his tone. *"I wanted you to know that, in case…"*

"Stop right there, Seth. Nothing is going to happen to you. Not today. You have to go into battle believing that. I'm almost to the entrance. They're opening it for us." There was a slight pause. *"People are coming out to help the elders. We're going to make it."* Another pause. *"I'm inside, Seth. They just closed the barrier. I'm heading up to the war room. Perhaps I can be of help there. And Seth…"* A shorter pause, this time. *"I care about you too. Be safe."*

"Seth, are you ready?" Hrardorr chose that moment to communicate.

"I'm just getting there. The guns are primed and ready to fire at my command," Seth reported, including Hrardorr, Genlitha, Gowan and Livia in his thoughts.

Livia would report to whoever was left at the Lair. Gowan and Genlitha would interface with the leaders of the dragon wings.

"We are ready," Genlitha reported.

"The enemy is lined up and making their first run. I'm going to start now," Hrardorr said. *"When they're at the mouth of the harbor, open fire, Seth. Genlitha, I believe the second and fourth ships in the first run have diamond bladed weapons. I can make out giant crossbows below decks, ready to be unveiled, and the ammunition has a crystal ring to it unlike anything else on any of these first five ships. In the second row, all five ships have that sound. In the third, only the middle three ships. Be warned."*

Seth was impressed with the quality of Hrardorr's reconnaissance. Ten ships with diamond bladed weapons in the first three waves was a lot for the dragons to evade. The harbor defenses and the lone half-sea dragon would have to bear the brunt of the fighting to avoid heavy dragon casualties.

Seth was finally in position. He stood on top of the rock-walled gun batteries, the unfamiliar weight of his new sword at his hip. He drew the blade. He'd use it to signal the gun crews. Raising it in the air, he watched the first wave of five ships approach. He saw the cannon crews on the nearest ship readying to fire.

They'd all get only one chance at this. Seth had to hold his own fire until the ships were in the optimal position. No sense wasting cannon balls or black powder. Not to mention the time it took for each cannon to reload.

The able-bodied men of the town, along with the guard and militia, were ready as well, hiding their numbers behind the rock walls of the harbor defenses. If any enemies did manage to make it to land, they would have a fight on their hands.

Seth watched the approaching ships, his heart racing as the

time for action drew near. The ships were proceeding all in a neat line, and then...

The middle ship swerved into the one next to it, colliding heavily and causing major damage.

"Hrardorr just took out the middle vessel," Seth reported to those who were waiting to hear in the Lair and in the sky above. *"The farthest ship is listing heavily to one side, probably taking on water, and the one next to it is tilting."*

In fact, it was hovering at an obscene angle, its mast clashing against the mast of the ship next to it that was already sinking.

"It's mast hit the other mast, and they're both going down."

Men began jumping into the water and swimming for the shore, but Seth had to worry about the two ships that were left, which were still moving quickly closer.

Closer...

Closer...

"Fire!" Seth dropped his sword, signaling the farthest cannon to fire even as the enemy opened fire on them. The volley of flame and iron went back and forth, causing destruction on both sides. The rock wall was built thick for a reason, but now, large chunks of it were scarred and missing. It held, but it was damaged.

More successful shots in the same spots would crumble it. It was up to them to make sure the enemy didn't get a second chance.

"The walls are holding for now," Seth reported.

Though out of practice, the harbor crews did a decent job. They were able to score several direct hits on the nearest vessel and at least one or two on the next closest, though it was somewhat blocked by the closer hull. Both began to list even as they sped past.

"Two slipped through, damaged, but still moving." Seth gave the signal to the guns farther into the harbor to take aim and fire at will. The harbormaster was in charge closer to the town, and he would see to them while Seth worked on the next wave of five ships, already on approach. *"Second wave is lining*

up."

The line was somewhat staggered this time by the need to navigate around the three ships that were lumbering slowly, heavily damaged. Good. The staggered approach would give Seth's gun teams more time and opportunities to fire. It would also mean the fresh gun crews on each of those ships would have the same, but there was Hrardorr to consider as well.

The moment Seth thought that, the farthest ship careened wildly off course, smashing into the vessel closest to it. And then, that one veered into the one next to it. Then that trio piled into the ships that were still limping along, sinking as they moved, from the first wave.

"Nice work, Hrardorr! Whatever you're doing, keep it up," Seth spared a moment to send.

"Messing with their rudders seems to be more effective than anything else, though poking holes in the hull is good fun," Hrardorr said with a hint of glee in his deep voice. The old bastard sounded like he was having fun, and Seth got a hint of how Hrardorr must've been before his injury, as a fighting dragon, taking on the enemy from the air.

"Keep having fun, by all means," Seth encouraged. *"You're well on your way to taking out most of the ships coming at us almost single-handedly. Just stay out of the line of fire. If we miss, the cannonballs sink at speed. I don't want you hit by accident."*

"Yes, mother," Hrardorr teased, in the best mood Seth had ever witnessed from the dragon. *"I'm going to work on the third wave now. Be aware of the smaller boats attached to the larger vessels. They're probably going to use them to come ashore and fight hand-to-hand."*

"Now who's acting like my mother?" Seth felt invigorated by the battle, the blood singing in his veins. He saw the small boats making for shore, along with the swimmers off the less fortunate ships. He knew they were going to be fighting shortly, man to man, sword to sword, and frankly, he couldn't wait.

How dare these pirates attack a peaceful town? How dare

they attack his people? His family? How *dare* they?

Hrardorr took out each and every one of the third wave of ships, effectively creating a blockage in the harbor mouth that the rest of the enemy fleet couldn't get through in their large vessels. They started sending the smaller boats out, filled with armed fighters, but Seth didn't see much more than that because, just then, the first of the enemy fighters made their way onto shore near him. Seth waited only to give the signal, loosing the reserve troops he'd had secreted behind the gun batteries.

And then, the battle was engaged.

Seth got to use his new sword, christening the sharp edge with enemy blood.

"I don't like this." Gowan grumbled to his dragon partner.

He detested hiding from the enemy arrows, but by the same token, he couldn't risk the dragons. For it was the dragons who would pay the price for confronting this pirate fleet without due thought and preparation.

"I don't either," Genlitha admitted, *"but it won't be for much longer. As soon as the ships with the dragon-killers on board sink, we'll go down and engage them in the harbor. You knights can shore up the fighters on land while we dragons burn the damaged ships where they sit, creating a more dangerous barrier to the rest of the enemy fleet."*

That was the best plan their leaders had come up with, but it still felt wrong to Gowan. He felt like he should be doing more.

"Hrardorr is going to have all the fun if we can't get down there soon. He's pretty amazing." Truth be told, Gowan was heartily impressed at what the blind dragon was accomplishing all by himself.

Gowan had no idea how Hrardorr could perceive anything underwater. It must be some sense other than sight, but what it was, he had no clue. Something specific to his sea dragon heritage, no doubt. Gowan thought there were going to be a lot of questions asked in the Lair when Hrardorr returned. Maybe he'd finally get a bit more respect from the other dragons after this day's work.

"Yes, he is." Genlitha sounded almost wistful. *"He always was. When he was younger..."* She trailed off as they watched yet another ship tilt wildly into its neighbor.

"They're engaging the ground troops now," Gowan observed. *"Come on. When are we going to get the order to join in?"*

"We should already be down there." Genlitha sounded as if she disapproved of the leaders' rather cautious battle plan. *"Seth is fighting a group of them,"* she reported, her sharp eyesight able to pick out individuals where Gowan could only see shapes of people from this distance. *"He's doing well, but when that other boat lands, they're going to be outnumbered."*

Gowan was through with waiting. *"Can you get me down there without putting yourself in too much danger?"*

"Yes."

"Then let's go. He needs help, and I'm sick of sitting on my ass, watching."

Genlitha launched from her perch on a rocky crag high above. Silently, she plummeted downward, using all her flying skill to get her down fast, before any weapons could be launched at her delicate wings. In fact, she kept her wings folded tight to her back until the last possible moment, increasing her speed beyond anything Gowan had experienced before, but he trusted her. She knew what he could handle. He never questioned her judgment when it came to flying. That was her expertise and he trusted it—and her—with his life.

Genlitha landed quickly, and Gowan jumped off her back, his sword already drawn. He hit the ground running, even as she lifted off again, riderless.

Gowan ran into the fray, swinging his sword and shouting his battle cry. It had been a long time since he'd been in a ground action, but it was something he had been doing most of his life. That was his area of expertise, and he didn't waste time finding his way to his newest, and perhaps most naturally talented, student's side.

"Nice of you to join us." Seth fought off an enemy soldier

even as Gowan reached him. They turned back to back, as Gowan had taught him, each one guarding each other's back.

"The so-called leaders are still hiding up top, but I figured I could be of better use down here. Can't let you have all the fun." Gowan grinned even as he faced a new opponent. The other man took one look at Gowan's face, and his well-worn and bloody sword, and backed down to seek an easier target.

Gowan let him go. He wouldn't be that easily lured away from Seth's unprotected back.

"The harbor is blocked. I'm going to do something about the rest of the fleet," Hrardorr reported.

Seth worried about what Hrardorr planned to do, but he was a little too busy fighting for his life to ask too many questions. Seth was glad Gowan had come down off the cliffs when he had. The militia was doing well, as were the town guard, but the townsfolk were a mixed lot, unused to fighting for the most part.

There was a serious shortage of trained soldiers, and having Gowan here helped even the odds. One Gowan was worth a score of townsfolk in battle.

CHAPTER SEVENTEEN

The mighty dragon rose from the sea. His dark wings shone with every color of the ocean—greens, blues, indigo, and even red and ochre. A dark rainbow of immense proportion, dripping with water while deep red flames shot from his mouth.

Flames that were aimed at the cloth sails of the rearmost of the enemy fleet, their weapons trained on the harbor or sky, not behind them at the open sea. They'd thought nothing could approach from open water. They'd thought they would see any dragon flying down from the cliffs and be able to track it as it came in for a flame run.

Nobody had ever heard of a sea dragon that could breathe fire. Nobody had ever heard of a sea dragon fighting alongside the folk of Draconia. And nobody had ever heard of a sea dragon, who was very obviously blind, doing so much damage.

The rear of the fleet was in flames when finally, somewhere far above, the leaders of the Lair gave the order for the dragons to do their worst. Arrows flew, but they mostly missed their marks as panic set in amongst the enemy sailors. Sailors feared nothing so much as fire aboard ship. Even surrounded by water, fire could destroy a ship and leave its crew at the mercy of the ocean.

The deadly diamond-tipped blades were mostly at the bottom of the harbor, except for those still hiding in the central mass of the badly disoriented fleet. They got off a few shots at the dragons, who were now swooping en masse, while the tight bunching of ships began to fall apart as captains broke ranks, turned their vessels around, and ran for their lives.

After his initial flame run, Hrardorr dove beneath the waves, out of reach of the diamond-tipped arrows and spears hastily aimed at him. But that left the opening for the rest of the dragon wings coming from the other direction.

Within a few minutes, half the enemy ships were on fire, and the rest were sailing away as fast as they could, no longer engaging in battle. The order came down from the Lair's leadership to let them go and concentrate on those still in the harbor. Knights were dropped on land to help the fighting men of Dragonscove while their dragons flew an aerial dance, evading the dangerous arrows and spears as best they could—unhindered by the need to keep a rider on their backs.

It was quite a sight to see, and Seth had to stop himself from being distracted as he fought back to back with Gowan. He could feel the tide of the battle turning, and he suspected it wouldn't be long before the fighters began to surrender.

Sure enough, it was only a few minutes more before the sailors realized they had lost and began to give up, refusing to fight when they saw that the townsfolk would have mercy on them. There was no way for them to win, and they knew it. They also learned they would not be summarily executed, so surrender was the smarter option at that moment.

Only problem was, the town jail couldn't handle quite this many people. Other arrangements would have to be devised, but that would be up to the town council and the harbormaster. The latter was used to impounding entire crews when dishonesty was discovered. He knew how to handle large groups of men and how to segregate them so they couldn't all plot together. He'd be able to advise the council on the best methods.

Seth's groggy mind was already planning ahead, he realized, even as the fight drew to an end all around him. The victors began to cheer—the town militia leading the shouting—but Seth just felt too weary to do much more than follow Gowan's lead as he began giving orders on how to deal with the prisoners...and the dead. At least Gowan had dealt with such things before and was willing to take charge on the battlefield. Seth was glad for his leadership just then. He'd had enough of command for one day.

For a man who, until yesterday, had been only a healer's apprentice, Seth had been well out of his expected role. He found he liked it. He had reveled in calling the fire sequence from atop the battlements. He thought he'd done a good job leading the ground-based firing teams, even though he'd never even contemplated doing such a thing before. And he'd proved himself adequately when it came to fighting one-on-one. He was still alive and mostly unharmed, which meant he'd done well.

But it wasn't anything he'd ever expected to do in his life. Not after he'd deliberately chosen to be Bronwyn's helper.

"You did well today." Gowan clapped Seth on the back, having returned from organizing the guard who were seeing to the prisoners.

"It was an honor to fight beside you," Seth replied, still feeling a bit numb after the hellacious battle.

"Same." Gowan grunted as they walked along the battlements, examining the dead. "These markings are not from anywhere near Draconia." He pointed to the designs carved into blades, scabbards and shields that were clearly of foreign origin.

"I believe the town council and the leaders of the Lair will have quite a few questions for the prisoners. In the meantime, I'd better use my training to help those who are injured and might be saved...unless you need me for anything else?" Seth almost hoped Gowan would say yes, which made Seth question once again where his true loyalties lie now that he'd had a chance to learn more about the fighting arts.

But Gowan simply nodded to him, letting him go, and Seth knew there were those in need who could use even his sometimes ham-fisted attempts at healing. Which reminded him…

"The battle is over." He sent the message directly to Livia.

"I know. Gowan told me. I'm glad you're both all right. And Hrardorr and Genlitha, too."

"Hrardorr was definitely the hero of the day," Seth agreed, giving credit where it was most definitely due.

"I'm so glad he got to prove himself. Maybe now he won't continue to feel so bad about being blind." It was a wish Seth shared with her, though he wasn't sure how Hrardorr was going to feel after all this. If he'd learned anything about the dragon, it was that he seldom did what everyone expected. *"Bronwyn and a delegation of those with basic healing skills are heading your way. They left as soon as Gowan gave the all clear."*

"Good. They'll be needed. I'm already sorting out those who need Bronwyn's skill and those that I can handle. Do you know if any dragons were badly injured? I couldn't see too much of the air battle from where I was, and I was, uh, somewhat busy."

He didn't know if she realized he'd been in the thick of the fighting, and he didn't feel like discussing his first real battle with anyone just at the moment. Even Livia.

Seth knew, deep down, that he had been forever changed by what he'd witnessed—and what he'd done—that day. He would see the faces of the men he'd killed for the rest of his life, in his mind's eye. He would remember the way they'd looked at him, clearly wanting to take his life, his riches and his land.

They'd left him little choice. He'd had to defend himself, his people, and his land from their attack. While he would rather have settled things peacefully, he knew now that when someone was intent on attacking you, for whatever reason they might have, there came a time when talk would not help. When words didn't work and they left you no choice, you had to fight for what was yours. For what was right.

Bullies could not go unanswered. Seth knew, beyond the

shadow of a doubt, that those men he'd killed that day would have happily killed him and every last person in Dragonscove before they were done with their evil deeds. They would have laid waste to the town and raped, pillaged and destroyed everything in their path, consuming like locusts on their way to wherever they were going next.

They'd had to be stopped.

The next hours passed in a blur of blood, sweat and work for Seth and all concerned in the clean-up of the harbor. Luckily, the fighting hadn't advanced too far into the town itself. Most of the damage was limited to the harbor area. And of course, the burning mass of timber in the harbor itself that had once been ships was still there, providing light and heat to those that worked long into the night on land.

The harbormaster had decided to let the enemy ships burn themselves out. Unless the wind changed direction or the current drew the burning wreckage too close, they were just going to let it be for now. There was too much else to do to set the town to rights and deal with the survivors.

Dragons were guarding the prisoners while their knights questioned each man in turn. Seth worked hard, rendering aid where he could, and instructing a few townsfolk in basic wound care while working on others.

Hrardorr was harvesting the bottom of the harbor floor for the diamond-bladed weapons. Such things were too dangerous to be left lying around for just anyone to fish out of the water, and the diamonds—once turned into faceted gemstones rather than blades—would go a long way toward paying for the rebuilding of the town and its harbor defenses.

Genlitha had been called before Sirs Jiffrey and Benrik to account for her movements during the battle. They chastised her for her solo run to drop Gowan off before the call to action had been given.

Genlitha wasn't one to stand by when hypocrisy paraded before her. Instead of answering the ludicrous charge, she had given the human leaders of the Lair a piece of her mind.

She criticized them for being too slow to act. She reminded the human leaders that, while they were old men, their dragons would live on long after they left this realm. By holding back until the last possible moment, they had taken the cowardly stance. She made them feel shame for doubting their dragon partners.

She made no bones about her belief that, rather than being the protectors of the realm they had once sworn to be, they had proven to be too old and too cautious to lead the Southern Lair any longer. She called for a vote of no confidence among the dragon council and the human knights, but that would have to wait for later, when they could all gather in sufficient numbers to cast a deciding vote. For the moment, her charges were on the table, so to speak, creating much debate among the knights and dragons alike.

Livia had come back down the mountain to Dragonscove and gathered up all the healing supplies in her father's warehouses. She had taken Rosie with her and dug right in, patching people up. Rosie had proven especially knowledgeable in treating cuts and the few burns they encountered. Seth crossed paths with the duo every few minutes on his way to his next patient.

Bronwyn was treating the dragons and the worst of the human injuries while Seth alternately saw to less severe injuries and helped Bronwyn with the more difficult cases. The losses, thankfully, weren't as great as they could have been. All in all, they'd gotten off lightly for such a large force arrayed against them.

According to the high-flying scouts, the remnants of the enemy fleet were on the run.

The answers elicited from questioning the prisoners began to form a clearer picture of why they'd been attacked. First, the leaders of this fleet had once been in business with King Lucan of Skithdron. They'd been the ones delivering the shipments of diamond-tipped blades Lucan had been using, only they hadn't delivered full cargoes on every trip. No, they'd been skimming some of the pricey weapons off of every shipment until they'd amassed quite an arsenal for themselves.

With King Lucan out of business, the fleet was at loose ends, with a stockpile of dangerous weapons that had really only one use—as dragon killers. Plus, it was widely known that the kingdom of Draconia was busy fighting in the north. The southern shore was seen as unprotected and ripe for the picking.

It made sense, really, though they all could have wished it didn't. The lesson had been driven home in the most brutal way. The south had to be prepared for invasion. Conflict had found them on too many fronts, and it would be up to the knights and dragons in each Lair to protect their own areas. They couldn't help on getting help from other Lairs. There was just too much going on in the kingdom, and the dragon knights were spread thinner than they ever had been in the history of the country.

"Are you sure about this?"

Livia had been running around ever since returning from the Lair, helping people. She and Rosie had done whatever they could, patching up friends and neighbors. Rosie was skilled in rendering aid. It had been part of her training as a nursemaid, after all. Few still remembered that Rosie had been hired as Livia's governess.

That hadn't worked out too well, due mostly to the fact that Livia had been a rebellious teen by the time Rose had come into the picture. Rosie's gruff nature hadn't helped either. They'd tolerated each other until they'd come to an understanding.

Rosie had been hired by Livia's father to be a combination of warden and maid while he was away, but they'd come to an uneasy truce before his first voyage ended. Rosie came to understand that Livia would not be dominated, and as long as Rosie did her job and didn't try to run Livia's life, she would keep her cushy job, for which she was paid a great deal by the richest man in town.

Over the years, their relationship had gone through changes. Rosie never lost her gruffness, but they'd learned to respect each other and rely on each other to keep the house running smoothly. Rosie had many skills—which was why Livia's father had hired her in the first place—so Livia left her working with the injured people while Livia saw to the hero of the hour, Hrardorr.

He was in the family boat shed again at the moment, and Livia was almost convinced he was...hiding?

"Yes, I'm sure," Hrardorr said, adding to the massive stack of glittering, diamond-tipped spears he had been steadily building along one wall. *"I don't trust anyone else with these. These blades are the only things that can slice through dragon scale. They have to be dismantled and ground down into other things as soon as possible. I trust you to do that above all others, Livia. Plus, you have experts working for your father's company, who can do the work quickly, and under your direct supervision. I want you to keep track of every last one of these. Will you do it? For me?"*

"Of course I will," she answered immediately. "I'll begin working on them immediately, in fact." She went over to the pile and picked up one of the spears, examining how to dismantle it and thinking about ways she could inventory each part. "But what I was really asking was, are you sure you should be hiding out down here? You're the undisputed hero of the hour, Hrardorr. I thought you'd want to enjoy that."

The dragon snorted, smoke rising from his nostrils. *"I've been in that position many times, and it is never a comfortable one for me, Livia. I'd rather work. Be useful. Let them fete the younger dragons who need it more."*

She stopped handling the spear and just looked at him. "You're pretty amazing, you know that, Hrardorr?"

The dragon seemed uncomfortable with her praise. *"There are more of these on the bottom of the harbor. I'm going to get them. Will there be room enough in here for twenty more, or should I find an alternate place to hide them for now?"*

Livia sighed inwardly. "You can put them in here. I'll stay and start dismantling them. The blades are only held on with leather bindings which I can cut through. There should be someone guarding the shed though," she thought aloud.

"You're right. I will talk with Genlitha. She may have some ideas of who best to utilize." Hrardorr lowered himself back into the water. *"I'll be back in an hour. Maybe less."*

"Be careful," she told him just before he slipped away under the surface of the water and was gone.

Livia spent the next hour using the first blade she'd taken from the spear head to slice through the leather bindings on the rest. With such a sharp edge, the work went faster than she'd thought it would. By the time Hrardorr returned with more, she'd already dismantled the first stack.

The wooden staves were stacked on one side of the boat shed, the diamond blades glittering darkly in a basket she'd emptied of fishing tackle. The new contents of that humble basket were worth a fortune, but it wasn't hers. She'd take only a small cut to pay the workers who would turn the dangerous blades into faceted gems and small tools. Never would any of these blades be left intact to harm a dragon. She vowed it.

She knew these giant diamond crystals were the rarest of the rare. Only one place in the world boasted so many of these giants. The only place these weapons could have come from—the magic mines on the eastern border of Skithdron.

For only magic could have forged a diamond so large and potentially deadly. Livia had to be careful in handling them. The slightest wrong move and she would slice easily through her skin. She'd put on a pair of old leather gloves that had been stored on one of the shelves. Now those same gloves had little slices all over the palms from her work with the diamonds, but better the gloves than her hands.

Hrardorr put the new supply of spears where she directed him, next to the original pile she had just finished. She would begin work on them as soon as she took a quick break.

"Can you stay here to guard these for a few minutes?" she asked the dragon. "I need to run up to the house and freshen up a bit. I'm also going to grab a sandwich and bring some food and drink down so I can continue working. Can I bring you anything?"

"I will stay. And I ate some fish while I was out hunting spears, so I am content. Thank you for asking. I regret putting you to such hard work, but this is vital, Livia."

"I understand," she told him. "Don't worry. I want these things rendered harmless as much as you do."

When Livia returned to the boat house, Hrardorr was dozing. He woke the moment she entered, and she smiled. He was a good guard, even as exhausted as he was from his exertions that day. Night had fallen, but the work in the town went on. Fires were lit everywhere, and the normal quiet of the night was broken by dragon snorts and the occasional intimidating burst of flame—coming from the square where they'd put all the prisoners under dragon guard—and people bustling about, carrying supplies and cleaning up after the battle.

The townsfolk had begun to return to reclaim their home. Livia was proud to see the way Dragonscove was bouncing back from the dreadful events of the day.

"Genlitha approaches. Can you open the sea doors for her? She is not very good at swimming underwater yet, but she can paddle around on the surface nicely." Hrardorr's observation caught Livia off guard. She hadn't realized Genlitha was coming to the boat shed. Good thing it was large enough to hold two dragons...just barely.

"I'll get the doors." Livia went to the far end of the tall shed, built between two wide piers to her father's exacting specifications. She tugged on the mechanism that opened the huge doors and stood back to secure them in the open position while searching the area for Genlitha.

Sure enough, she was making her way toward them at a steady paddle. She wasn't kicking up any water, so her movements were mostly soundless, which was good, though her light color stood out a bit against the dark water.

"Thank you, Livia," Genlitha said as she paddled through

the open doors. Livia closed them behind the sky blue dragon. *"Oh, this is cozy."*

"I'm sorry it's not more comfortable. This place was designed to shelter my sailboat, not dragons," Livia explained as she walked back down the left side pier toward Hrardorr while Genlitha pulled herself out of the water onto the right pier and padded up toward the main deck where Hrardorr was sitting.

"It's fine, Livia. Plenty of room for us," Genlitha insisted graciously. Her large head rotated, craning on her long neck as she looked all around the boathouse. *"You've made quick work of those spears. Well done. Hrardorr, did you know Livia has already taken apart so many of those awful weapons? You two are to be commended for acting so fast."* She shuddered as she arrived at the main deck that was much wider than the piers. *"I hate to think what could happen if the wrong people get their hands on those things."*

"I intend to get my most trusted craftsmen working as soon as possible to turn the blades into something a lot more harmless and much prettier," Livia said with a grin. "We can sell the majority to pay for the damages to the town, but if you want one as a souvenir, I'm sure that can be arranged as well."

"I'll have to think about that." Genlitha winked one great eye at her. *"I'd want to be sure the townsfolk had enough of the proceeds first before we did anything frivolous, but all girls do like sparkly things, don't we, Livia?"*

Livia had to laugh as she agreed with the pretty dragon.

"We will stay here tonight to guard the diamonds," Hrardorr stated, bringing them back to the matter at hand. *"I will dive again to check for more of the weapons, once I've rested a little longer. It was a big day."*

"You've got that right." Gowan's voice came to them from the doorway. Livia spun to find both Gowan and Seth entering the boathouse. She went to them, hugging each of them tightly.

Gowan walked over to the basket where she'd been placing the diamond spearheads and let out a long, low whistle. "That's quite a sight, isn't it?" he asked Seth, who had joined him, one arm still around Livia.

"I've never even seen one diamond crystal that large, much less a basket full," Seth agreed.

"Genlitha told me the plan for dealing with this," Gowan said. "I think it's great that you'll be financing the rebuilding of the town from the enemy's weapons."

"It's sort of poetic justice," Seth agreed.

"I've already decided to commission new and better harbor gun emplacements, regardless of what the town council says." Livia was adamant about that. The state the defenses had been allowed to fall into was shameful.

"A wise move. I'd be happy to share my thoughts on what would work after the day I just had. I saw some areas where we could've used a cannon or two," Seth mused. "And I bet Petr, the smith from the Lair, and the town smiths would have some advice for you as well."

"Excellent ideas, Seth. I'm going to talk to them tomorrow. Or as soon as everyone has a chance to catch their breath a bit." She decided on quick action then and there.

"If I know Petr, he'll already be working on it before you even speak to him. He's proactive that way. As are most of the smiths I've known."

Seth smiled at her, and her knees went a little wobbly. She wanted so much to just lean on these men after the hell they'd all been through earlier. They were her strength right now. Her security in the storm.

"Will you two stay with me tonight?" she blurted out the thought foremost in her mind, blushing hotly after she realized what she'd said.

The men looked at each other and then back at her. It was Gowan who spoke first.

"Genlitha is staying here with Hrardorr, so I have no reason to go back to the Lair just yet. The leaders got an earful from Gen earlier, and I think I should probably hide out for a bit before going back to face their wrath." Gowan chuckled, and Livia understood he was mostly joking.

Genlitha chuckled too, smoke rising toward the rafters of the boathouse. "I would be honored to stay at your home tonight, and I thank you for the invitation." Gowan bowed graciously, reminding her in a somewhat comical way of the manners he must've been raised with as the son of a lord.

"I already told Bronwyn I'd be staying in town tonight," Seth added. "There's much work to do here, but I do need a place to sleep. I'd be thankful if you'd allow me to stay, Mistress O'Dare." The twinkle in his blue eyes belied his formal words.

She knew, if the men stayed in her house, they would also be in her bed, for which she was immensely thankful. She didn't want to be alone. Not tonight. And though it was still odd to be part of a trio, it felt...right. Somehow.

She'd have to pay Rosie extra to keep her mouth shut about this one when Father returned, but it would be worth it. *So* worth it.

The dragons stayed in the boathouse while the trio shared Livia's bed. They celebrated victory and just being alive.

Livia was too keyed up to sleep, even after the languorous lovemaking. Seth had taken her first, hard and fast, burning off all that battlefield energy that had been sustaining him for hours. When he collapsed at her side, it had been Gowan's turn.

A more seasoned soldier, Gowan was better able to deal with the built-up stress. He stretched out the love play, finally making her beg him for completion, which he gladly gave. Of the two, Gowan was the more controlled when it came to making love. Someday, she dreamed, she might make him lose that epic control of his.

But when?

These moments were stolen out of regular time, she knew. Once her father heard about the attack, he'd be on his way home in a flash. He was not without feeling for her. Quite the contrary. He stayed away so long more because of the memories of her mother than a dislike of his daughter.

He was in mourning. Livia understood that. And leaving was his way of dealing with it, though she could have wished he'd stay with her and help her through her own loss. But he didn't see it. He was too far gone in his own grief to really understand what his absence meant to his only child.

She'd thought most males were selfish like her father when it came to grief, but now that she'd come to know Hrardorr, her opinions had changed. Hrardorr had shown her that everyone grieved in their own way—some self-destructive, at times.

Helping Hrardorr, and becoming his friend, had helped her more than anything. She now understood that loss is something everyone comes to know at some point in their lives, though some feel it more than others. For dragons, who had to lose their soul-bonded knights over and over, the loss was no less profound than her own loss of her mother.

They'd shared their stories out there on the water, where nobody else could hear and no one would judge them. They'd bonded over those stories and the shared sorrow. And they'd both begun to heal a bit, she thought.

"What happens now?" she whispered, not really sure anybody else was awake to hear her, but Seth rolled over to face her. He bent one elbow, supporting his head with his hand and just looked at her.

"I've been lying here, wondering that myself."

"The town continues to clean up and recover," Gowan added, his deep voice coming from her other side. "You facilitate the grinding of those diamond blades into something harmless. We do the debrief at the Lair and set some things in motion to change the way they run things up there. Seth comes out and tells his parents he is a fighting man after all, though I don't see why he can't keep helping Bronwyn too." Gowan paused, lifting his head to look over at Seth. "I expect you in training from now on, my friend. You've proven yourself even more able than most of the young knights. You've been blooded. You've been in battle. You need to take your rightful place among the fighting ranks, even if you aren't a knight."

Why did she hear an unsaid *yet* on the end of his sentence? Or was that just wishful thinking?

Things would be so much easier if both men were knights. Then, she might...just might...be able to keep them both. If their dragons agreed, of course.

But at least it would be in the realm of possibility then. For now, this trio was a stolen moment. Something not to be repeated unless under extraordinary circumstances. She knew that, but it still broke her heart a little.

Seth sighed, smiling faintly. "I'll show up, but I may have to knock a few heads together to prove I belong there. The Lair has gotten used to me being Bronwyn's errand boy. I don't think they'll accept me as a soldier easily now."

"Are you kidding?" Gowan scoffed. "Anyone who saw you leading the fight from the battlements knows you're the real deal, my friend. And we *all* saw it. While Jiffrey and Benrik held us back, we were all wishing we were down there in the midst of it with you, supporting your valiant defense of the city. You made quite an impression, and when you finally make it back to the Lair, I expect your fathers will have a few words to say to you. As will many others."

Seth's face reddened, and he lowered his head to the pillow, directing his gaze up at the ceiling. Was he embarrassed by Gowan's praise? Livia thought so, but she also knew the words were well deserved. She rolled toward Seth and put her hand over his heart, her cheek resting against his shoulder.

"You were so brave. I can't imagine what you went through, facing those broadsides from the enemy ships the way you did." She reached up and kissed his stubbly cheek. "You're my hero. And the town's hero, if I'm any judge. Many were speaking your praises as I worked among them earlier. Prepare yourself. Things are changing for you, Seth. Even I can see that." She smiled at him before placing a deeper kiss on his lips, which he returned full force.

From there, things heated up quickly. She climbed over

him to get better access to his mouth...and to other parts. She sank down on his hard cock as if coming home. He felt so good inside her. She felt incomplete without one or the other of them in her yearning core.

The bed shifted, and she felt something slippery enter her rear hole, along with Gowan's fingers. *Was he?*

Oh, dear. He was.

She moaned as he slid his cock into her backside, unused to the stretching, the tightness and the unexpected pleasure of it all. *Oh, yes.* This was something she could come to yearn. It felt so good, so right. These two men were her everything in that moment, her all, her reason to be.

Then, they started to move.

Gowan directed the motion and did most of the work, pushing into her, which made her slide upward, making Seth's cock retreat a bit. Then, as Gowan retreated, his motion guided her downward, fully onto Seth again. It was ingenious. It was incredible. It was heaven itself.

There was no moment when she wasn't filled one way or the other, and it didn't take long to take her to a peak of pleasure that made her cry out. But they kept moving. And another climax hit her out of the blue. Then another.

She called their names. She begged for...something. She wasn't even sure what.

Gowan came, followed swiftly by Seth, filling her, surrounding her, loving her with their bodies in a way that meant the world to her. Gowan collapsed for a moment, squishing her between his heavy body and Seth's strong muscles, but she didn't mind at all. In fact, she loved the feeling of being sandwiched between these two incredible men.

They were so good to her. So loving. So caring.

She was very much afraid she'd lost her heart. To both of them.

Gowan rolled away, taking her with him. He placed her gently in the center of the bed while they all recovered a bit. Sometime later, after his breathing had returned to normal, he rose and cleaned up using the water pitcher and bowl on her dresser. Dipping the small towel into the clean water, he came over and took care of her too.

Such a sweet gesture, though embarrassing to her at first, but he insisted and made her feel comfortable with the way he handled her body. He sat between her legs, splaying them wide as he ran the soft cloth over her, and even within her, which shocked her gaze to his. He only smiled, rubbing over her clit with the towel, then with his warm fingers.

And then...with his mouth.

She came again, under his lips, and didn't know anything further until morning.

Both men were gone from her bed when she woke. Washing and dressing quickly, she went to find them, hoping they hadn't left yet. She wanted every last second of this stolen time with them before they had to face the real world again.

She found Seth in the kitchen with Rosie. He had somehow managed to get on Rosie's good side. Probably by his heroics and then ministering to the injured the day before. Either way, Rosie was actually not frowning at him, which was a big thing for her. Frowning was her normal mode. If she wasn't frowning, that was like a full, beaming smile from someone else.

Rosie was dishing up breakfast, and Livia was pleased to see she had set three places in the dining room. Seth was in the kitchen, helping Rosie carry the heavier things out, which normally would've made Rosie growl at anyone else. Today, she merely grunted at Seth, which was another milestone as far as Livia was concerned.

When Seth saw her, he deposited the heavy tray on the table and came over to give her a good morning kiss. Rosie bustled out of the room, back to the kitchen, and Livia let the kiss evolve as much as Seth wanted. Unfortunately, he let her go far too soon.

"I can't stay much longer than breakfast, I'm afraid. I have to help Bronwyn again today. A few dragons were injured yesterday, and they'll need their wounds tended, which isn't always easy for her. I tend to do most of the work under her instruction."

Was he nervous? Was that why he was so chatty?

"I know," she told him simply, holding his hand and trying to convey her understanding. She'd known their time together was short, but she didn't regret a single minute of it. "Where's Gowan?"

"He went down to the boathouse, but he'll be back any minute."

"Have you been to see the dragons this morning?" Livia walked around to her place at the table, motioning for Seth to do the same as Rosie brought in the last of the trays of food and scurried away.

"First thing. They passed the night well. Genlitha rearranged a few things to make it more comfortable for them. I told her you probably wouldn't mind."

"Not at all. I'm just glad it was big enough for both of them."

Gowan arrived in the dining room at that moment, pausing by Livia's chair to bestow a fiery kiss on her lips. He sat down on her other side and began serving himself, as the other two had done.

"They were fine," Gowan assured Livia, joining the conversation already in progress. "Snug as two birds in a nest."

They all laughed as they started to eat heartily of the massive breakfast Rosie had prepared.

"They're dragons, not birds," Livia chided. "And it's a boathouse, not a nest."

More laughter masked the entrance of another male into the room, but when he dropped his sword with a clang on the side table, everyone looked up.

Livia's father—Captain O'Dare—had come home.

# # #

ABOUT THE AUTHOR

Bianca D'Arc has run a laboratory, climbed the corporate ladder in the shark-infested streets of lower Manhattan, studied and taught martial arts, and earned the right to put a whole bunch of letters after her name, but she's always enjoyed writing more than any of her other pursuits. She grew up and still lives on Long Island, where she keeps busy with an extensive garden, several aquariums full of very demanding fish, and writing her favorite genres of paranormal, fantasy and sci-fi romance.

Bianca loves to hear from readers and can be reached through Twitter (@BiancaDArc), Facebook (BiancaDArcAuthor) or through the various links on her website.

WELCOME TO THE D'ARC SIDE...
WWW.BIANCADARC.COM

OTHER BOOKS BY BIANCA D'ARC

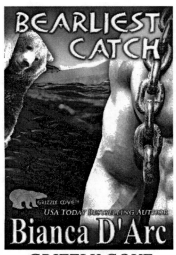

GRIZZLY COVE
BEARLIEST CATCH

A woman of mystery...

Jetty is a huntress of the deep ocean who finds herself fascinated by a man—a shifter—who sets anchor in her realm day after day. She is obliged to watch him, not fully understanding the fascination the handsome stranger compels within her battered heart.

A man with hidden scars...

Recovery from major injury isn't easy. While Drew's physical problems have been addressed and cured, the emotional scars from his battlefield catastrophe are harder to heal. He seeks the solace of the ocean even more than the welcome company of his former military comrades in the town of Grizzly Cove. When they give him a mission to make contact with an elusive mermaid, he's more than willing to give it a try.

A people in danger...

Jetty and Drew will have to work together if they are to bring the mer people into the protection of the cove. They will both face the terror of the deep. Will they be strong enough to overcome its evil? And will their love be strong enough to overcome the injuries of the past that have left them both slightly broken in different ways?

JIT'SUKU CHRONICLES ~ ARCANA
DIVA

She needs only one name...Diva. Galactic superstar. Brilliant musician. Chanteuse extraordinaire. But she has a number of deep, dark secrets. For a woman who lives her life in the spotlight of a billion lenses, she managed to lead a double life, full of intrigue.

When her path crosses that of Captain John Starbridge everything changes. Here is a man who sees beneath the mask she wears for the public. Here is a man in love with the woman behind the music into which she pours her soul. Here is a man who could be hers...if they didn't both have duties that must be fulfilled.

John's allegiance has always been to the human race and his band of Spec Ops brothers, but the music of the woman known only as Diva has accompanied him on every deep space mission he's ever undertaken. Her voice croons him to sleep in his lonely bunk each night and her intense lyrics haunt him throughout his days. When he finally meets the object of his fascination, he realizes there is even more depth to the woman than he expected. He gives her his heart, though he knows it's likely a futile gesture. What would a superstar like her want with a plain old soldier like him?

Circumstances throw them together and tear them apart, while enemy forces gather to invade the galaxy they both try—in their own ways—to protect. She will have to walk into the lion's den in order to save the galaxy...and perhaps, the man she loves. If there's a way, she'll find it, but it might just be the mission that finally breaks them both once and for all.

Or not...

WWW.BIANCADARC.COM